THE
LAST
WILD

THE
LAST
WILD

PIERS TORDAY

VIKING
An Imprint of Penguin Group (USA)

VIKING
Published by the Penguin Group
Penguin Group (USA) LLC
375 Hudson Street
New York, New York 10014, U.S.A.

USA ° Canada ° UK ° Ireland ° Australia ° New Zealand ° India ° South Africa ° China

penguin.com
A Penguin Random House Company

Originally published in Great Britain in a slightly different form by Quercus Books, 2013
First published in the United States of America by Viking,
an imprint of Penguin Young Readers Group, 2014

LIBRARY OF CONGRESS CATALOGING-IN-PUBLICATION DATA IS AVAILABLE
ISBN: 978-0-670-01554-2

Printed in the USA

1   3   5   7   9   10   8   6   4   2

Designed by Eileen Savage
Set in Mercury Text

o o o o o

To my parents

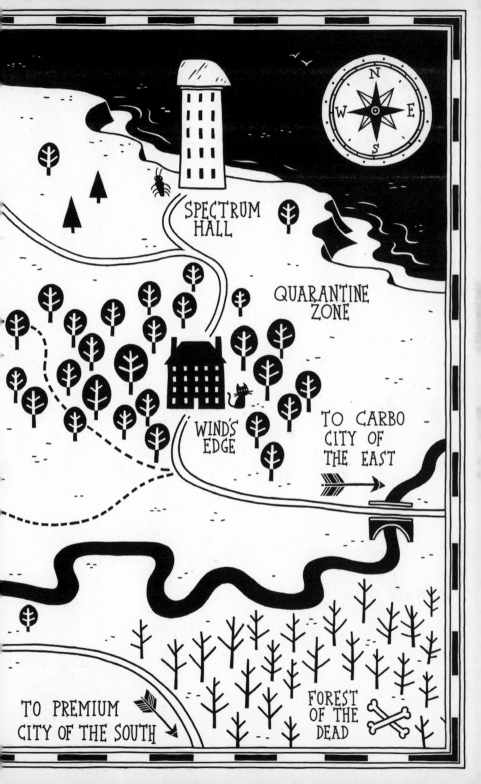

THE
LAST
WILD

PART 1
SPECTRUM HALL

My story begins with me sitting on a bed, looking out the window.

I know that doesn't sound like much. But let me tell you where the bed is, and what I can see from it. This bed is right in the corner of a room only just big enough for it, and the bed is only just big enough for a kid my age.

(Twelve—just about to be thirteen—and skinny.)

The window is the size of the whole wall, made of special tinted glass that means the room stays the same temperature all the time. The room is locked shut and you need an electronic keycard to open the door. If you could open it, you would be in a long corridor with absolutely *nothing* in it apart from cameras in the ceiling and a fat man in a purple jacket and trousers sitting opposite on a plastic chair. Sleeping, most likely.

This fat man is called a *Warden*. And there are lots of them here. But I think he is probably the fattest.

The corridor with the cameras and the fat Warden is on the seventh floor of a building that is like a big upside-down boat made of glass and metal. Everywhere you look there are reflections—of you, other faces, the storm clouds. The curved glass walls stretch all the way down to the edge of some very high cliffs—only grass and mud for miles around, with rocks and sea below. The cliffs are in the north of the Island, in the middle of the Quarantine Zone—far away from the city and my home.

The name of this building is Spectrum Hall.

Or in full: Spectrum Hall Academy for Challenging Children.

It's just like a big school, really. Only the most boring school in the world, that you can never, ever leave.

And as for what I can see out of the window?

I know that what is really there is sea and sky and rocks, but the light in the ceiling bounces off the glass into my eyes. So when I look out into the dark sky all I can actually see is my reflection. That and the hairy grey varmint flapping about in the corner. A "moth" is what they call this kind—with antennae and spotted grey wings. I shoo him away, only to send him circling round the light above.

I try to ignore the flittering noise above me and carry on with my practise. "Bed," "chair" (one, screwed to the floor), "window," "my watch"—loads of words to practise with. You see, I know what the words mean. I know how to write them. I just can't say them. No more than the moth can.

Not since Mum died.

I look at my watch again. The chunky green digital one she gave me. The last present I ever got from her. My favourite present I ever got from her. Even Dad nicked it once, because he thought it was "nifty," and I had to hassle him to give it back.

I'm lucky to still have it—we aren't meant to keep anything personal at the Hall, but I kicked and bit so they couldn't take it. I flick the picture onto the screen.

It's a summer afternoon in our garden, behind our house in the city. You can just see the sun shining on the River Ams, gleaming beyond the top of the back wall, and far away on the other side, the skyline of tall glass towers.

Premium.

City of the south, and capital city of the Island. When the rest of the world grew too hot, and cracked open in the sun, everyone came to live on this cold grey rock—the Island—in their hundreds and thousands. If only it was hot *here* sometimes. The weather is never good. But for me this picture has just always been where our home is, where Dad is—and where, one day, I know I'll return.

Right now, though, I'm more interested in the person in the garden.

It's my mum, Laura, before she got sick. She has long curly hair the colour of shiny new coins, and she's laughing at something Dad or I have said.

I used to be able to talk normal, you see, like everyone. Mum and I talked a lot. Dad and I talked a bit. Now, though, it's like trying to learn the hardest language in the world.

I know I can inside; it's just when I try to speak—nothing happens. The more I try, the harder it gets.

They want to make me talk again here—Doctor Fredericks with his tests—but it's not working. People here stare at you funny as you go red in the face, or sometimes they laugh and make up what they think you were going to say.

I'd rather try and talk to a varmint, thanks. There's enough of them—that's for sure. Flapping moths that circle round lights, like the one in my room right now, and spiders lurking in corners, or cockroaches scuttling around by the bins. All the useless insects and pests that the red-eye left behind. We don't even bother with their real names half the time. Varmints is all they are.

And I have practised talking at them, as it happens. Not that you're meant to go near them—even though everyone knows they're the only thing that can't get the virus. So I haven't reported this flapping one in my room. Because I like practising with him there buzzing around. He won't talk back. But at least he doesn't laugh or stare—I can almost pretend he's listening.

I do that a lot.

Right, varmint, I say to myself in my head, *let's see what you think I'm saying this time.*

So I'm just about to have a go at saying "b-e-d" again—or at least the "b," or even a noise that sounds like a "b"—when the round speaker hidden in the ceiling splutters into life. You can almost see the spit fly out of the holes. The varmint whirls angrily away; he doesn't like it any more than I do.

"Calling all, ah, students. Your first meal of the day is, ah, served, in the Yard. You have t-t-ten minutes."

There's a clank as he replaces the microphone in its stand, and a hum as he forgets to turn it off, and I hear his heavy breathing for a minute before he remembers and flicks the switch.

Doctor Fredericks, the Governor.

He can give himself as many titles as he likes; he's still just an ugly man in a white coat with a comb-over, whose breath smells of sweets. The day after they brought me here—bundled out of my home in the middle of the night—I gathered with all the new kids in the Yard while he stood behind a lectern reading words off a screen, his jacket flapping in the air-con.

"Good afternoon, ahm, boys and, er, girls. Welcome to S-Spectrum, ah, Hall. You have been sent here because your parents want to, ahm, f-f-forget about you. Your, ah, schools can no longer t-t-tolerate you, so they have asked us to help. Because we are a special institution, dealing with special c-c-cases like yours. And I'll tell you now how it's going to, ahm, work." His amplified words bounced off the walls. "Look behind you at the sea. It is the filthiest and most p-p-polluted sea in the world, we're told."

He stared down at us through his bottle-top glasses and flicked away a loose strand of greasy hair as we gazed out the glass walls behind us, at the waves chopping and crashing at the cliffs.

But I didn't believe that Dad wanted to forget about me.

Six years later, I still don't.

"There are t-t-two ways, ah, out of here. Through our front gates, as an improved and functioning member of society. Or off these bally c-c-cliffs and into the, ahm, sea. So either learn to, ah, m-m-modify your behaviour, or jolly well learn to, ah, dive!"

I haven't learnt to do either yet.

I pull on my sweatpants, shove my feet into my sneakers, and strap on my watch. Then there's a beep, and the light in my door goes red, orange, then green, before sliding open with a hiss. The fat Warden is standing there in his crumpled purple jacket and trousers, my door keycard dangling on a strap from around his wrist.

"Come on, Jaynes," he mutters, scratching his hairy chin. "I haven't got all day."

I'm not surprised, with so much sitting on your bum and sleeping to do, I think. That's one of the advantages of not being able to speak—you never get in bother for talking back. I step out into the corridor and wait.

One by one, the other doors along from mine beep and slide open. And out come the other inhabitants of Corridor 7, boys and girls my age, all in T-shirts and sweatpants and sneakers like me, their hair unbrushed, their faces blank. We look at each other, and then the Warden silently points to the other end of the corridor.

I feel his eyes boring into my back as we walk past him along the passage and into the open lift.

o o o o o o o o

The Yard is full of noise, which gets right inside my head. Most of it from the queue for the servery, a polished counter set into the wall, lined with pots. Metal pots full of pink slop, which some women with grey hair and greyer faces are busy dishing out, all of them wearing purple tunics with a big "F" stamped on the front.

"F" for Factorium. The world's biggest food company. More like the only food company now, since the red-eye came and killed all the animals. Every last one, apart from the varmints.

So Facto started making formula for us to eat instead. Which now makes them the only *company*, full stop—they run *everything*. First the government asked them to take care of the red-eye, and then they ended up taking care of the government. They run the country now, from hospitals to schools. Including this one. I don't know why making food or killing animals makes you good at running schools as well, but the first thing you learn in a Facto school is: never argue with Facto.

"What's the flavour, miss?" shouts Wavy J, waving his plastic bowl in the air, somehow first in the queue already. That's why he's called Wavy—he's always at the front of every line, waving. I don't even know his real name.

Behind him is Big Brenda, a fat girl with hair in bunches, who has to sleep on a reinforced bed. She's here because she ate her mum and dad out of house and home—even during the food shortage—and got so big they couldn't look after her anymore. That pale-faced kid with bags under his eyes is Tony—who got in trouble for stealing tins of food. And now he's here, quietly nicking some headphones out of the bag belonging to Justine, who is here because she was caught being part of a gang. A gang of thieves who got around everywhere on bikes, who nicked not just tins of food but anything they could get their hands on. Like music players and headphones. That little kid she's talking to with spiky hair and a devil grin—that's Maze, who has an attention deficiency. The kind of attention deficiency that makes you chase your mum around the kitchen with a knife. And then right at the back, behind them all, is me.

I know their names. I listen to their conversations. I know why they're here.

But I don't know why I am.

"Chicken'n'Chips," announces the grey lady behind the hatch, who looks like a big door on legs, with hairy arms. "Today's flavour is Chicken *and* Chips." Her name is Denise, which doesn't rhyme with "arms," so instead the others have made up a song about her hairy knees, which aren't actually that hairy. It doesn't matter what Denise or any of the women say, though—Sausage'n'Mash, Ham'n'Eggs, Pie'n'Peas—everything they serve looks exactly the same: bright pink gloop that spills over the edge of the bowl and only ever tastes of one thing: prawn-cocktail crisps.

"Formul-A," they want us to call it, pronouncing the "A" like in "day," but no one does. It's just *formula*. First the animals we eat went, and then the bees went, and then the crops and fruit went. Vegetables were contaminated. So there were rations, and you had to measure out butter in a spoon, or milk in a cup. Then all the fresh and frozen food went. We lived out of tins. Oily, meaty, fishy, or veggie mush out of tins. The tins began to run out too. People started eating anything. Even varmints. Rats. Cockroaches.

Then, one day—I was here by now—they just started serving us formula, and that was it—no more normal food. "It's gone," Denise had said, "and it ain't coming back. That's all you need to know." Instead we got given a meal replacement that "satisfies all your daily nutritional needs."

If you like prawn-cocktail crisps.

"Jaynes! Do you want feeding or a crack on that dumb skull of yours?"

Hairy Denise empties a ladle of pink slop into my bowl, and I walk back past the others, already stuffing their faces where they stand. Big Brenda smiles at me as I pass, and so I stop. She's all right, Bren—perhaps because people laugh at her all the time for being fat, she doesn't laugh at other people so much.

"All right, Dumbinga?" she says, putting away half of her formula dose in a single spoonful. Dumb *and* ginger. I'm a gift for a nickname, I am.

I shrug and stir the formula round in my bowl.

Then there's a head-full of spiky hair in my face, and Maze is leering up at me.

"Hello, Dumbinga. What's the chat?"

I avoid his gaze and look down at the pink gloop.

"Bit quiet, is it?" he says.

"Leave him alone," says Bren, her mouth full of Chicken'n'Chips.

But he doesn't. "Nah. He's only pretending. Aren't you,

Dumbinga?" I shake my head, already resigned to what happens next. Maze puts his bowl down and rolls his sleeves up. "Look, Bren—I'll show you. I bet you if I give Dumbinga a dead arm, he'll scream his little head off. Won't you, Dumbinga?"

No, I won't.

(A) Because I can't, and—

(B) I'm not in the mood for this today.

So holding my bowl close to my chest, like a shield, I press past him and the others.

I hear Maze spit with disgust on the ground behind me and laugh, and even though it's the worst thing to do—it's impossible not to—I turn back round. They're all just staring at me.

"Freak," says Maze. And flashes his little devil grin.

I have to remember that I gave up trying to be like the talkers a long time ago. So, shaking my head, trying to pretend like it doesn't matter, playing the big man—I turn back and take the bowl to go and sit in My Corner.

My Corner isn't really *my* corner, of course. It's just a part of the Yard, underneath one of the metal walkways between classrooms, where there's more metal and concrete than glass, where they pile up the empty formula kegs from the kitchen, next to a drain. A quiet and dark place, somewhere good to go if you don't want to be bothered by spiky-haired idiots. I put the bowl of fluorescent pink down on the ground and turn one of the kegs over.

FACTORIUM IS A SELWYN STONE ENTERPRISE

is engraved on the bottom. Whatever. No one's ever seen Selwyn Stone for real. He probably doesn't even exist. It's hard to see people when they're always behind a smoked-glass car window or disappearing into a sky-scraper surrounded by crowds of photographers and bodyguards. The head of Facto, the man who invented formula. The head of the whole Island now, the man who made up all the new rules. Don't touch this, don't eat that, don't live here—well, right now, I don't care for his stupid rules. And to prove it, I sit right down on top of his stupid name, pick up my bowl, and wait.

You see, I'm not going to eat it myself.

Well, maybe a bit—but it is properly foul. I'm going to give it to someone else. Someone who should be here right about . . . now.

And sure enough, there on the edge of the shadows by the drain, I can just see two antennae poking out, curling, and tasting the air. Two orangey-red antennae belonging to an insect about the length of my thumb. An insect with a flat head, lots of bristly legs, and—silently chewing at the front—a pair of jaws.

Another varmint. A cockroach.

The antennae sniff the air, and, checking that no one else is around, he carefully scuttles out into the open, revealing the two large white stripes across his back.

I give him a smile. Not that he can smile back; he's a cockroach. But he likes to come and nibble at spoonfuls of my formula, so I let him. And he's OK to hang out with. He doesn't thump your leg and say, "How about if I give you a dead leg instead? Will you scream *then*?" (No.) He doesn't grab both your arms behind your back, while his mate tries to tickle you to death, saying, "What, you can't even laugh, either?" (Again, no.) And he certainly never, ever jeers or points when you do try, as hard as you can, to say a word.

He just sort of *listens*.

I scoop a bit of formula in my spoon, and, checking no one is watching, lay it down on the ground by my feet. He scurries over and starts to lap it up.

No one knows why the cockroaches didn't catch the red-eye. Dad used to say he wasn't surprised they survived—apparently even if you dropped a nuclear bomb on everything, they would be the only ones left.

(That's what happens when you have a scientist for a Dad. You don't need school or exams when his lab is in the basement and he lets you watch him work, muttering to himself as he does. Your head is full of useless facts from the get-go.)

The red-eye wasn't a nuclear bomb, though; it was a disease. A disease worse than a nuclear bomb, if you ask me. "Like . . . animal flu," Dad said. A flu that turned animal bodies and brains to mush and, just before they died, made their eyes burn bright red like they were on fire inside.

Dad thought it had started on a cattle farm, but no one really knew where it had come from. And before anyone could find out, the virus had spread everywhere. Not just to the animals we eat, but to nearly every living creature—

wild animals, pets, animals in zoos—right around the world it went, till the jungles were full of bodies, birds fell out of the air, and fish floated in silvery slicks on top of the sea.

It killed all the animals in the world.

All, that is, apart from the useless ones. The ones we couldn't eat, the ones that didn't pollinate crops or eat pests. Just the pests themselves—the varmints. Like this smelly cockroach slurping at my spoon of formula. Even though they can't get the virus, you're still not meant to touch them. Because humans can get the virus. That's why Facto declared the whole countryside a Quarantine Zone and forced everyone to move to the cities, where they can keep them safe—and why we live here under an upside-down glass boat. Just in case, Selwyn Stone says.

I don't care. I lean over, put my hand out, and let the varmint crawl into my hand.

He's a big guy. Perhaps the biggest I've ever seen. Other kids here would freak out, but not me. And I look around at the damp empty patch of shade I'm sitting in, at the gang on the other side of the Yard, laughing and joking over their food, and I think perhaps "freak" is a good choice of word by Maze.

Because he's right. That's what I am. I didn't choose it, I didn't ask for it, but that's what I've become—a genuine freak, mute, with only varmints for friends.

There's a blast of cold from the air-con, and I shiver, feeling all of a sudden very alone. The most alone I've felt for a long time. Like I'm not even really here in the Yard anymore, like I'm just sort of floating about in space, cast adrift in the sky above. It's weird, but I kind of enjoy feeling sad sometimes. I deliberately think of all the sad things that have happened—the animals going, then Mum, and being taken away from Dad, dumped and forgotten about in here. Like it's all been done on purpose just to make my life as rubbish as it could ever be, and there's a kind of warm feeling rising up inside my chest, filling up behind my eyes, because I hate it, I hate everything, including myself for feeling like this, and I think I'm going to cry, when—

I hear it. A noise.

Strong, loud, and clear, the strangest noise I've ever heard: faint and crackly, like an old-fashioned radio in a film. A noise that slowly, definitely, turns into a word.

Help!

That's it—nothing else. It comes again.

Help!

There's no one else here. The Wardens are inside, probably dozing. Back over by the servery, Big Brenda seems to have Tony in a headlock and is trying to steal his bowl of formula, but they're miles away. And then the voice speaks again, with more words, so faint I can only just make them out.

Kester! Help!

Whoever is speaking has a very deep voice—it's not a kid's voice at all, or even a man's—it rasps and echoes, like a rock rattling down a metal pipe.

Please. You must help.

Almost not human.

Then slowly, with a knot in my stomach, I realize whose voice it is. The only possible answer, however impossible it seems. Looking straight at me, his little varmint antennae waving—

The cockroach.

No—I must be making this up. We're not in a cartoon. The cockroach hasn't got massive eyes, or a hat, and he isn't singing a song. I definitely don't think he's going to grant me a wish. He's just an insect sitting in my hand.

And yet I can hear him. He's trying to speak to me.

The cockroach flicks his antennae impatiently—before we are both plunged into shadow. The shadow of a Warden looming above us, a heavy hand on my collar, hauling me to my feet, as the varmint tumbles to the ground and scurries back to the drain. He pauses on the edge, looks at me one last time, and then dives down inside the hole without another word.

What was I thinking? Cockroaches can't talk. I can't talk. Nothing has changed.

Which is when the Warden says the words no kid at Spectrum Hall ever wants to hear: "The Doctor will see you now."

There are some places you aren't ever allowed into without being asked first.

The Doctor's rooms are different from the rest of the hall. They don't have glass walls to look at the sea through. They're underground, and you have to enter a special code in the lift to get there. The lift opens out into a long white corridor, like in a hospital. There are rooms off either side, and the whole place stinks of toilet cleaner.

This room is clean and bare, almost empty apart from a plastic chair in front of a desk, and a sink in the corner. On the wall behind the desk there is a picture of Selwyn Stone.

A picture I've found myself staring at many times before. He has such a strange face. Something weird about it that I can't explain—like he doesn't look quite real. Apart from his eyes, which stare straight through you, seeing everything.

I look away.

The thing you notice most about the rooms, once the

lift has beeped shut again and the Wardens have turned off the lights behind them, is that there's almost no noise. There are no screams and shouts from the Yard, just every now and then the *squeak squeak* of rubber shoes along the corridor outside.

I know it's only me down here, sitting on a plastic chair facing an empty desk, but you hear things in the quiet, you see. The sound of something shifting its weight on the ceiling above, or a gust of air that could so easily be a breath. Then, out of the corner of your eye, a shadow seems to bend and slide along the floor—a shadow with eight legs. Another varmint.

A black spider tapping about the floor.

I hate spiders. How it got in here, the most sterilized part of the whole Hall, I don't know. I just sit still, count to ten, and hope it doesn't come near me. When I get out, I'll tell Dad about the rooms. How they leave you there, all on your own in the dark, for hours, just to wind you up. You can't admit you're afraid of the dark here because that makes you a wuss, but I am. If Dad knew, he'd never allow it; I know he wouldn't.

It was raining that night, raining a lot, hitting the windows in noisy splats. It wasn't properly dark, because of the moon. I was woken up by a strange sound from downstairs. I still remember how the toys on my shelf looked cross, with the shadows of the raindrops flicking across them, as I turned on the light to make the darkness go away.

For a moment everything in my room—the clothes in a mess on the floor, the toys on the shelf—all looked normal and happy.

But then I heard the door downstairs ripping open.

I got out of bed to go and get Dad. The landing was pitch-black, and I couldn't find the light switch. The door ripped again, and I wanted to cry out for him, but I couldn't. I knew I'd have to go into his room to wake him up by shaking his shoulder.

Perhaps he just left the door open, I thought, and started to go down the stairs extra quietly so as not to wake him up.

I got halfway down when I heard a whispering noise that came in with a wind, blowing across my face and making my cheeks cold.

The door was definitely open. At the bottom of the stairs I tiptoed across the room to shut it.

I turned around and started to go back upstairs.

There was a squeak on the floor behind me. I looked back, and the door had come open again. This time there was a man standing there in the doorway. I couldn't see his face because of the darkness.

I felt more frightened than I'd ever felt in my whole life. "Kester Jaynes?" he said quietly.

I nodded, not knowing what else to do.

"You're coming with me."

A noise in my head snaps me back to the present. Not the metallic rasping I heard in the Yard, more a high-pitched whistle, like a boiling kettle. A whistle that seems to contain words at the same time.

There is no one else down here.

I shake my head, as if the noise was a buzzing fly, but it doesn't go away. And I force myself to look at the spider, sitting calmly on the floor, every one of its eight eyes watching me. The whistling gets louder and louder in my head, as if the kettle is about to explode, until the ear-piercing shriek begins to slowly form into a word.

A word, floating and twisting inside my mind. *Listen.*

So I do, but all I can hear is the *slap slap* of sandals coming down the corridor, and the door sliding open, while the spider scuttles back into the shadows and squeezes through a super-thin crack into the wall. I think I am beginning to go mad. They said this would happen if I didn't talk to anyone, that I would start making stuff up.

Imaginary friends.

Doctor Fredericks turns on an overhead lamp, shining it right in my face. I squirm away from the blinding light towards the floor, trying not to look at his chipped toenails. He doesn't say anything like "Hello" or "How are you today?" He's called a doctor, but he isn't the kind of doctor who makes you stick your tongue out and puts a cold stethoscope on your chest. He does wear a white coat, it's true, but that's the only thing doctorish about him.

I catch a whiff of blackcurrant. The pockets of the Doctor's white coat are full of blackcurrant cough sweets, and there's always one in his mouth. He turns on the tap in the corner and begins to scrub his hands.

"Name?" he says, his mouth full of lozenge.

He knows I can't speak. *He knows.*

"Name?" he says again.

I just look blankly at him. Doctor Fredericks sighs. "Jaynes, Kester. You, ahm, were seen handling a, ah, varmint in the Yard."

He's drying his hands on a sheet of paper towel. I know what's coming, but I don't care. The cockroach doesn't have a virus. The cockroach is my friend. It tried to speak to me. I think.

"Did you, or did you not, ahm, handle a restricted insect, young man?"

I stare straight ahead. A bristly hand knocks me round the back of the neck. I continue to stare straight ahead, trying not to wince.

The Doctor sighs and sits down behind his desk, like he's still waiting for me to say something. After what feels like forever, he gives a long drawn-out breath and begins to pick at his nails, still not looking at me. His voice is softer this time, trying to sound casual.

"Do you know why you're here, Kester? Haven't you ever wondered?"

I can't help but smile and shake my head. I'm not going to show him that I care. The less you give away in here, the better. He waves his hand crossly at the world above our heads.

"Do you think all of this is a joke? The Q-q-quarantine Zone, the glass roofs? Do you think Mr. Stone"—he turns and glances at the picture of his boss on the wall behind him—"is having a, ah, jolly g-g-good laugh?"

He leans forward suddenly. Now he's looking at me. I catch a glimpse of bloodshot eyes behind the thick glasses.

"Does it never, ah, occur to you, that you might be here for your own g-g-good? That we might actually be, ah, trying to, dash it to blazes, p-p-protect you?"

I shrug and stare through him as blankly as I can. The Doctor leans back in his chair and glances up at the ceiling again.

"There's still so much we don't know about the, ah, virus. Where it came from, how it spread so jolly quickly. All we do know is that it mutates. Without any sign, or any, ah, warning. From animal to animal." He fixes me with his bleary gaze. "To humans. To varmints one day, our best scientists are sure of it. It's not a question of if, but w-w-when. Do you understand me, boy?"

I shrug. I've heard the lecture many times before.

"So, I'm going to ask you one more time. Why were you handling a, ahm, v-v-varmint in the Yard? Is there anything you would like to t-t-tell me?"

He waits.

I try to speak. To tell him something, just any word—not

what actually happened in the Yard—just a simple word, to keep him happy.

I do. I try so hard.

But no word comes.

My body sinks into the chair with the effort.

"Well?"

He waits.

"Nothing? Ah well. What a shame. What a d-d-dashed pity."

He stands and begins to pace up and down the room. "So, young, ah, Jaynes—the son of the great Professor Jaynes."

Here it comes.

"Do you think that makes you different? Do you think that makes you better than anyone else, eh?" He leans into my face, and his whiskers brush my cheek. "Do you think it makes you s-special?"

I look down at his big white toes in their sandals and think, You're pretty special yourself, Doctor, but he grabs my chin and twists it back up so I have to stare at him.

"Your, ah, dear f-f-father also thinks he's better, you see, than the rest of us." He laughs, although it sounds more like hiccups. "Us, ah, less honourable scientists," he continues through the hiccupy laughs, "doomed to spend our jolly old days working with wretched specimens such as yourself."

I don't know why he keeps calling Dad an "honourable scientist." He was just doing his job, as a vet. A very good vet, mind, perhaps the best in the country, Mum said. He had "the magic touch"—that's what they called it. "No animal too small, no disease too big," he always said. Animals in farms, animals from the house next door, animals on the other side of the world. Until the virus came.

"And all I am trying to, ah, jolly well do is keep my little d-d-delinquent, ah, charges safe and, ahm, sound." He gives me a big smile, and it looks like his fraggly yellow teeth are running a competition to see which one can fall out of his mouth first. "Which is why I have no choice, I'm afraid."

I look at the shut door. At the picture of scowling Selwyn Stone. None of them offers any advice or any help as the Doctor gives me my sentence.

"You touched a restricted insect. You know the rules."

He presses a button under the desk, and the door slides open to reveal two Wardens in the corridor, waiting for me.

"Take him, ah, back to his room," says Doctor Fredericks with a wave of his hand. "Q-q-quarantined for seven days. Total isolation."

The Wardens haul me back to my room and lock the door behind me as if nothing had happened.

Seven days. Stuck in here. Because I thought an insect was talking to me.

Sitting up against the wall, clutching my pillow to my chest, I try to focus on the world beyond the window. A solid black sky, but no rain.

I try to think of happy things—like being back at home. I'm helping Mum unpack the shopping. I've said something to make her laugh. Then Dad comes in holding his favourite mug, full of tea, and joins in. And we're laughing and cooking dinner and we're happy. Everything's normal again.

I don't know how long I stay like that, curled up on my bed, clutching my pillow. At supper time they shove a bowl of Eggs'n'Ham formula through a hatch in the door, but I don't feel hungry.

While I sleep and stare, untouched formula bowls pile up on the floor—that is how my life is until seven grey skies have been and gone since I was taken to the Doctor's rooms.

That evening, I have the strangest dream.

I'm dreaming that I'm asleep in my room at home, when there's a faint noise at the window.

A *tap-tap-tapping*.

I try to ignore it, and roll over. But the noise just keeps on getting louder and louder.

My head is pulsing—half dreaming, half awake, I toss and turn, feeling my pillows, the cold wall behind, confused as to whether I'm at home or in the Hall. The *tap tapping* grows louder and louder, like a drill inside my brain.

Then, with a jolt, I wake up. I'm definitely in my room at Spectrum Hall.

And I'm freezing.

I'm freezing because the window wall has a jagged hole smashed right through it, and in the moonlight I can see shards of broken glass all over the floor. Carefully I climb out of bed, trying not to step on the jagged edges, when some feathers hit me on the head.

Dark and wet feathers, flapping round the room.

I raise my arm over my eyes, and another thing hits me from the opposite direction. Flying in through the window, flying at me from all sides, is a flock of birds. They flap manically, showering me with freezing water from their wings.

In the half light I catch a glimpse of their huge eyes and purple-grey chests.

Pigeons. My room is full of flying varmints.

I grab my chair, ready to bat the birds back out again, back to wherever they came from, when they start to speak—all of them talking together in a deep voice, more like singing than talking. Like a choir, direct in my head— just like the crackle from the cockroach in the Yard, or the whistle from the spider in the Doctor's room, only this time there are hundreds of voices speaking at once.

And I really can hear what they're saying.

Kester Jaynes, we have been sent to find you.

But it's a talking choir without perfect timing. Because as most of them finish, I notice a higher-pitched voice join in late, making even less sense than the others—

Yes, Kester Jaynes, you have been sent to find us.

All their heads turn to look at me: what looks like at least a hundred pairs of eyes and beaks swivelling in my direction as if they're synchronized. A hundred pigeons at least—in my room.

Kester—we know you can hear us.

It's true. I can. But I don't understand how or why. *You can talk to us. Let your mind go free. Let us in, Kester. Let us hear your thoughts.*

I don't want to let anything into my head. The pigeons flutter about in the pale blue light. It looks like most of them are dark grey, with white speckles. But there's one white bird with pink feet and orange eyes. Ninety-nine dark grey pigeons and a single white one, the one with the high-pitched voice. The one who can't say words properly. Like me.

Kester Jaynes, the time has come, say the ninety-nine grey pigeons.

Kester Jaynes, have you got the time? adds the one white pigeon.

You have a special gift. Only you can save us.

Yes. We've saved a special gift, only for you.

I think spending so long on my own has sent me crazy. And then, without thinking, words start to form in my head.

Yes, *words*—actual words.

After six whole years, six years since I spoke a single one. And now, as if that had been yesterday, as if we were still in the hospital, as if Mum was still lying there, they come again: words.

The last words I ever spoke were to Mum. The night that she—

She was lying there, sort of looking at me, more looking past me, holding my hand so lightly, like just to keep hers on top of mine was an effort, her breathing rickety, her skin yellow—so all I said was—

"Will you come back?"

She shook her head ever so slightly, from side to side, gave *what was maybe a smile, and then said—in fact whispered—so soft, so I had to lean in, smelling her breath, sweet and stale—"Tell Dad." Another pause, a big breath. "Tell Dad he has to tell you."*

But she never said what.

The pigeons peck in—

Kester! Kester! You must save us!

Mum disappears, and instead there are just words—forming, circling in my mind, pulses of sound trying to connect.

There's a silence. While I think, and try to speak.

Yes, Kester, save yourself from us! squeaks the white pigeon.

The other grey pigeons shake their heads and peck at the white one so much he falls off the end of my bed with a squawk.

But it helps. I realize I can speak. Like in my head before, to the moth in my room, to the cockroach in the Yard—only it's different this time. Because I know they're listening and understanding. So I say the first new words of my new talking.

Get out of my face, birds!

(No one said the words had to be polite.)

The pigeons cock their heads. Like they don't care what I say or think. The white one picks himself up off the floor with a shake of his head and hops back on to the end of my bed, scratching furiously at his wingpit with his beak. Ignoring him, the grey ones fill my head with their singsong, wailing like ghosts.

They are coming, Kester Jaynes, they are coming. They are coming for you! Prepare yourself!

I want to clap my hands and clear the craziness from my head. But I don't have to. My brain crackles once more, and my eyes grow heavy as my thoughts slide back down into the darkness. The last thing I hear is the squeak of the white pigeon.

Coming? I thought we were going? Oh—

And then flapping, and then—nothing.

When I wake up again, it's still night.

There are no birds. Just the sheets on my bed, the chair in the corner. Everything in the same place it has been for the past six years, apart from the window—which is still smashed, cold air blowing in.

Immediately everything feels different. The fuzziness in my head has cleared and the moonlight coming through the window seems somehow whiter and sharper than before. The shadows cast by the lines of the frame are crisper than I've ever seen.

I don't even feel tired. I feel awake and ready for a fight, but I don't know who with. Which is when I realize that I didn't just wake up again. Something woke me up, something *in the room*.

A *crisk-crack* noise.

I pull the duvet up tight under my chin.

Crisking and *cracking* noises made by things I can't see, things that just crawled onto the bed and up my leg. The floor is alive and crawling all over me—on my stomach, along my legs, across my arms, and up my neck. An army of bristly feet marches robotically over my chest. Tiny quivering jaws chewing air only millimetres above my skin.

Cockroaches.

A *lot* of cockroaches.

One of them crawls right up over my duvet, right onto my bare neck, and its feathery antennae brush my lips. *Are you ready?* says a voice. A deep voice.

I recognize that voice. The voice I last heard only as a metallic rattle, now getting clearer with every word.

Are you ready? it says again.

Am I ready for what?

I still can't believe I'm talking to them. Just like that.

He pauses and sighs. I didn't know cockroaches could sigh. For a moment I wonder if he's going to bite me. It would be a weird way to thank me for all that formula, I reckon.

Kester Jaynes! I thought the fool pigeons warned you we were coming. I'm not going to ask you again. Are you ready to leave?

I start to laugh.

Leave where—my bed? To sit on a chair covered with cockroaches? No, thanks!

A *crisk-crack* noise. The cockroach shakes his antennae impatiently.

No, to leave this place altogether.

He barks some orders to the others. A ripple moves across them, and there's some scurrying by the door. *Who are you? What are you doing?*

Silence! snaps the cockroach. *You will learn soon enough.*

His head turns to face the doorway, like he's waiting for something.

I follow his gaze to the thin line of light underneath the steel door. There are the outlines of roaches coming and going underneath, and then they are passing an object along, from one to another, an object about the size of each insect: a white plastic rectangle. It comes closer and closer to us over the sea of shells until I see what it is.

A keycard—the one normally dangling from the belt of the snoring Warden outside.

Now I sit up, and some of the roaches tumble off the bed.

But the one I fed in the Yard remains where he is on my chest. They pass the card up the line until it reaches him, and with his jaws he carefully lays it down on my stomach.

A keycard covered in roach spit. I wipe it on my sleeve and pick it up, turning it over in the blue moonlight.

One swipe and the door is open—but then where? The cockroach is just staring at me. Not that he has eyes I can see. But I can feel him scanning me, looking for something.

Come with us now, Kester Jaynes. Or rot here forever. The choice is yours.

I must sit there for only a few seconds or less, staring at the keycard in my hand, but it feels like hours. The cockroach is bristling mad to get going and taps me with his jaws again.

Like a switch has gone on inside me, a switch that I didn't flick, I reach under the bed and pull on my sneakers. Then I take them off, shake out the cockroaches, and start again. Walking over to the cupboard, trying very hard to not tread on any insects—and it is very hard—I get out my things.

My only things.

(1) Red Spectrum Hall–issue anorak
(2) Striped Mum-and-Dad-issue scarf
(3) Green watch

Come on, come on! barks the cockroach.

I slip the watch on and fix the strap tight around my wrist.

One last look around the room, a deep breath—and I slide the keycard into the slot. The lights change, and with a soft hiss the door slides open.

I'm going home.

The cockroaches power into the corridor, filling the floor with a black flood of shells.

The Warden is fast asleep in his chair, his hands flopped in his lap, his fat chin tucked into his neck. The loop that once held the keycard dangles empty from his belt. Those cockroaches must have seriously strong jaws.

He mutters and stirs in his sleep, making me nervously step back. I begin to realize this could actually be dangerous, but as Mum would have said, "You've done it now."

There's a movement on my shoulder. I look down. *How did you get there? I didn't even—*

Hurry, says the cockroach. *Not all the men who guard this place will be as idle as him.*

In the ceiling above, the black ball begins to swivel towards us slowly.

In that case, I say, *we need to do something about that camera.*

The animal voice still sounds strange in my head.

The cockroach barks again and there's a flurry of noise at the other end of the corridor. The grey curtains covering the window dissolve into fragments and fly quietly towards us. It's only as they get closer that I realize they're not bits of curtain at all.

They're moths—lots of moths. Just like the one from my room.

I shrink back, but they're gone in a moment, flying up to the round camera swivelling in the ceiling. Locking their wings together, they swarm all over it till not one bit of shiny lens is left visible.

How did you . . . ? I start, but my arm is empty. The cockroach leader is already scuttling along the floor towards the lift, the others making way for him as he does. Just before he gets to the open doors, he turns around and rears up, snapping at me.

What are you waiting for? Quick march!

First I feed him, and now he's giving me orders. Climbing into the lift, I hold out my hand and the cockroach clambers into it. I bring him up to eye level and examine the insect again, looking at the white stripes across his back.

I'm going to call you the General, I say.

If you wish, he replies.

Do you not have a name?

His antennae flick quickly.

Just because you can speak our tongue, it does not mean you understand all our ways. Now, are you going to make this cage move or are we just going to sit here and wait for that oaf to wake up?

What floor? I ask.

The ground! And he rattles off my hand onto the floor, as if that is the most normal thing for a cockroach to say. As if it's normal for cockroaches to speak, anyway. I bang the green button on the side panel, and the lift doors slam shut.

Slowly we begin to clang our way down. Beneath the drone of the lift there's a really tense silence. I fiddle with my watch. The General eyes it suspiciously.

What is that magical device?

I'll show you.

I think I still remember which button activates the camera. Angling my wrist at the cockroach, there's a soft whirr and a flash, bouncing off the glass walls. The General flicks his head away from the sudden bright light, and all of the roaches sweep into the corner.

Was that entirely necessary? he asks.

I'm just chuffed the camera still works. I look at the picture. If you can call an out-of-focus shot of a blurred cockroach, turned half-white by the flash, a picture.

Everything is so quiet—no alarms, nothing. Perhaps it's too quiet. I realize exactly what I should have asked him only when we hit the ground with a bump and the roaches all swirl crazily around the floor.

Open the doors, please, he commands.

My hand hovers over the buttons. *Wait—tell me how we're getting out of here first.*

You shall discover in good time.

I'm not going unless you tell me.

He stamps several of his feet.

It is not permitted. You must have faith in us. We have come to take you from this place.

Not until you tell me how.

You're behaving like a child!

Maybe that's because I am one!

The General looks like he's ready to nip me on the ankle.

And perhaps it is time you stopped being one. Now. Open. The. Doors!

I look at him. And at the rest of his roach army, on the floor, on the walls, all over the doors, their antennae quivering, waiting—one against thousands, I guess. I press the button.

The doors slide open and I follow the cockroaches out into the main hall.

A red light flashes on the wall, and a whooping siren echoes in our ears. The Warden must have woken up. I can hear shouts and boots thundering towards us.

Quickly! urges the General as we scramble out towards the Yard. I have to run as fast as I can to keep up with the insects scurrying ahead. We hurry through the darkness, trying as best we can to avoid the roaming searchlights. The alarm, much louder out here, shudders in my head. I follow the insects round to my corner, where I first heard the cockroach. They start to disappear, streaming straight into the drain, like it's swallowing them up.

Chop, chop! says the General, suddenly on my arm. I've never looked at the drain properly before now. It's a badly dug hole in the ground—not a me-sized hole: an insect-sized hole.

You are joking, right?

It's our only way out.

I kneel down and the cockroach jumps off my arm. I feel the edges. Perhaps if I could make them a bit wider . . .

You have to hurry.

I kick at the sides of the hole, and some earth tumbles down on top of the stream of roaches still pouring in.

Hey—look out! calls a roach voice from down below.

Sitting on the side, I try to get my legs in. It's a very tight fit, but with a bit of pushing I manage it as far as my waist. I can't see what lies below, or feel anything except my legs thrashing about in empty air. The stink coming up from the pipe below is something else.

The General is not being helpful.

We thought you were thinner.

I place my hands against the sides and push as hard as I can, my nails digging into the muddy ground around the hole. But I don't move at all.

You have to get into the tunnel. Otherwise our plan will not work.

Do you have a Plan B?

He cocks his head and chews for a moment.

What's a Plan B?

I shake my head and keep on pushing.

"JAYNES!"

Five Wardens skid to a halt in a circle around me, torches flying. Gloved hands grab me by the wrist, and the Wardens grunt buckets of sweat trying to heave me out. I kick my legs one last time, and chunks of earth tumble away into the tunnel below, with me following, slipping out of the Wardens' hands like a bar of soap and through the hole, down into the dark below.

I land with a massive splash in a puddle.

There's a disco display of torch beams going on over my head, but the Wardens can't get down. "Come on!" says one of them, and then I hear their boots running overhead as their lights move away.

I'm in total darkness, with hundreds of cockroaches clicking and scratching around me. I start crawling after them. I wish I were brave, like a soldier walking through a minefield. Then maybe crawling through this tunnel— full of muddy water, cockroach slime, and something that smells really bad—would be easier.

I say "crawling," but actually it's more like swimming, the water is so deep. I didn't even know cockroaches could swim, and here they are paddling alongside me. They don't speak, not even to one another, or stop to rest, just keep on pushing forward. The Wardens' thumping feet have totally faded away now, and all I can hear is my own breath echoing off the wet walls and the occasional *crisk-crack* from a roach.

This tunnel isn't a smooth pipe. It's jagged and uneven, and I keep cutting my hands on the rocks. It might be my imagination, but the farther we go, the deeper the water seems to be getting.

As the water rises, I can feel the floor of rocks fall away from my feet, and I start to bump and scratch my head as the roof of the tunnel gets closer and closer. I'm working hard just to stay afloat.

Slowly and steadily, more and more water, tasting of soil and dishwater, starts to splash into my mouth as my arms grow tired.

Slow down! I call out into the blackness. *I can't keep up.*

There's no reply, just quiet splashing. Then, very faintly, some distance up ahead, I hear a deep voice, like the beat of a drum.

We must keep going. There is no time to lose.

But the ceiling of the tunnel has dropped down right in front of me. Tracing the outline of rock through the water with my hands, I try to search for the narrow layer of air between it and the water that they expect me to swim through.

Except there isn't one. The tunnel from here is completely *underwater*.

I take the deepest breath I've ever taken and plunge under the surface. I struggle to squeeze through the gap, my legs kick, and I feel the weed-covered walls of the tunnel draw closer and closer in.

Water goes up my nose, burning—the last drops of

oxygen leak out of my lungs. My chest wants to *explode*.

Panicking, I think I should go back, but it's too late.

I give one last feeble kick with my legs.

The tunnel of water breaks into a torrent, turning and tumbling me like I'm in a washing machine before finally spitting me out, bouncing and scraping against the edges of a filthy pipe, down some slippery rocks and onto a wet patch of grass.

I can see stars.

I mean, not cartoon stars around my head, but actual stars in the sky. My chest heaving, I fight to catch my breath, turn onto my belly, and cough up some water. As I raise myself onto my elbows, a light shines straight into my eyes, and beneath that I can just make out a pair of feet.

A grimy pair of feet, in sandals.

Doctor Fredericks stands in front of a line of Wardens. Behind them, the curved glass of the Hall, lit up with searchlights. We're outside, in the Quarantine Zone. But no one's wearing a suit or a mask. There's no air-con, no special glass roof, no electric doors sealing us in. We're just out here, in the wet and the wild, where the red-eye rules.

I turn around to see what lies behind, although I already know.

The small patch of grass slopes down towards the edge of the cliff, beyond which is nothing but rocks, sea, and big, big trouble.

His glasses speckled with rain, Doctor Fredericks takes a step towards me, holding a syringe in his hand.

"One little prick!" he shouts, to be heard above the gale blowing around our heads. "One little p-p-prick and we'll, ah, put this unfortunate episode behind us!"

This is it, I say to myself. There's only one way out. And it looks a very long way down.

The General trots up my arm, out of nowhere, and into my anorak pocket. *You think we haven't planned this down to the last detail?* he barks. *No time to explain. Just jump whenever you're ready.*

Doctor Fredericks takes another step towards me.

I take a step back, towards the edge of the cliff, carefully balancing with my arms outstretched.

"Careful there, young lad, we don't want an, um, unfortunate accident now, do we?"

I look up at Spectrum Hall, the lights crisscrossing through the upside-down tinted-glass boat. A breeze of wet spray flicks the back of my neck from the sea below.

Whenever you're ready, says the General. *You have to trust us.*

I close my eyes and take one step back. Then two steps.

"K-k-kester," says the Doctor. "Look—I'll even put this down. Let's talk. I'll explain everything." He places the syringe on the ground between us. "P-p-please."

I smile. I got the Doctor to say please. It was worth it for that, if nothing else.

I take a last step back, and as he lunges for my legs, crying out—

I fall back into the air.

But I don't fall onto rocks and sea.

Hooks in the air catch me—moving, flying hooks—the beaks and claws of a hundred pigeons. The ones from my room, grey and one white. They really hurt, grabbing not just at my clothes, my soaking anorak and scarf, but my hair, the skin on my hands, even my ears.

At first we sink down, the pigeons straining with my weight, the icy spray of the waves flicking at my ankles, but then slowly, surely, they begin to flap up into the sky, pulling us farther and farther away from the rocks, the sea, and Spectrum Hall.

Wind and water whip around us, lashing at my face— weather. Seeing it out of my window was one thing, feeling and tasting it is very different—I try to twist away, but it's coming from all sides—impossible to avoid.

There's a scrabbling inside my jacket, and the General sticks his head out. *Look,* he says proudly.

I glance back at the clifftop and see the other cockroaches swarming over Doctor Fredericks and the Wardens, pouring out of the ground and up their trousers, making them jump and wriggle and yell—but then I can't see any more, as the pigeons wheel me sharply round and begin to fly north from the Hall.

Hey! I shout up. *That's not the way home!*

The birds don't say anything, but just flap their wings even harder.

I thought you were taking me home!

There's no reply, not even a squeak from the white pigeon.

I twist my head to see the lights of Spectrum Hall dwindling to a faint glow on the horizon behind us. But we're going farther north, not south. We're flying away from Premium. I jerk my arms, trying to turn the birds around. *You said you were getting me out of this place. I want you to take me home, right now!*

Take my advice, soldier, says the General firmly from my pocket. *Stop struggling and get some sleep while you can. We have a long journey ahead.*

Despite myself, I feel my eyes grow heavy and part of me wants to sleep, but I don't dare. Every time I start to drift off, a gust of freezing wind stings me awake.

And besides, there's so much to see, looking down between my feet.

We're flying right over the countryside, over places I have never seen before. Places no one is allowed in—the Quarantine Zone. Miles and miles of deserted open country shut down by Facto, to contain the red-eye and stop it from spreading to the cities—nine years ago now.

At Spectrum Hall, there were rumours of outsiders. People who didn't believe the warnings, people who took their own chances with the red-eye and tried to forage what food was left behind after the animals went.

But if such people exist, there is no sign of them from up here.

Everything is so dark. No lights from houses, villages, or towns—just the faint outlines of empty buildings here and there in the moonlight, like scattered boulders. Miles and miles of rocky shores and clifftops, their jagged edges only just visible. Directly beneath us, the only signs of life are buoys tossing about on the dark waves below, their orange lights blinking.

Once, far off in the distance, we see the white glow of a city. Factorium-run, disease- and animal-free, beaming rays of light into the night from their glass skyscrapers. From here the towers look like glowing white crystals reaching up into the stars.

Four great cities, built to contain the world's refugees. Our home—Premium, the city of the south and the largest, divided in half by the River Ams. A coastal city of the west, Portus, and the industrial city of the east, Carbo. This must be the city of the north, the city built among cold peaks and steep valleys—Mons.

The four cities that grew and spread and spread until, on the satellite maps, all that was left of the countryside was just a narrow strip of green enclosed by big blotches of thermal reds and yellows.

I try and swing my legs towards the distant city glow to see if I can steer the birds—but it only seems to make them fly faster and harder in the opposite direction. Farther and farther we fly, till it feels like I will never touch solid land again, as we head—

Straight into a cloud.

As if someone turned out the lights, I can't see a thing anymore. Water and dust clog my eyes and nose, making it hard to breathe, and my clothes—which had begun to dry out after the tunnel—are instantly drenched again.

When I look up, even the birds are hard to see through the fog—

On and on the clouds go, leaving me gasping for air—

The dust choking and filling my throat, as everything grows thicker and greyer—

And then black.

I snap open my eyes, shuddering and staring wildly around.

I have no idea where we are, or how long we have been flying for. I must have been asleep.

Any clouds are long behind us. There's a pink light on the horizon that woke me up, filling and warming the sky, showing the masses of green weed that cover the clifftops below. The sea beneath us sounds louder in the light some-how, roaring and crashing against the rocks.

It feels like we're in a different land altogether, but I don't think we are. We're just right at the end of the country. Right on the edge of the Quarantine Zone, on the tip of the Island, surrounded by the world's ocean, the huge sea that now covers most of the planet.

Finally we begin to turn back towards this deserted land, dropping lower in the sky as we do.

The air rushes faster and faster past my face. Now we're flying over moors, over an old house, with half its roof missing—

A bridge with chunks blown clean out of it, like bites. I grab a glimpse of more ruined buildings with no back wall, yellow flowers sprouting out of the empty windows—

The countryside. Deserted and no longer open to humans.

And I'm heading straight for it.

PART 2

WHAT IS THIS PLACE?

Flying lower and lower all the time now, so my feet scrape an old wire fence, covered with red-and-white signs, which we pass too quickly to read. And then we're over a circle of trees, flying very fast now, the treetops catching the soles of my shoes, and I can see water—

And then we're falling, falling out of the sky.

We crash onto the ground.

Imagine landing with a parachute that collapses all over you, your insides jumping up into your head as you hit the wet earth, while you can't see anything because of the giant tent you're under—a giant tent of oily feathers and claws that yanks itself free and flaps back off into the sky.

Every bit of me is aching. They pulled my hair, they tore my clothes, they pinched my skin, but they got me here. Brushing feathers off my face and grit out of my streaming eyes, and untangling myself from my scarf, I look around.

Until I went to Spectrum Hall, I'd never even left Premium. And I never left the Hall till now.

I have never seen anywhere like this before.

It certainly isn't anything like home. There's a massive pond, more like a lake, with only tiny spots of sun able to squeeze through the leaves above, making the water glitter. Silvery trees line the edge, with ferns and reeds clustered around their base. Not trees I've ever seen before. Everything looks all . . . old. Proper old, in fact. And—I don't want to say the word, but there's no one here to tease me for saying it—it looks beautiful.

There are no beeping doors, no shouts in the Yard, and no spluttering Doctor. I can hear my own thoughts bouncing off the logs and the still surface of the water. They aren't all good ones. I look at the pigeons quietly resting in the treetops above my head, their heads tucked into their wings.

Where are we? What are we doing here?

They don't answer. Instead the General clambers out of my jacket pocket and down my leg onto the ground. *The first part of our plan is successfully achieved,* he announces, and then, as he darts under the nearest rock—*With flying colours, I might add. By the Order of Cockroach Merit, I am now awarding myself a long afternoon nap.*

Fine, I think to myself—suit yourself. I've got other things to worry about.

First, I stink. That tunnel was not good. There are dirty

splodges all over my red anorak, making me look like a ladybird. My sweatpants are soaking and my striped scarf is stiff with encrusted yuck.

The sun is out, though. I look at the lake.

I can't help but wonder what else might be in there, and remember the pictures we all watched on the news of dead fish floating in the water, piling up in rotten heaps on the banks of rivers. I don't want to get the red-eye. But this isn't a river. This is a lake, hidden behind trees, far from any-where. The animals went years ago. It must be safe by now, whatever Facto says.

Yanking off my jacket and sweatpants, I step along the boggy shore, splashing down into the shallows with my clothes bundled in my arms, trying not to slip or step on a sharp rock.

The water's dark. I start to wade in quickly, taking deep breaths to fight off the cold.

The farther I go in, the darker and deeper it gets.

I look down at my bare feet, only just visible through the murk, and start to imagine dead fish rising suddenly to the top in an explosion of bubbles, their lifeless red eyes rolling at me. Glancing over my shoulder, I see that the pigeons are watching me intensely. I've probably never washed myself so quickly, scooping up handfuls of water as fast as I can over my head, relieved there aren't dozens of diseased fish in each one, before giving my clothes a quick soak and wad-ing noisily back to the shore.

The birds are curious. *What made you hurry?*

Clutching my dripping clothes in front of me, I say, *I thought . . . I thought there might be infected fish in there.*

But there are no fish left. Not in this lake, not anywhere.

They sound so sad. Then the white pigeon hops down from his tree, strutting about on pink claws, his little head bobbing up and down. In daylight I can now see that the feathers on his scalp are skew-whiff, like he just got out of pigeon-bed.

Yeah, he sneers, *no fish in this cake, stupid.*

The others coo, hiding him from me with their wings, like he embarrasses them—but he's right. I do feel stupid. Naked and stupid.

Why don't you tell me what's going on, instead of laughing at me? You brought me all the way out here. Why don't you do something useful? Like take me home!

But before I even reach the end of my sentence, I discover I'm talking to nobody. They've all clapped off into the air. There's a distant flapping, and then nothing.

General? I say, but the only reply I get is some loud snores coming from under a rock.

As the birds all disappear I notice how knackered I am as well. I badly want to lie down. Anywhere would do right now.

Just by the edge of the water there's a large rock with a flat top. Its size is ideal for drying wet clothes on, and a shaft of sunlight makes it look as white as a sheet. Sunlight like I never saw at the Hall.

I've never slept outside before. I just tell myself that there are no animals left, so it will be fine. Varmints can't give you the virus yet, and besides—it's almost comfortable. It's definitely *very* warm and *very* quiet.

I can feel my eyes slowly closing, and I'm just drifting off to sleep when something makes me sit bolt upright. Wide-eyed, I look around, but the water is as calm and steady as it was before. There are no floating, swollen fish. There are only the pigeons, who have returned and are sitting on the tufts of grass around the big white boulder, pecking about beneath it. They make me feel safe for a moment, before I remember that they brought me *here* rather than taking me home.

You snore more than your guard did, soldier, says a snarky voice in my lap.

Like you can talk! I want to say back, but I don't. Instead I brush the General away without even replying, and am about to lie down again when a rock tumbles and crashes out of the trees into the bog.

Not a big rock.

But a rock just big enough to get knocked by something moving through the silver trees. A rock followed by a little avalanche of pebbles hissing down through the ferns in between.

There's someone in the forest. Someone—or something— heading our way.

The pigeons flurry up into the branches, and the General scurries under my boulder while I roll off it, grabbing my clothes. Crouching down, I peer over the top.

The intruder suddenly breaks through the undergrowth and emerges into the light. It's not a person. It's not meant to exist. It's meant to be dead. Only it's here, close enough for me to see its blinking eyes and four tall, unsteady legs. The fur on its back, the soft ears—it can't be, except it is.

An animal. A living, breathing one.

Whatever he is, he's certainly not a very big one. In fact, he seems more nervous than we are, looking warily about before trotting farther down the slope towards the water's edge. He stumbles into the swamp and topples over onto his side with a soft splash. Then he hauls himself up and continues before coming to a jerky stop about a hundred metres away from us. He sniffs the air and twitches his ears, like he's waiting.

The first other living creature I have ever seen for real that doesn't live under a rock or feed off our rubbish. The General emerges from under his rock and perches on top of it.

Look at him, General! I whisper, pointing at the animal by the lake. *A baby horse!*

Not quite, soldier, he hisses. *It's a deer, and it's a she.*

Soon another one joins the lonely limping she-deer, edging its way around the water's edge. Before long the shores of the lake are alive with deer, a shuffling, manky line of furry red-brown backs. I can't see any red eyes, there is no wind, and they are quite far away, but I put my hand over my mouth just in case they are infected. As if they can tell, they stiffen as one, looking up—and I dive back down behind the rock. They're not looking at me, though; they're looking at the other creatures crashing towards us through the trees. My first impulse is to run, but I can't take my eyes off the new arrivals. A whole family, it looks like, of creatures with black-and-white striped heads and pale pink snouts, blinking in the bright light.

Weasels!

No, badgers. The General is beginning to sound genuinely cross with me. Like I'm meant to be an encyclopedia.

The badgers join the red-brown line, and at first some of the deer skid and stumble away, as if they're scared of them—but the badgers don't attack. They just snuffle along the shore, perhaps looking for food that isn't there.

Now it's not just them, either. The whole shoreline as far as I can see is starting to fill up with animals. There are large white rabbits hopping towards us from the other end of the lake. *Hares, actually,* the General chips in before I can even say anything.

Through a gap in the branches, up in the sky above I see other birds join the pigeons. The biggest, with their wings blocking out the sun as they fly past it, must be golden eagles, I reckon—even I know that much. There are also some noisy birds, which I think are seagulls, as well as some funny-looking blue-and-grey crows and some little fat birds that look like brown tennis balls. I even see what looks like a bat dangling from a tree, but I can't be sure.

Nearer to the ground, there are butterflies, bees, and dragonflies buzzing over the reeds in the water. A line of reddish ants marches out from under a log. This whole place, which a moment ago seemed dead and empty, has become as busy and as noisy as the Yard at feeding time.

A badger says to another, *It will never hold, it's unnatural* —and I wonder what *it* is.

More and more animals keep joining the crowd. There are goats with twisted horns, scruffy-looking cats that are definitely bigger than any pet I ever heard of, and I think I might have even spotted a snake with a zigzag pattern winding its way between the mass of legs and tails. But they all have one thing in common.

They're alive.

Living animals, right in front of me, and not a red eye to be seen.

I look at my watch. The screen is cracked and smeared with mud from the tunnel, but it still works. Hiding behind my boulder, I take as many pictures as I can of all the different creatures. Dad is never going to believe this. I only stop pointing and clicking when I feel the pigeons gathering behind me, cooing crossly.

You have to tell me properly now, I say to them. *What is this place?*

You are in the last place we have left, says an old voice.

That didn't sound like the pigeons, or the General. It sounded more like my grandad.

No human has been here since we first discovered it. You are the first.

I turn around to see a deer much bigger than any of the others.

Our stag, whispers the General.

A stag. I had heard of them, but to see a real one— enormous, dark brown, right in front of me . . . He is twice the height of any other animal here, with wide horns, jabbing and curving in all different directions. He takes a few steps towards me and all the other creatures part to make way for him, like he's the king.

He lowers his head. I flinch back against the rock, trying to not breathe or touch him. But he doesn't gore me. He sniffs me. He sniffs my hair and face and hands, all over, inhaling every inch. When he next speaks, his voice is soft.

This old stag humbly asks for your forgiveness, but I am the one who summoned you here. I sent the pigeons to help the cockroach.

I don't understand—why? I mean, how are you even still— But I can't say the word. It sounds wrong.

The stag raises himself to his full height once more. It's hard to read his face. I can't tell if he's smiling or frowning.

Alive? Look around you, man-child. Tell me what you see.

A lake, a load of animals— I swallow, not daring to look him in the eye. The next words come out in a whisper. *Animals that should be dead.*

He makes a noise at the back of his throat, part cough, part chuckle, and looks out over the crowd. *Yes, we should be. But we are not. At least, not yet.* He tosses his head towards the forest we just flew over, the horns catching the sun. His words are strange and old-fashioned, almost like he's speaking a different language. *I am the Wildness, and these creatures are my wild, the last such gathering of animals left alive. Once we roamed far and wide for many strides all over this island—until your sickness came and destroyed so many. The creatures you see before you are the last who remain, each sent by their kind to form this wild and keep their blood alive, in response to my call. I led us as far north as the ground went, and found this hide-all—a Ring of Trees, free from humans and disease. It is all we have left. We are the last. The last wild.* He pauses and must see the expression on my face. *You are surprised, I think, to hear me call it your sickness?*

Right now that's the least of my worries. *I'm surprised you brought me here. I thought the birds were going to take me home.*

Fear not—we do not expect you to stay here. Even if you desired so, we would not permit it. No, the reason I have had you brought to us will soon be plain to see. He looks down at the ground. *We thought we had found safety here, we thought we were protected—but we were wrong.*

I get a bad feeling in the bottom of my stomach and step back.

The stag bellows deep from his chest. A barking roar, which sounds half like he's in pain, half like he's super-angry. This close up, it's definitely deafening. His teeth are all cracked and worn down, with scraps of twig stuck between them.

In response to his bark there's a kerfuffle of barging and pushing among the crowd of animals, as they make way for some new arrivals. Another deer, a badger, a goat, and a scruffy black bird with huge wings dragging along the ground line up in front of the stag, their heads bowed—like they're embarrassed about something. I hadn't noticed these ones before; it's like they were hiding at the back of the crowd, out of sight. He stalks up to them, touches each one of them gently with his snout, and turns back to me.

Two moons ago, a fierce wind blew in what we feared the most.

I don't want to know. I don't want to look.

You have nothing to fear. Please—come.

I put my sleeve over my nose and mouth, and edge round to the other side of the rock. I don't want to go any closer, and I don't need to. I'm not my dad, I'm no vet, but even I can see from here that these animals are not well. They aren't hanging their heads in shame, they're hanging their heads because they're weak and exhausted. I thought the first deer I saw looked a bit skinny, but these poor things have fur and feathers coming out in great clumps. The skin underneath looks yellow and flaky, bones pressing against it.

Look closer still, commands the stag in his craggy voice. *You cannot catch it from looking.* Still barely daring to breathe, I go a few steps nearer. As I do, they all look up—the deer, the badger, the goat, and the bedraggled black bird. I stop dead in my tracks as I see their eyes.

The eyes that are all red—bright red and burning with light.

Our name for it is the berry-eye, says the stag. *The berry eyes are themselves the final mark before a great heat savages them from within. These ones do not have long. The plague moves from beast to beast with the greatest of ease. No water, no leaf, no amount of rest can bring relief.*

As if the virus itself is listening, the she-deer standing in front of him is racked by a huge cough, her skinny body spasming and shuddering before her legs give way and she collapses onto the ground. The other deer crowd round, nudging her back up again while the stag watches.

It is a mystery to us in every way—but we cannot allow it to spread further. After these have gone, then it will be the turn of others, and then we will all be gone. This sickness will not stop until it has driven us from the earth, and then— He stops abruptly, like he was going to say something else, but he doesn't. He just looks up at the sky through the trees. Beyond their leaves are glimpses of the first bright sky I have seen for years, the first sky filled with sunlight rather than dark clouds.

I can't believe he's saying that they're going to die right in front of them, but the infected animals don't even blink. I take a step back.

Why are you showing me? What do you expect me to do about it?

The words sound harder outside my head than they did inside, but I didn't mean them to. The stag shakes his head, like he's astonished. A murmur runs through the crowd.

Why do you think, young human? Because you can help us—to find a cure.

But I'm just a boy. I mean, the best scientists in the world, they've tried—

You are a boy who can hear us and speak for us. You can tell your fellow men that the last wild still lives and bring us a cure—a special cure from your human magic.

Human magic that has failed so far.

But I can't. Talk to other humans, I mean.

The human has many ways of making himself understood, of that I am sure. The stag bends his head and front legs, like he's bowing. *But we only have you.*

I have one last try. *I still don't understand why you chose me.*

You spoke to us. You spoke to the moth, the cockroach. You have the gift of the voice.

I shake my head. That's what the pigeons said in my room, but I don't have any gift. Apart from getting farther and farther away from home, it seems.

The stag fixes me squarely in the eye. *When we heard that there was a boy who tried to talk to us, we decided to summon you here.*

I wasn't trying to talk to them. I was . . . The words falter in my head before they are out as I look at the last animals left in the world, led by a great stag—all waiting on me.

He repeats himself one more time. *The question is, now you are here—will you help us?*

I look around at the rock behind me, the dark water beyond, the silver trees stretching for miles around its edge. The middle of nowhere, full of animals with the red-eye, animals who will die if I don't help them. The last animals ever. A wild, he called them.

I think. I think some more.

There is one small chance. So small—but it is the only chance they have. I take a step towards the stag and I say it. *I don't have the magic to find a cure for the berry-eye.* The animals cry out in despair. *But my father is a famous scientist—a human magician who works with animals. He might be able to help.*

A buzz of chatter sweeps through the wild. The stag quiets them down and turns to me again.

You are sure of this? You are sure your father's magic can cure the berry-eye?

No, I'm not. Six years have passed, and I have heard nothing. People still live in cities under glass roofs, eating Facto-made formula. The countryside is still a quarantine zone, and as I can see right in front of me, the virus is still very much raging. But maybe, in six years, Dad has made some progress. I just nod, and to my surprise the animals scatter. The stag barks again. But they don't listen. They're panicking, stampeding. The sound of animals of all kinds trampling and splashing across the shore fills the air. What did I say? The stag lowers his head and growls, like he's going to charge at me.

Kester! call all the pigeons from above. *Look out!* It's too late.

A creature thumps straight into me from behind, sending me flying to the ground, the wind knocked clean out of my chest so I can barely breathe. I try to move, but heavy sharp claws are pressing into my back. There's a smell of rotten meat. Just behind my ear, a low, hoarse voice whispers with a hiss—

Who did this? Who let a human into the Ring of Trees?

I gasp for air. The weight crushes me farther and farther into the pulpy ground.

Let the man-child go, orders the stag. The creature just presses his heavy foot farther down onto my back, growling deep in his throat. I try to twist my head round and catch a glimpse of a long snout, the black lips pulled back over the teeth.

No human may enter the Ring of Trees, it snarls. A wet nose runs all over my back and neck, snuffling and sucking. *There is no point talking to this thing.* Then another hissing breath. *We must destroy it.*

My head pressed into the mulch, all I can see out of the corner of my eye is the stag bowing his huge head of horns.

Noble guardian—the blame lies with me. I summoned the man-child here. We discovered he had the voice. I sent the pigeons and the cockroaches to collect him. He will go to the humans and tell them that the last wild still lives. That it is not too late to save us. His father is a great human who will deliver a magic cure.

The beast on my back grunts and sniffs me once more. *No human has ever been allowed within the Ring of Trees since we first arrived. It is only our vigilance that has kept us alive till now. We are the guardians charged with keeping this wild safe—you are only its leader.*

He grinds his paw deeper down into my back. I want to tell him that the berry-eye arrived before I did, and I try to speak, but nothing comes out.

What if the human in question has come to help us? asks the stag.

The only help a human can ever offer us will be the kind that aids our own destruction.

The stag peers down at me, trapped face down on the ground. I'm choking on moss and mud. He paces around for a moment, like he's thinking, before saying to the beast—

Very well—then I will fight you for him.

The snouted creature heaves his body round and gives a high-pitched howl. Other whines come back at him from all sides. There are more of these things, whatever they are.

Then the thing lifts his foot off me and air rushes back into my lungs. I manage to crawl out of the light to the edge of the woods. My sight slowly swims back to normal, everything coming into focus. I can just make out the stag to my right, pawing the ground, his head lowered. Behind him, the last wild huddles together for safety, reaching far back along the shore.

I can see why they are scared of the thing that knocked me to the ground, the thing about to take on the stag. He's the leader of a seven-strong pack, animals I have only ever seen once before, on a screen in Dad's lab. I take a quick picture of them with my watch, just to be sure I'm not dreaming.

Wolves—they're definitely wolves.

Their fur is greyish brown. They have long snouts and sharp teeth and even sharper-looking claws on their giant padded feet. The largest one, the one who jumped me, has grizzled fur around his jaw. It's a miracle he didn't snap me in half.

The youngest of the pack, a cub about half the size of the others, looks ready to take us all on and win. A pink tongue darts out between his bared teeth, under his velvety black muzzle.

He shouts angrily, his eyes flashing straight at me. *You will see! You cannot win against my father, he is the best fighter in the whole world!* He thinks for a moment. *And you smell strange!*

Some of the watching animals titter, but the grizzled wolf snaps at the cub to be quiet and then pulls back on his haunches, ears pointed, hackles raised and teeth bared. He growls, a deep, shuddering sound. Just a few metres in front of him, the stag paws the earth and lowers his head.

There's a *flitter-flutter* behind me and I turn to see the pigeons, who have dropped down into the grass behind.

Can't you stop this? I ask them.

It is the animal way.

But what about the berry-eye—the reason you brought me here? What about me? What will happen if the stag loses?

Then you will belong to the wolf.

I stagger up. My voice sounds light and faraway, like it's coming out of a hole in the ground. I wave woozily at the stag.

Stop—listen to me. You have to stop this.

He mutters under his breath. *Do not interfere in our affairs. This is our custom.*

Suddenly the wolf launches himself at the stag with a

roar that must have been heard all the way to Spectrum Hall. The stag tosses his horns and deflects him, but an outstretched paw catches his rear flank, scoring a long and glistening red gash down the side. He cries out in pain.

The grizzled wolf, knocked about but not down, snarls and prepares for his next blow.

I have to do something. The last animals in the whole world. I have to take them to Dad.

I take a few dizzy steps forward. From the grass the pigeons coo with worry.

Please don't do anything you might regret, Kester!

Kester! I don't regret anything! shouts the white pigeon proudly.

The stag runs for a second time at the wolf, who lunges right back, drawing blood from his neck. The clunk of stag horns against the thick muscle of the wolf sounds like a sword hitting a wooden block.

The other members of the wolf's pack start to draw in. I notice the young cub hang back, as if he is uncertain what to do, his green eyes flicking anxiously from me to the stag and to his father and back.

Maybe the pigeons are right, but it's either "Do something you might regret" time or "Get torn apart limb from limb" time.

I stand up and walk between them. There are gasps from the animal audience.

The grizzled wolf roars, *Get out of the way, human, or face your fate now!*

The stag, even though he's wounded, nods slowly. *Have faith in me, boy. Let us settle this our way.*

No! Look at yourselves. Look at what you're doing. Look at all these sick animals.

I point to the group of moulting creatures watching us from a distance. The gaggle of cowering badgers, shivering deer, and eagles with drooping necks.

Look at them! They need your help. What good does it do if you tear each other apart?

The wolf stalks towards me. I find myself staring him right in the mouth. A mouth curled up with hate.

You brought about this disease, human. He doesn't know that; no one knows how the disease started. *That is all humans bring with them: disease and death. So first I will destroy the traitor who brought you here. It is the duty of a Wildness only to lead his wild to safety, not invite intruders in.* He licks his lips with a purple tongue. *And then we will destroy you.*

The other six wolves crowd behind him in a semicircle, growling and flashing their teeth.

But what if the human magic could help? asks the stag.

Lies! Lies and trickery! Like this human child talking in our common tongue! The wolf spits. *You are just the leader, not the guardian! Wolves are and always have been responsible for a wild's protection from the outside world, by common consent of this one and many wilds before it.*

Murmurs ripple through the crowd.

Then why have you not protected us from the berry-eye? calls out a snake, his tongue flicking.

Yes! comes a cry from an owl in the treetops. *You cannot save us from that. Only the human magic can!*

The grizzled wolf turns on them all. *Silence! Where is your faith? We have protected you all till now, have we not? The natural order must be maintained, whatever the cost.*

The animals shuffle edgily. Then one voice rings out from the crowd, a high, weak voice—it's the young she-deer, the first one I saw come down to the lake.

You only want to keep us for your prey. You do not understand. This plague will kill all of us—and then where will your natural order be?

There is uproar. An oversized, scruffy cat shouts her down. *Have faith! Our guardians will protect us!* Some of the birds begin to wail. One of the wolf pack yells at them to be quiet, but they can't be calmed.

We are doomed! . . . What will become of our wild?

A boar trots up onto the white boulder behind me, his tusks bristling. *I have taken to the white rock. So hear me.*

The animals slowly shut up.

The boar looks out at them and continues. *The guardians are right! This human child cannot and should not help us. I for one do not believe the old dreams about the voice. The humans have been killing us and driving us from their land since they learnt to live apart. Why should they try to find a cure?*

The grizzled wolf gives a condescending smile to the boar.

But he has the voice! calls out another from the crowd. *The old dreams must be right.*

In among the cries and arguments, I barely hear the stag whispering in my head.

Jump on my back—now!

I don't take in what he says at first. I can't take my eyes off the wolf, who's turned his back to us, his hackles raised as far as they will go, trying to calm the animals down. The stag is insistent. His dark eyes flash and he kneels down in front of me.

Now, Kester! he says. *Now or never.*

Everything I've ever been taught about not touching animals is forgotten in an instant, and I haul myself onto his back, grabbing a tuft of fur between my hands. It's tangled with seeds and dried mud. I can smell the hot, sweet tang of blood from his injured leg.

Hold on! he warns.

The stag takes a breath and then, with a giant leap, jumps clean over the head of the grizzled wolf, landing with a leafy thump in the ferns on the other side. I half slide off his furred back, only just clinging on. The pigeons flock up from the ground into the sky.

Cowards! pipes up a voice from my jacket pocket. I look down to see two orange antennae curling out of it.

Stop them! roars the grizzled wolf from the shore. *Hunt them down!*

And the wolves, all seven of them, begin to run after us, their howls rising into the air.

I barely have time to pull myself back up before the stag is galloping away through the trees. He runs in big strides, and every time he leaps I rise in the air before coming down hard on his spine. The trees are narrow and close together, and the deer's horns are so wide I flinch as we scrape through. He weaves and turns, like he's following an invisible path through the undergrowth, sniffing the way—but all I can see are ferns, and all I can smell is fear.

Bravo! yells the General as we narrowly escape being whacked in the chest by a fallen trunk. *The chase is on! Full march ahead!*

Stay down! urges the stag. *Get as low as you can.*

There's a crashing behind us, the sound of breaking wood. I turn around and see the wolves spread out in a line, piling through the trees. The ground rises and falls beneath us. There's a snarl to my left—the grizzled wolf is running just behind us, not even out of breath—but laughing.

You know that if you desert your precious animals now, we will never allow you to return.

The stag ignores him and suddenly veers off to the right, jumping down into a huge ditch. Tricked, the wolf tries to do a sharp turn but slips in a pile of leaves and tumbles over before righting himself and pounding hard on our tail.

Fastest is not always best! jeers the General after him as we shoot away down the gully.

But with a triumphant snarl, the grizzled wolf skids to a halt and calls after us—

It does not matter. You cannot escape now.

We soon see why. The gully ahead is blocked by a wall of boulders covered in twisting creepers, looking like they've just been thrown there on top of one another. Six very hungry wolves are bearing down on us from behind. I can see the young cub yapping at their tails, his lips pulled back in rage. If I could just talk to him, perhaps I could . . .

But before I can say anything, the stag has begun to clamber up over the boulders, scraping his hoofs against the stones. He slips, he slides, his horns bash the side of the rocks, but with an extra kick we stumble to the top. He immediately trips over a knotted root crossing the rocks, hung with dead leaves, and I bang into his horns with a jolt.

We must be far away from the lake by now, but we're still surrounded by forest on all sides. The Ring of Trees.

The wolves can't climb up the boulders so easily. They keep leaping up and skidding off. I can hear them arguing about the best way up. Beneath me, the stag heaves for breath. Everything around us is silvery and soft, the light coming through the leaves in patches. Ahead of us are rows and rows of trees, like streets, all leading in different directions. I look at them, hoping to see the bright light of the outside world shining at the end of one, but they all seem to go on for miles.

Do you know the way out? I ask the stag as he stands surveying the corridors of green in front of us. There are more snarls and howls from below.

Our old deer walk-upons finish here. We have not been this close to the edge of the Ring since we came here. He turns his head towards me and I notice how deep and brown his eyes are. *No one has. Do you think your magic instrument could tell you?*

I have no idea what he's on about.

The coloured device you wear around your paw. He must mean my watch. Pressing the various buttons, I'm hoping a magic map of the forest will just appear. It doesn't. Only all the photos I've taken—of the General, the sick animals, the wolves.

Let us stand our ground and fight to the death! declares the cockroach from my pocket.

There's a sound of scrabbling very close behind us, followed by a husky howl.

Or, er, on second thought—perhaps you should use the magic green device, soldier, says the General. *And that's an order. You gave your word you would help us.*

I look at the watch, look at the photo of Mum, pretend to study it closely, and then . . . the strangest thing happens. The screen starts to shudder and shimmer, like a signal is being interrupted, and the photo I took of the General in the lift, perched on my hand and staring at me, reappears. Then the picture flickers and disappears again. I must have knocked the watch in the tunnel or somewhere and sent it haywire.

But it reminds me that the General is right. I said I would help them. They're looking to me. All I can think is—what would Dad do? What would Dad want me to do? Not let them down.

This way! I point straight ahead. Without another word the stag gallops straight on down the wide avenue of trees.

Faster! Faster! whoops the General.

I look over my shoulder. The line of trampled bushes behind us is empty. The stag leaps on.

Are you sure this is the way? he calls.

Yes, yes! I shout, caught up in the moment, the air rushing past my face.

In fact, the dark green of the tunnel of trees does seem to be lightening up ahead. The thorns and brambles criss-crossing our path like ropes seem to be curling back. Maybe I was actually right. Maybe I guessed our way out.

"Just say something," Dad used to say, "even if you don't know the answer . . . have a guess."

The air is getting lighter. I can feel a warm breeze. The

trees begin to fall away. And then with a short, sharp shout, the stag rears back, lifting his hoofs in the air like a bucking horse. I grab on to tufts of fur where I can, squeezing as tight as I can with my knees so I don't fall off.

He staggers and crashes back down to the ground. Pulling myself up, I can see why. The alleyway of trees has ended. But so has the ground. Behind us, a tangled mess of fallen trees and mangled undergrowth. In front of us, a leafy, thorny fringe marks a slab of sheer rock, falling hundreds of metres down to where a river roars over a bed of stones.

A twig snaps. Slowly I twist around.

There, approaching us through the shadows, is the semicircle of wolves. Slouched down low, the hunters approach us, balanced on the very edge of their world.

For a moment the only thing I can hear is the rush of water from far below, along with the blood rushing in my head. The leader of the wolves breaks the line and steps forward. There is still a growl to his voice, but his tone is softer.

Noble Wildness—my quarrel is not with you. Give up the human child and we shall let you return in peace. The stag doesn't reply at first. He stares straight ahead. His nostrils quiver. Puffy breaths curl out of them into the sky.

Guardian, you know that I am the last of my kind.

Yes, Wildness, this is why we shall let you live. Our duty is only to protect the last wild, to preserve the natural order.

The stag neatly turns so he is facing the dripping jaws

of the wolf pack. Even the half-sized cub looks like he could take a big chunk out of him. There is a new emotion in the stag's voice when he speaks, though—anger.

Yes, a natural order that suits you the most—to have us all at your disposal as your prey. But we now all face a far greater danger than you. That is why we have joined forces and sought human help.

The grizzled wolf shakes his muzzle gruffly.

We will survive this as we have other threats in the past. Why do you not have faith in the way of the wild?

You know as well as I that this danger is different from any that we have faced before. It will be the end of all of us unless we get help from the humans.

I do not want to destroy such a good and wise creature as yourself—the wolf braces his legs, as if getting ready to pounce—*but you give me no choice. Throw the child off and we shall let you go in peace.*

The stag takes a half step back towards the valley edge. His hoofs dislodge a couple of loose stones, which tumble noisily into the chasm below, their clatter echoing all around.

The wolf tries one last time. He sounds as if he is losing patience.

I will not tell you again, Wildness. Let beasts be beasts and men be men. That has always been our way. That is how we have survived until now.

And that time has passed, replies the stag, glancing up at the sky. He is about to say something else when there is a noisy scuffle in the trees above. We all look up. The grey pigeons burst through the branches in an explosion of leaves.

A way out! they sing excitedly. *We have found the way out beyond the trees.*

These trees are way out! says the white pigeon, arriving late behind them. *Beyond way out!*

They weren't cowards at all. They were looking.

Then everything happens quickly. The grizzled wolf leaps at us with a blasting roar. The stag leaps too. As he does, he tilts his head. With a sickening crunch, we collide in midair. Gored in his side by the stag's horns, the wolf yelps with pain. Too late to stop, he falls over the edge, slithering down the slope, flecking the white stones with bright red blood.

The stag doesn't pause. He leaps in a single move over the other wolves and ploughs on once again into the forest. I twist on his back and see the cub peering over the edge of the chasm, his tail between his legs.

Follow us, follow us, trill the birds, soaring on ahead.

The stag never falters, never tires, but keeps running, his breathing loud and strong. The pigeons keep on calling, occasionally looking back to check on us. The wolves don't give up either, panting and sweating with the effort, but always close behind.

Trust pigeons to lead us the long way out, grumbles the General from my pocket.

The light starts to change just up ahead. It slips from

grey to white. Cool air blows on my face. The last few trees are in sight, but I can feel the stag beginning to slow down. His back and sides are slippery with sweat, and even from on top I can sense his heart hammering away like a steam engine. Then, with one final leap, we break through the last line of trees.

Before us stands the wire fence that runs round the whole Ring, a jagged hole torn right through it, and beyond that—the edge of a moor.

I duck and the stag plunges through the hole. Then, heaving for breath, he skids to a halt immediately.

But the guardians? I'm convinced we're finally about to become their lunch.

See . . . for . . . yourself, he says between gulps of air. I look back.

The wolves are standing at the edge of the forest, only leaps behind, howling to the sky. They paw the ground and swipe chunks out of the earth with their claws—but they don't follow us.

Why?

They are the guardians. Animals who have sworn an oath to protect the wild against all intruders. They cannot pass beyond the Ring of Trees while the others still live within.

I look at them quickly, their green eyes flashing and tongues hanging out. The cub is there too, standing between the bigger ones. He catches my eye and holds it—but I look away. I'm not going to feel guilty about the grizzled wolf. He wanted me dead.

Instead I get my first proper look at the Ring from the outside.

The wild's guardians stare at us through a fence of rusting barbed wire, curving all the way round, as tall as the grey and whippy trees. Between the concrete posts that hold the fence up hangs a series of old, white wooden signs with red words painted on them. Half of the signs have rotted away with wind or rain, but there are enough of them left for me to make out a few letters:

EFENCE

IRING RANGE

EP OUT

Somehow I don't think it was just the guardians keeping humans out of the Ring of Trees.

And you—as their Wildness—will you be allowed to return?

We look behind us. The wolves have melted away and we are on our own once again. The shadows of the wood stretch out along the ground like crooked black fingers.

Certainly not. The wolves would tear me apart. You must lead us all to your father's magic. And then, spoken in a way that is impossible to argue with—*We must go on alone. We will form our own wild to save those we left behind.* He digs his hoofs into the ground. *They must be saved.*

I look out over the moors, shading my eyes. Inside the Ring everything looked all soft and blurry, but out here in the open the light is so clear, the edges so sharp, it kind of burns your eyes. We can't go back. Yet at the same time . . . I turn to the stag. *You have no idea. There are other humans out there, humans who will want you dead. They send out patrols. They kill anything that moves.*

Cullers. Former soldiers sent in the early days to try and stop the virus by slaughtering contaminated herds or packs. When that failed, their orders changed. They were told to kill anything non-human that moved—and they did.

I jump off the stag. *Stay here with your wild—let me go. I will make my own way home to my city and find you your cure.*

Even though I've no idea how to get there. The stag doesn't reply at first. Instead he straightens his long neck and gazes at the horizon. All I can see are miles and miles of empty moor stretching ahead, and then just beyond them, through a blue haze, the rocky tips of a mountain range—so much *outdoors*, like I've never seen before.

He looks like he's seeing something else, something far away, inside his mind.

The Great Open, he says at last. *We lost so many on this land as we made our way here. Some from the plague, others at the hands of those you describe. I made a promise in their memory. That I would keep those who survived the journey safe, as long as I had breath in my body.* He wheels about to face me. *And if that means I must carry you all the way into the heart of the human land itself— then so be it.*

The pigeons dance about in the sky like crazy, while the General clambers out of my pocket and with a flutter of his little wings buzzes onto the stag's horns.

That's the spirit, Stag! he chirps. *Let's see what you're really made of—stag or mouse!*

The deer growls angrily and shakes his head from side to side, trying to tip him off, but the General clings on.

They're both missing the point. I try one last time.

Stag, the Quarantine Zone—it's too dangerous. I'm not even allowed to be out here. I know it's a long way, but I'm small, I can hide, I'll find help—

I made a promise, says the stag bluntly, and lowers his horns at me. I'm not going to disagree with them. So I climb back onto him.

The General gives a cheer and scuttles up to the very

highest tip of the horns, shouting, in such a deep voice that the pigeons nearly fall out of the sky in surprise, *So be it—let the journey begin!*

Now then, says the stag to me, warmer than before, *where is this famous city of yours?*

Once again I realize I have no answer to his question. I don't even know where we are. But this time I'm not going to make the same mistake as in the Ring of Trees and just guess. I think of where we lived and what Dad taught me—before I got taken away.

On the tip of a map—in the south, I think.

Can you guide us south, birds? he calls out to the pigeons.

I doubt it's going to be that easy.

But they yell out, *It is enough!* before speeding off over the moors. Correction: the grey pigeons speed off over the moors away from the Ring; the white pigeon flaps up into the air and heads straight back towards the forest.

He realizes his mistake in time and spins around, going as fast as he can to catch up with the others, muttering to himself, *You say north, I'll fly north; you say south, I'll fly—*

North? suggests the stag as the little bird passes overhead.

I dig my knees in tight, and he sets off across the fields without another word. Just like that. The pigeons seemed to know automatically which way south is, and the stag only sniffed the air before following fast behind.

I've never seen the world from the back of a deer before.

The country is so smooth and wide, nothing but open land for miles. As the stag pounds across the ground, the pigeons fly above our heads, occasionally disappearing over the top of a hill in the distance.

Riding along, the animals tell me things I never knew before. The grey pigeons swoop down to tell me how they never forget a tree or a face, and the white pigeon tells me what a forgettable face I have. How they always know which way is north, south, east, or west. They don't even need to see the sun or the moon. The stag tells me about all the different scents he can smell: here was a fox a long time ago, these are old sheep walk-upons, and there is good grass for grazing over there. He uses his nose more than his eyes.

And what about me? I ask.

I don't follow, says the stag, sweeping down a grassy slope.

I mean, you can do all these things—that's what you do, you're animals. But how can I talk to you? I still don't understand.

Your voice is a gift, he says simply.

You keep saying that. It's not normal, though. How did it happen? How come I can talk to you and no one else can? I can't even talk to other people.

He suddenly stops on a hillock of reeds the colour of rusty metal, looking down at the valley below and sniffing the air. He doesn't answer my question.

Was it something I said? I ask the General.

But he doesn't reply either. He's following the gaze of

the stag, his antennae bristling. I can't see what they're looking at that's so special.

Stretching over the dip in between the hills are four crumbling walls, connected together to form a square. Each wall is made of huge jagged rocks, each one at least twice the size of me. To try and lift even just one would be impossible.

As the stag slowly approaches the first wall of heavy rocks, only loosely still held together, I can see dry and crusty layers of moss spread across the top, which the pigeons immediately settle on and start pecking at. The white pigeon joins them but loses his balance and tumbles over the other side in a cloud of feathers.

Look carefully, Kester, say the grey birds, gesturing with their wings at the walls. *This is the First Fold. It has been here since man first kept beasts as his own,* they sing together, strands of moss dangling from their beaks.

There is one small gap between the walls, marked by two slabs of stones jammed upright in the ground. Going closer, I can see that these stones are inscribed. Dotted lines, circles within circles, arrows and pointed letters, none of which makes any sense to me. And blowing in the wind, caught in a crack between two rocks, one fraying strand, damp and sour to smell—wool.

What have some old sheep walls got to do with my gift?

A storm cloud passes overhead, and for a moment we are in shadow. The grey birds have turned black and their eyes sparkle as they tell me.

Everything. The dream of your gift begins here.

Yes, says the white pigeon, clambering back onto the wall as the cloud moves on. *Here is your gift—some old sheep.*

The other birds peck at him crossly, knocking him off again. They're very solemn and serious when they turn back to me, though.

This is the very spot where man first surrounded sheep with walls of stone, so he could wear their wool and eat their young.

So? I shrug. *What's that got to do with anything?*

Do you not know the old dreams? they ask, sounding amazed.

Of course I don't.

They jump down off the top of the wall and beckon me to sit down. I find the driest patch of ground I can, leaning against the old stones to be out of the wind, and they gather around my feet in a circle.

Animals only believe in two things, they explain, *in calls and in dreams. Calls, which are*—they pause, as if trying to think of the right words—*well, you might think of them as songs. They are how beasts summon one another in a time of need, and how we let one another know our deepest feelings. The stag called the last wild together, and the cockroach's call first led us to Spectrum Hall—to you.*

I try to imagine the General singing. *And dreams?*

Dreams are our stories—how we learn about animals before us, dreams which have been passed down from beast to beast, since the very first to walk upon this land. And there is one dream we tell each other the most.*

What dream is that?

They hesitate, glancing at each other nervously, as if they shouldn't be discussing this.

Well, come on, I say. *You've got to tell me now.* The grey pigeons burst out, in a fluster—

It's yours.

I stare at them in confusion as the stag steps back from where he has been looking sharply up and down at the field beyond the Fold.

And you are not permitted to hear it, he snaps. *That is sacred animal knowledge, for animals alone. Perhaps one day—*

I've had about enough of their secrets and strange ways. *You have to tell me something! I'm the one trying to help you. Like—why do you keep looking at the sky, for example?*

He sighs and looks back up at the gathering clouds. *Whenever an animal dies, wherever we are, we shall know, because the sky weeps tears,* he says. Every time an animal dies, it rains. I never knew. It certainly explains why the weather has been so terrible for the last six years. *And when the last animal on the earth dies, the dream tells us that there will be the storm of storms, and—* The stag stops suddenly, his nose twitching. *Humans,* he says. *There have been beast-hunters here.*

How long ago? I ask.

Half a sun at most—but I can still smell them. The stag

is amazing. I can't smell anything except his fur and the dampness of the air. *And they're coming back.*

With that, a large van comes over the brow of the hill opposite on six giant off-road tyres. Long, with a rocket-shaped front, it looks like a giant, blind varmint that has crawled out of the earth, spattered with mud, a tinted windscreen hiding the people inside. The machine gives a growl as it tips up over the top of the hill before coming down with a crash, the tyres gouging muddy ditches out of the earth. I clamber back on the stag and without another word he leaps over the Fold and we are bounding off down the grassy slope, towards the nearest trees.

We head *swiftly* through the cluster of trees and rocks, going downhill all the time. My heart is in my mouth and I keep looking back, but there is no crashing or roaring of wheels coming after us, only line after line of trees that seem to close up behind as we charge through. I want to ask the stag if he thinks we were spotted, but he seems so silent and lost in his head that I don't.

If the stag is in no mood to talk, the General is only too keen to show off. He peers out of my jacket as we bump along, teaching me more about animal ways as I fire questions at him.

What do you call those grey trees over there?

What you call a tree, we call a tall-home.

OK. So what is the name of those red berries on that bush?

He pauses, as if not sure what to answer at first. *You might not understand with our name.*

Try me.

We call those berries—food.

The long antennae disappear back into my pocket. As the sun begins to set, the pigeons call down from above.

Come on, come on—we must travel as far as we can before night falls.

Yet again I feel like the animals can see things I can't, know things that I don't. A shiver of fear runs down my spine. *Why? Is the human machine catching up with us?*

No—we just can't see as well in the dark.

We ride out of the trees and find ourselves surrounded by the edges of mountaintops, dark blue against the evening light. It feels much colder, and I pull my scarf tight around me, the darkness getting deeper and blacker around us. Each clash of the stag's hoofs against the rock-hard ground vibrates right through him. My neck, shoulders, and thighs are in agony from clinging on for so long, and I think my stomach is beginning to eat itself.

I am very tired and hungry, Stag.

He seems to ignore me, skipping down to some rocks and up again.

I feel my eyelids begin to droop, and my head sinks lower and lower onto my chest till I am nothing more than a nodding sack.

It's hard to tell whether it's five minutes or an hour later, but with a jerk I am sliding down his sleek side onto the damp ground. We're standing right on the edge of a valley, looking down. It's just possible to make out, in the moonlight, thousands of black treetops marching on for miles like an army in formation and, right in the distance, the silver flash of a river.

Here and there, the light catches a pale roof or a darkened window. There are houses and barns scattered like dice across the floor of the valley, but no electric lights and no people to be seen. I make out collapsed walls and, in places, the gleam of an abandoned vehicle. There is not a noise to be heard anywhere, apart from our breathing and the wind running over the grass. I'm hoping the stag will suggest that we go down and explore—there might be old tins of food, beds . . . anything. But all he says is, *You may rest here for a while.*

I look around. I don't see a bed or anything looking like one.

You don't look properly. Look with your hands and feet.

I've got no other option. So half crouching, half sliding, I feel my way over the edge. The short damp grass gives way to a large overhang of earth, and patting the ground beneath, it feels drier and warmer. Crawling under it, I draw my knees tight against my chest and rest my head against my shoulder, like the pigeons did by the water.

I've no idea how many hours I sleep under the overhang, but when I wake up it's still dark. Water dribbles down my chin and into my mouth and something sour and furry is nuzzling me.

I push it roughly away.

Calm, says the stag. *I brought you water from a fresh spring. Drink.*

He's giving me water from his mouth. Water from an actual deer.

You must drink, he says firmly.

I don't want something that's been in your mouth!

You must drink, he repeats. *This water is straight from the ground. The purest there is.*

My mouth is so dry, and his eyes aren't red in the least—so I do. I expect the water to be utterly rank, but it's actually clean. And nice.

As I wipe my chin, two of the grey pigeons leap onto my lap.

And we found you some food, Kester.

Then they drop branches of berries and beak-loads of nuts into my hands. But before I can even look at them properly, the white pigeon snatches the juiciest bunch of berries back between his beak.

Kester! You found us some food! he says, dragging them behind him into a corner of the overhang, before being attacked by the others and disappearing in a puff of feathers and berries.

They're welcome to it. I sniff the berries I have left.

They smell strange and acidic, even though they are the ones the General described as food. The nuts are in a hard shell, and I've nothing to open them with. The memory of

prawn cocktail–flavoured Chicken'n'Chips comes painfully back to me and my empty stomach.

I'm not like you! I can't eat this stuff.

Very well, says the stag, sniffing the air, never not
watching out for a moment. *As you please. But we must
continue with our journey. Dawn will come soon and we need
all the hours of light we can get.*

He raises himself to his full height and stands there
waiting. They are all watching and waiting for me.

Shaking my head because I can't believe I'm actually
eating something they just found in the outdoors, I slowly
put one of the berries first against the tip of my tongue,
then in my mouth. It's sweeter than I was expecting.
Almost juicy. Slowly, berry by berry, I eat as many of the
bunches left by the white pigeon as possible. Then I take
the nut shells and, smashing them against the underside
of the rock, manage to get some of the sweet green-white
mush out from inside. They taste better than they look.

I leave the rest for the General, who polishes it all off in
about minus eight seconds.

The stag watches us both stuff our gobs with his usual
intense stare, barely waiting for us to finish before barking,
We should not delay any further. Climb on.

Still feeling half asleep, I haul myself onto his back,
and then we are off, zigzagging down the boulder-strewn
sides of the valley towards the forest. It's slowly getting
lighter too, so it should be easier to see, but white clouds

are rolling down from the mountains and making the air thicker and thicker.

I'm starting not to feel so great. A blinding pain flashes behind my eyes, and my stomach keeps clenching. Each time it's more painful, but I just have to keep going, clinging on to the stag's soaking fur. It's cold all around, but there is a strange heat flushing through my body that I try to not think about.

For the first time on our journey, the stag nearly trips, and I lurch to the side, my stomach heaving. I see why he stumbled—suddenly there is fog behind us, fog ahead of us, fog everywhere I look, like boiling clouds steaming up from a kettle. Through the white, I notice the walls of our valley have closed in on us, and the grass has turned to rock. The stag clatters over piles of loose stones.

Our every move echoes around the steep walls. The General peers out of my pocket and tests the air.

I do not like this valley of rock, he says. *It is too easy for us to get crushed in such country.*

A valley of rock has been smashed and carved out of the earth. Through the curls of mist I can see the shadows of crane arms drooped with dripping chains, and digging machines seized up with rust. On the far side a steel cabin stands abandoned, the door hanging wide open, creaking gently in the wind. And everywhere, piles and piles of glistening wet purple slate. Slate that begins to swim before my eyes, until from behind the foggy clouds I hear a *crack*.

The *crack* of one slate stone hitting another.

Did you hear that? I whisper to the stag.

He doesn't answer my question but picks his way even more slowly and carefully between heaps of slippery slate and toffee-coloured puddles. The pigeons have disappeared above us, hidden behind layers of mist that are as white and thin as tissues.

Then there's another *crack* from the rocky sides of the valley stretching away over our heads. The stag stops dead, not moving apart from his nose, sniffing the air. It's incredible how still he can make himself, as if he was made of the slate we stand on, rather than flesh and blood.

I am not made of slate, though, and I can't help but sneeze. A sneeze that echoes off the rocks around us.

The stag doesn't move or say a word.

There is another *crack*. A *crack* made by something no farther than two metres away. I think of the metal beast-hunter van with the tinted windscreen, and shiver. Then there's another *crack*—louder, nearer, definitely not accidental. Something is making the stones move.

The stag just stands stock still, sniffing.

There's a scrabbling noise behind us, the noise of something or someone sliding down the rocks.

A pause, then another tiny landslide of pebbles. I freeze as much as I can, my breath caught in my throat—

Come on! Why don't you run away?

A great stag never runs away from his fate.

Then, to my amazement, he slowly clip-clops over the floor of smashed slate till we are facing the direction of the sound. I want to jump off and get out of the way, but I can't. I feel rooted where I sit, paralysed by fear—fear of what lurks in the grey mist.

All is well, the stag says suddenly, but he's not speaking to us; he's speaking to the thing, the thing in the fog. *All is well,* he repeats. *You may show yourself now.*

The swirls and puffs of fog begin to slowly lift into the air like a paper curtain, and stepping out from underneath is not a human beast-hunter. More like a beast human-hunter. Pale flecks of mud dotting his coal-black head, his ears pinned back and his tail trailing down behind him with exhaustion—it's the wolf-cub from the Ring of Trees.

PART 3
THE MAN WITH CRUTCHES

I shrink back, expecting the cub to jump up and lash out at the stag. But he doesn't do anything wolf-like at all—the total opposite in fact. He shrinks into himself, like he's frightened of *us*.

Well tracked, young cub, says the stag.

The wolf-cub's green eyes dart nervously between the stag and me. *I come in peace, noble Wildness . . .*

I know you do, the stag replies, his deep voice bouncing off the rocks.

I left in darkness after you—we made an evening kill—I can see the stag wince—*and I took my fill, enough to let me hunt for a whole moon if I wished. Then I left by the same hole as you in the Ring of Trees. After that I picked up your scent along the Great Open and by the First Fold—*

Yes, yes, all this I know, says the stag. *I smelt your scent from afar, when I woke the boy under the rock.* He chuckles. *I think perhaps you still have some way to go as a hunter?*

The wolf-cub snaps and bares his teeth. *I am a fine hunter! My father said I would grow to be the greatest hunter of them all! I am not frightened of you! I am a guardian from the Ring of Trees! My father—* He stops for a moment and gulps.

How is your father? asks the stag gently.

The cub shakes his head. *We do not know. He tumbled into the valley and was lost from view.* Anger flares suddenly in his green eyes. *They have sworn to avenge him—do you know that?*

The stag is not laughing now. He is listening.

Yes, I can imagine. And you, what about you, Cub—do you wish to kill me now, to avenge your father?

My father will be avenged, says the cub quietly. He looks down at the wet slate beneath his paws. *But he was wrong. We were all wrong. Even before the sunset after you fled, more of the wild had been lost to the berry-eye. Now all the eagles are afflicted, and more of the badgers too—everyone is so fearful. Some say that the end of all things is approaching, as in the dreams—* He glances anxiously at the swirling sky above.

The stag closes his eyes and shakes his head. *Not yet, Cub, while blood still runs through these veins. So why have you come, if not to avenge your father?*

Because the wild I have sworn from my first breath to protect is dying. I . . . I have come to help you in your quest, Wildness.

I slide off the stag and take a step towards the cub.

I want to stroke him. But he suddenly growls, bristling, and I jerk my hand away.

But I will not help the human! I can never help a human! he snarls.

Then you may not travel with us. We need the human's help.

The wolf-cub stares straight at me, eyes open wide. I hold my hands up in the air, trying to make peace.

I want to help you, I promise, I say. *I won't harm you.*

Ha! he says, his ears pinned back. *Have no fear of that. But you had better watch out for me. I will always be watching your back!*

I'm confused.

Now the wolf-cub is confused too, looking to the stag for advice. He tries again. *No, I mean, that is . . . you should watch your back! That's all I'm saying.*

I will try, I say, trying not to let him see my smile as I get back on the stag. I can feel the cub watching my every move, and we wait.

Finally the stag breaks the silence. *So, Cub, will you join us all in peace?*

The wolf-cub snorts and, glancing at me, licks his nose sulkily.

In that case you are most welcome, says the stag, nuzzling the cub softly on the top of his head.

And then we are off again, marching back into the fog, the pigeons guiding us out with shouts and cries, the wolf-cub trotting behind as if he has been with us all along—

which, in a way, I suppose he has. He is quiet, though, treading suspiciously over the broken slates one by one like they might suddenly attack him.

There is a steady series of soft snores coming from my jacket pocket. I can't believe the General slept through a wolf-cub arriving.

I would give anything to be able to lie down and sleep now. My head is boiling and pounding at the same time, and every step the stag takes makes me want to throw up.

The walls of rock give way to green slopes overgrown with rolls of spiky bush hidden behind yellow flowers, which look nice but scratch at the stag's sides and my legs. As he picks his way along a path of muddy earth and roots, the ground rises steeply until we find ourselves on top of a small knoll overlooking a dark green forest. And beyond, poking out above the trees, only just visible against the grey sky but definitely there, dead ahead—a row of six chimneys sticking up from a roof.

I have seen other houses and chimney tops throughout our journey, but these chimneys on this house have something none of the others had.

Smoke.

Sparks start to fly in my brain. If there are smoking chimneys, then underneath them there must be fire—and warmth. And perhaps a bed, not a rock, that I can lie on.

I don't say much of that, though. My head and stomach feel carved clean out, hollow, and every word is an effort.

Look. Smoke.

The stag grunts and turns around before starting to clop back the way we have come, along the rocky ridge, heading once more into the low white mist. I grab at the tufts of thick fur around the base of his neck.

Wait! What are you doing? You're going the wrong way.

We do not know what we might find there.

But I don't feel well. I want to lie down.

He stops and gives a long sigh. *My animals are not well either. And if we do not find a cure for them, they will all die. We cannot be discovered.*

This is a joke. Checking around for any sharp rocks and not seeing any, I bounce off him onto the hard ground, my head spinning as I do. The wolf-cub ducks out of my way, ears pricking. The stag keeps on walking, but a few strides ahead he sighs and stops before turning round to glower at me. You forget when you're on top of him, but he is really massive.

I reach down and grab a dead branch off the ground, holding it like a sword. My hands might be tingling from the cold, but there's a fire burning in my stomach that rushes up my throat, a shower of sparks behind my eyes, making me dizzy.

Please, Stag! I feel really sick. I'm the one who's going to die if you don't take me to the house.

Then the stag speaks gently. Soft. I wish he wasn't so soft. You can't hit anything with a stick when it's being soft.

Very well. We can rest here a while, if you wish.

I look at the stones jutting out of the earth, the spiky

bushes. *I don't want to lie on a rock! I want to lie on a bed—I need to lie down.*

He nods slowly, chewing, not saying a word. I try again. *If you're worried about meeting people—well, you'll have to meet plenty of them in Premium—*

I will enter your land to meet with your father and his magic. But first we need to get there alive.

The pigeons flutter down onto his horns, blinking at me.

You must understand—we do not trust other humans like we do you.

Yes. Don't trust me, human, says the white pigeon, popping up on the stag's back from nowhere.

But there's a fire—I could get warm, I say, my head feeling dizzier and dizzier by the second.

Yes, reply the grey pigeons, *and humans only make fires so they can roast pigeons in them. That's the reason you made them to begin with.*

It is a great honour that we trust you at all, says the wolf-cub, trying to copy the stag and sound older than he is.

But the old deer puts his foot down. He shakes his head gruffly, sending the pigeons tumbling off into the bushes while the wolf-cub cowers behind him.

Enough of this—you are all behaving like fawns. We take another walk-upon.

As I listen to them bicker, a thought charges up out of nowhere like a battering ram. The fire behind my eyes, the shakes, the sickness in my stomach—my brain and body are burning up. I should never have gone near these animals; I should never have agreed to any of this or left the safety of the Hall with them. There's a reason the countryside is abandoned and all the animals are gone. An infectious, deadly reason. And now I've got it.

That's it. I've got the red-eye. That's the only explanation. I drop the stick, shaking. Sweat trickles down my sides.

I was wrong. I can't help you.

The stag lowers his head without a word.

The stomach fire crackles and roars behind my eyes.

Do you understand? This is all your fault!

But they all just stare at me silently. Almost like they're just animals again and we can no longer talk. Fine—that's probably for the best. So I turn on my heel and run away from them, down the hill, slipping and sliding on the flattened grass, in the direction of the chimneys, running faster and faster, away from the animals, towards the house. I don't look back. I can't.

Because I know they're not coming after me.

I keep on running, down through the forest of spiky trees.

My scarf catches on a branch—

I fall over on my front, right into the mud—

Hit my knee on a rock and get straight up again—I'm going so fast. Just have to keep breathing and stay upright.

Stars begin to dance across my eyes. The more they do, the more I get used to them, like they're normal.

A twig snaps behind me, or maybe I snapped it. Don't care. Don't care if someone does find me. I need help, medicine, a doctor—anything.

The soft ground turns into a gravelly track—that leads through two crumbling old pillars.

I'm dizzy with excitement and confusion. There are some words on the pillars—old-looking words carved into them, which keep blurring. I trace their ridges with my finger, saying each sound.

WIND'S EDGE

Looking between the pillars, over a rambling field dotted with stooping trees, I can see the house beneath the chimneys, so big and old it could be a museum. It must have a hundred windows and doors.

As long as behind one of the doors is a bed, I don't care.

There are no lights in the windows and the paint is peeling off the wooden doors. The track turns into a paved circle, with threads of weed tangling in between the cracks.

I stagger up the uneven stairs to the tall doors, each step a massive effort.

The door is locked. I rattle the handle and see there's

an old-fashioned doorbell, which I press—but nothing happens. I hammer on the door as hard as I can. It sounds as weak as a twig tapping against a window. Forcing myself to knock again, all I can hear is the sound of my own fist echoing against the wood inside.

I turn away from the door and push on round the corner, shivering like crazy, and wobble across an overgrown orchard, past blackened piles of long-rotten fruit. Just going near them, the sweet stink clouds my head in a rush that makes me want to puke—*deep breaths, deep breaths.*

It's no good.

Everything is shut up and fastened down. There's no way in. One of the fire-snakes in my stomach slides down my leg and scurries over to the rotten fruit. Only it's not a fire-snake.

General, I just manage to say, *I thought . . .*

The General doesn't look up from the fruit. But when he speaks, his mouth sounds full. *I'd like to say I came along to protect you, but that wouldn't be entirely true.*

He's now totally coated in rotten apple from top to bottom. I try to speak, but the words don't come out properly.

The General sighs. *What are my orders now?*

Unable to speak at all anymore, I just point at a line of sheds tacked onto the side of the house. The cockroach looks at me, looks at the mushy apples, and makes a hissing noise. Then he darts between my legs and under the door of the nearest outbuilding.

I wait unsteadily, using every ounce of concentration I have left to stay upright.

After what seems like forever, there's a rattling noise from inside. The door swings open, banging in the wind, and perched on the rusting lock is the General.

Did you ever wonder how cockroaches get absolutely everywhere? Well, now you know.

I shake my head and follow him into the shed. It's damp and smells of old tomatoes and something else—armpits. *A fragrance of true beauty,* the General says happily, before scuttling along rows of tall metal shelves, weaving in and out of old flowerpots. Groggily I stumble against them—

Mind where you go, soldier! the cockroach calls out, and, stepping over him, I fall against a door in the wall, which opens with a gentle click into the house beyond.

In the dark I feel my way along the walls and edge carefully round till I find the ridges of another door, which twists open. I can hear something else now—not the General—

A crying noise.

What is that infernal wailing? mutters the General, but I'm hardly listening to him. Whatever it is, I'm heading for it as fast as I can. I know crying doesn't mean food. But it means someone, something living. I don't care how dangerous it is. I need help. Stumbling along a corridor lined with paintings, down steps curving round a corner towards a warm glow of electric light . . .

Just try to be quiet and stay out of sight for longer than *ten seconds,** I whisper to the cockroach. He scuttles up my leg and into my pocket.

The crying is high and painful to listen to, like a screaming baby.

I reach the bottom of the stairs and find myself looking into a dimly lit room. The light comes from a low lamp hanging over a long wooden table. A table covered in glass-topped boxes, each one filled with a collection of pebbles or rocks or shells. And a brass microscope next to row after row of bottles stoppered with corks, filled with a muddy liquid.

There's a globe, an old-fashioned ticking clock, and towering piles of leather-bound books. Everything is covered in a thick layer of dust. It really is like a museum in here.

Some of the books are spread open, showing pages with dead brown leaves stuck to them, and flaking flowers, all marked with tiny handwritten labels. And curled up right in the middle of one of the books is the crying thing.

I take one jerky step after another across the deep carpet.

The thing should be dead, not sitting here crying. Thin, white, and fluffy, curled up on an old book, it's a kind of pet people used to have—a cat. The white fur glitters under the light. I stumble towards it, confused—

*I wouldn't do that if I was you,** she snaps in a snotty voice, stopping her sobbing abruptly. The cat twists her head at me and bares her little sharp teeth and pink gums.

But I'm not looking at her teeth. I'm looking at her eyes. Her burning red eyes.

The confusion spins faster and faster in my head. This isn't the Ring of Trees—how is she even still alive, how is she . . . ?

I have to take a picture. I point my wrist, a quick flash, then—

"Hands off my cat," says a voice. "Turn around! Now!"

I turn around to see a girl with dark hair curled up on her head and fierce eyes staring at me over a small, angry mouth. A girl wearing blue wellies. And carrying a gun, pointed at me.

With a yowl the cat leaps off the table, sending bottles and books flying in a billowing cloud of dust.

"Sit down!" barks the girl, waving her gleaming rifle at me. "Are you a kidnapper?"

I don't know, I—all I can do is slump to the floor.

She calmly sits down opposite me, resting the gun across her knees. An outsider. So the rumours were true.

"If you've come to kidnap Sidney, I'm not going to let you." She picks up the gun and squints down the telescopic sight, frowning at me. "Just because she's the last cat ever. I don't care how much money you want for her. We won't pay."

I look at the dark hole of the gun barrel, and at the cat, now stalking in and out of my legs.

Sidney's a weird name for a girl cat, isn't it?

But Sidney the female cat just snarls. *I didn't choose

the name. *Talk to her—tell her what you want,** she says, flashing her teeth. **You can see she knows how to use that thing.**

I believe her.

I can't talk to people, only animals. I'm sick. I just want to get better . . .

Oh, we all want that, she says, narrowing her burning red eyes and turning her back on me with a flick of her tail.

"Put your hands where I can see them," says the girl. I hold them out, palms up.

"On your head!" she snaps.

Leaving the gun resting on her knees, but her eyes on me, she reaches into one of the boxes piled up behind her, finds a water bottle, unscrews the cap, and takes a long, slurping sip.

All I can feel is my dry throat, my glued-together lips. The girl puts the bottle back down.

We sit, staring at each other over the gun, neither of us daring to blink first.

Then I look away—and lunge suddenly for her bottle of water—

But she is too quick for me, snatching it out of reach.

"No! Tell me what you want first, and then you can have a sip." She drums her wellies on the floor and the gun jumps. I point to my dry lips and gums, waving my hands across one another for "no." She stares at me, not understanding, until eventually a light dawns in her eyes.

"You can't talk? Well, you can't be very good as a kidnapper if you can't talk! How do you issue your orders?"

There's a silent standoff, broken only by the sound of Sidney, now curled up in her lap, purring softly. I feel the General bristling for action in my pocket.

"OK," says the girl, like she's answering a question I haven't asked. "Let's try this another way." Rummaging about in the sea of junk around us, she shoves a battered rectangular box across the floor to me. I wonder what weird or rotting specimen lies inside.

"Go on! Open it!"

I rest the box on my knees and prise the lid off. But there's nothing rotting inside—just a folded board, which opens out into a series of differently coloured and labelled squares. There are some racks and a drawstring bag.

I just look at her.

"Well, go on, Kidnapper! You must play, don't you?"

Confused, I empty the bag into the box, and a jumble of lettered tiles falls out.

The girl jabs at the board with her foot. "Tell me your name at least, and I'll give you a sip of water."

Beginning to understand, I stick my hand into the pile. Scrabbling around, I grab a fistful of letters, find the ones I need, and lay them out on the board.

The girl peers over her knees at the tiles. I'm keeping an eye on the gun.

KESTER

"That's only ten points, Kidnapper, and you haven't even got a double word score."

I shrug and hold my hand out for the water. She pauses and then passes it over. I unscrew the lid and take a long, long swig. Possibly the best drink I've ever had in my life.

"I don't even know where you're from, Kester the Kidnapper. You could be anybody. You know you're not allowed through here." She glances out of the window behind her. "They tried to make us leave. But it's our family home, you see. And has been for gen-er-ations." She pronounces the word slowly, like she's still getting used to saying it right. "The last time they came, we hid in the attic."

Don't remind me, says Sidney, with a cough that rattles her skinny body like a massive electric shock. *She put me in a suitcase so they wouldn't hear anything. Me—in a suitcase! Can you imagine?*

I can. It sounds like quite a good idea.

"Well, go on!" says the girl, nearly taking my eye out with the end of the gun. "Tell me where you're from, Kidnapper." Her eyes never leave me for a second while I rummage among the tiles.

She cranes her head to read and sniffs.

KESTER
P
E
C
T
R
U
M
H
A
L
L

"The Facto school? It's certainly high-scoring." She edgily eyes the gun, still resting on her knees and pointed at me. "You must definitely be dangerous if you've escaped from there." A glance at the board again and then back at me, dead in the eye. "I'm going to ask you this one more time, and the answer had better be good. Why are you out here in the Zone?"

Taking a deep breath, I start to spell out a number of words across the board, moving and rearranging tiles till my story is told.

"I hope you're sticking to the rules. It won't work unless you stick to the rules."

I take a last look at my attempt and swivel the board around so she can see. The girl studies it closely for a moment, and then looks up and shakes her head.

"That is the stupidest story I ever heard. Talking animals? I'm not that gullible, you know. Even if they could talk, which they can't, there's none left. Sidney's the last one left in the whole world, which is why she's so precious. And you're not precious, you're just a dirty little boy."

She stands up and points the gun, which is twice her size, right up my nose.

"Now, for the last time, tell me the truth about why you're here. Or get out of my house."

I can't go back out there. I need a doctor. There's no way to convince her, unless—

Sidney! I force the words out. *Sidney—you have to help me.*

The cat stretches and, eyelids half-lowered, looks down her nose at me. *And pray why, exactly? I'm not just any cat, you see. I, my dear, am a prize-winning cat. Once upon a time I was Best in Show, Best in Section, Best Groomed—*

Sidney! I'm actually shaking with frustration. *None of that matters anymore. Don't you understand? I've come from the Ring of Trees.*

At this, Sidney leaps onto her front, hackles raised. The girl's eyes dart between us, unsure what is going on.

Impossible! That place doesn't even exist. It was only ever a rumour.

It's true. Ask the General.

Who?

I point to the cockroach, who is now perched on the table above, idly nibbling at the edge of a dead fern in a scrapbook but listening with deadly attention.

It is true, Cat. The last wild live there, with a great stag as their Wildness. We summoned this boy to help us find a cure for the plague.

Sidney snorts. *Even if you expect me to believe this bug, what do you want me to do about it?*

Tell . . . I realize I still don't know the girl's name.

You may call her Polly, purrs the cat.

Tell Polly I'm not a kidnapper. Explain how I can talk to animals, and that I need her help.

Sidney is racked by more coughs. *How can I explain anything to her? She can't talk to animals—thankfully. I'd never hear the end of it if she could—can you imagine?*

Just prove to her that I can! Move pieces around on the board. Spell it out!

Her red eyes oozing a little, the cat looks down at the board and sniffs. *Just because I win prizes doesn't mean I* *do tricks, you know.** I'm about to throw the whole bag of letters at her when she gives a flick of her tail and trots up onto the board.

All right, all right, my dear. Keep your fur on.

As coolly as if she had been playing the game with us all morning, Sidney starts to push the letters around with her paws. She moves a couple of tiles, stops, and then adds a couple more before stepping back to examine her efforts.

I look down and shake my head. *Very helpful,* I say. "Those words aren't in the dictionary," says Polly. The cat has written:

Well, it's the truth, my dear. Like it or not, says Sidney. *That's cat spelling, anyhow.*

Go on, Sidney. Please. Tell her. Tell her the truth.

Sidney sighs. She swipes her paw across the board, scattering all the other pieces, and starts again, clawing more tiles out of the drawstring bag, arranging cat-spelled word after cat-spelled word, until the board is full.

As Polly reads what the cat has written, she looks no

longer flushed with anger but white. Like she's seen a ghost. "You've got the red-eye?"

Finally. Feverish and exhausted, I can only just nod.

"You're absolutely sure? Your animals have given you the virus? The same one as Sidney?"

Look at my sweating red face, I want to scream. *Feel my forehead!* I don't know how much more ill I need to be.

I half expect her to run away, but instead Polly just purses her lips and shakes her head. She picks up the tiles and puts them back in the bag, drawing it tight and folding up the board before putting them both away neatly in the box. Then she lays the gun carefully on the floor, grabs a magnifying glass off the table, and examines me closely, peering in my eyes and feeling my forehead and my wrist.

"And you left these animals at the top of the valley? That's where you came from?"

I nod. Although who knows where they could be by now. But Polly seems satisfied with this answer. She scans me all over one more time before rummaging in her pocket, pulling out a pair of tweezers, leaning forward, and plucking a piece of muck off my cuff. She holds the scrap of muck up to the light with the tweezers in one hand and studies it with the magnifying glass in the other. She nods to herself, as if answering a question no one has asked, raises an eyebrow in my direction, and says—

"You don't have the virus." She picks up the gun and digs it in my belly. "And I'll show you why."

The kitchen of Wind's Edge is bigger than any I've ever seen and messier too. In the light squeezing through the shuttered windows I can see pans, mugs, and dishes piled up in a sink full of water. Bundles of spoons dangle from wooden bars, hanging low on ropes attached to the high ceiling, along with bunches of dried leaves and blackened twigs. The walls are lined with crooked shelves, crammed with jars of powders and seeds and glass bottles holding puddles of oily liquids.

"Sit down," says Polly, simultaneously pointing the gun at a chair and tossing the word game onto the table. As I collapse onto the seat, the General whizzes off down my leg.

Right! he barks. *It is essential that I carry out a reconnaissance for any possible enemy armies.*

You mean the kind of "enemy armies" that you can eat?

Do not interfere in military matters, he snaps back, before scuttling off over the rubbish-strewn floor.

Ignoring him, Polly leans her rifle against the wall and pulls out a notebook from underneath a tottering pile of newspapers, sending the whole lot flying—and Sidney running.

The book is old and covered with wrinkled black leather. As she flicks through the pages I peer over her shoulder. It's full of drawings and diagrams—of plants and petals and leaves. Trees, from diagrams of their tangled roots to close-up sketches of their crinkly bark. Bunches of berries, nuts, and weeds. More plants than I've ever seen, every kind, there must be—drawn this way, then that way, cut in half, and covered with scribbled notes.

Polly finds the page she wants, begins to study it—then senses me watching and whips the book away. She stamps over to the sink and fills up an old kettle, setting it to boil on a stove in the corner. Standing on a stool, she reaches up to pull at the dangling bunches of twigs, examining and sniffing each one until she has a carefully selected pile in her palm.

She crumbles them into a stone bowl, followed by a scoop of powder from a jar and a squirt of some oily green liquid. She takes a wooden spoon and bangs and pounds the different ingredients together until a bitter smell rises into the air, making my stomach turn. The kettle begins to hiss and scream on the stove—and rinsing out a mug from the pile in the sink, Polly tips the crushed mess in, before topping it up with boiling water and plonking down the cup in front of me.

I take one look at the steaming potion and gag, pushing it away.

Polly shakes her head. "Headache?" she asks. I nod. "Stomach cramps?" I nod again. "Feeling sick and dizzy?" I just close my eyes to try to stop the spinning.

With a look of triumph she digs around in her pocket for her tweezers, and drops the piece of muck from my sleeve onto the table. Except, peering at it, I can now see that the piece of muck is in fact half a squashed berry. One of the berries the pigeons gave me, now blackened by mud.

I still don't get it.

"Briary berries," she says, sliding the notebook across the table. It's open at a page covered with a drawing of berries—the ones I ate. "The woods you came from are full of them. I made the same mistake once too—they're so pretty to look at, and so juicy. But you can't eat them." She thinks for a moment. "Well, humans can't—they're poison-ous to us. Not enough to kill you, but enough to make you very sick."

I look at the potion and feel the bile rise in my throat, but Polly pushes it towards me. "This will make you feel better. Charcoal and flaxseed tea. But you have to drink it. Every last drop." She folds her arms. "You haven't got the red-eye. Trust me."

I see the General watching us from the floor. *How was I to know you couldn't eat them?* He bristles.

I look down into the steaming mug, close my eyes, pinch my nose with one hand, and take a gulp. It's black and claggy, and every mouthful makes me want to retch, but somehow I get a bit down.

I shudder at the taste, but my stomach feels calmer already.

"It was only luck that I saw that berry really," Polly says. "It could have been anything. The woods round here are full of poisonous things you mustn't eat. But I always knew it wasn't the red-eye."

I don't understand. She reaches under the table and picks up Sidney, all bony and lopsided, with red eyes burning, holding her tight to her chest, burying her face in the white fur till Sidney wriggles free onto the floor, yowling with disgust.

For goodness' sake, boy, I'm ill enough as it is—can't you make her stop?

But I only have ears for Polly.

"Look at her. She's been sick for two weeks and I hold her every day, but I'm as healthy as can be." I look at her, not believing what I'm hearing. "Facto is lying to you all. Humans can't get the virus."

Over more sips of charcoal tea, which begins to taste much nicer and more warming than I could ever have imagined, Polly tells me her story. Sidney falls asleep, stretched out across the table only mewing and coughing occasionally, but the General perches silently on my shoulder, not missing a word.

"I was very little, so I don't remember it starting," she says. "When they ordered everyone to leave the countryside and declared it a Quarantine Zone, we stayed. Mum didn't want to leave the house she grew up in, you see—anything could have happened to it."

Looking around at the peeling window frames and filthy kitchen, I'm not sure what else could have happened to it.

"We ate everything in the larder, in rations, and then we rinsed out the empty tins and packets and made soup from the scraps. When the formula came, we never got any. We weren't meant to still be here, you see. They only gave it to people in the cities." I never knew that. "Facto destroyed the vegetables and crops, saying they were contaminated. Every potato plant, every apple tree, the wheat and barley fields—everything. So Dad said if we were to stay, we had to learn everything there was about the plants. The wild ones. The ones they either left or didn't know about." She waves the leather notebook in front of me. "We had lots of old books in the library. Mum and Dad are historians, you see. Of the way we used to live—right back to the first human beings ever. We studied the books together. I know about all the plants in the woods around here—which mushrooms and berries are safe to eat, and which ones aren't. Even soup made out of nettles—we ate anything we could get our hands on."

I'm not sure that sounds much better than my charcoal tea, but I take her word for it.

"Even so, Dad always said that we must never let Sidney outside, in case she came into contact with any infected animals." She looks over at the coughing cat. "We just couldn't keep an eye on her all the time, so she got it eventually." Polly rests her hand on Sidney's belly and her eyes have a faraway look. "But I haven't."

She must read my face.

"My parents haven't either—at least, not as far as I know. She's been feverish for ages, and they were fine when they left, which was just before her eyes went red. We ran out of nice things to make from weeds and bark, you see, so last week Mum and Dad decided to go to Mons to try to get some formula. They said they would only be a day. I thought you might be them, you see, and when you weren't—"

Polly looks exhausted, her fingers propping up her cheek as she tries not to let her head drop onto the table, her dark hair coming down untidily all over her face. I realize we've been "talking" for hours.

"I'm starving," she says, and goes over to a large sack stuffed under the sink. Digging her hand in, she scoops out a pile of dusty-looking biscuits and holds them out in her palm.

I look amazed. They still have real food left.

She sees my expression and laughs. "Don't be silly—they're not normal food. They're Sidney's cat biscuits. They're very old and have the worst taste in the world, but they're all we've got. I've been living off them since Mum and Dad left."

And with that, she chucks a handful in her mouth.

Just seeing her eat makes my stomach start to rumble again.

"Want some?" she says, with her mouth half-full, offering me a pile.

Anything. Anything to eat.

It turns out cat biscuits do have the worst taste in the world, but as I crunch through them, I slowly start to feel like I might be able to move again. We've been up all night long, and now rays of light are beginning to slide in through the tops of the windows. Finishing my biscuit breakfast, I walk over to open the stiff shutters. Rubbing the moisture off the glass, I can make out the paved yard down below, the posh field and the crumbling pillars. I want to see a shadowy outline of a high back and horns, maybe some blurry dots flapping around in the sky above—but there's nothing—just the empty wood of spiky trees beyond.

I wonder where they are.

"Why did you leave them?"

I turn around. Polly's rubbing her eyes and stretching out a yawn.

"I don't understand. If there really are animals who are still alive, and who are your friends, why did you leave them? I would never leave Sidney."

I don't know now. I look at the floor.

"Do you think you could rescue Sidney too? I think she would quite like that."

I stand breathing on the glass, tracing an outline with my finger and thinking. I made a promise. I look at my watch again, hoping it will give me an answer. I flick idly through the pictures, trying to work out what to do.

And then the watch flickers again. Just like it did at the Ring of Trees.

The pictures I took of the animals judder up and down on the screen, and it's like there's another picture trying to get through—black and white, an outline of someone or something—but it's no good. I shake the watch, hold it close to the window . . . and the interference clears. A single word appears. Just that. One word, black and white on my screen.

HELP

I stare at it. Then, just as quickly as it appeared, the word has vanished. No matter what buttons I press, or how many times I shake the watch, it doesn't return. I don't know what it means. But it's helped me make my decision.

I turn around.

Polly stands up to face me, tired and unsteady. "What are you doing? Are you going to rescue us?"

I look at her exhausted face. She helped me. I look at Sidney, racked with coughs. I made a *promise*.

I nod and grab the game box, but before I can get out a single letter tile, Polly has clapped her hands with excitement.

"An adventure! I love adventures. Now, we'll take the game so you can talk to people as well, and I'll get a torch. We won't be long, will we? As long as we're back by dinner, I'm sure they won't mind—"

And she's gone, out of the kitchen, clattering up some stairs, still talking as she goes.

Woken, Sidney stands up on the table, her shadow curling out behind her.

I don't think I want to die, my dear—there are so many prizes still left to win.

I stroke her back and she flinches.

You'll have to ride on a stag, I say.

Is he terribly rough and uncouth and brutish?

I nod.

Well, that's some consolation, I suppose, she says, whisking her tail.

Scooping her up in my arms, I walk out of the kitchen, straight into Polly, who now has a bulging rucksack slung over her shoulder. She's wide awake, her cheeks flushed, opening the bag for me to inspect it.

"I think I've got everything. Your letter tiles, some extra cat biscuits to eat in an emergency, binoculars, and the magnifying glass in case we need to examine anything more closely." I feel the General prickle in my pocket. "And my notebook, of course. We might even discover some new plants to eat! I grabbed some plastic specimen jars and bags if we do—and left a note for Mum and Dad in their bedroom—do you think we'll be *very* long?"

But the words die in her mouth as we both hear the noise.

A noise I haven't heard for such a long time—the noise of a car engine, pulling to a halt across the stone circle outside.

Polly and I freeze in the doorway of the kitchen, staring at each other. Barely daring to breathe, we listen to the steady hum of the engine from down below.

Then she is off again, flying down the passage, yelling—"They're back!"

With Sidney over my shoulder and the General in my pocket, I run after her as fast as I can, through the maze of corridors and stairs. I find Polly at the end of a stone hallway, clutching a bunch of keys and straining to open about fifteen different locks on a very heavy door.

"I should have got blankets or something; they're bound to be cold after their journey. But they'll have brought formula so we can probably have a feast tonight!"

A feast of pink Chicken'n'Chips slop. I wonder what her parents will make of the silent boy covered in mud who broke into their house with a cockroach.

Polly loosens a padlocked chain, draws a wooden beam back, and struggles to pull open the door.

"Don't just stand there, Kidnapper! Help me!"

Together we force open the heavy door across the stone.

Polly rushes out, full of words. The sky is filling up with grey clouds, but there is no rain yet.

She stops dead in her tracks halfway down the steps outside, looking at the machine in the courtyard, its engine quietly humming. It doesn't look like much close up, all dented with scratches down the side, smoke pumping noisily out of the rusty exhaust. But there is no mistaking it. The six large wheels, ridged with mud, the purple panels, all painted with a yellow "F" in a circle—the machine the stag first saw in the Great Open.

"Maybe they gave Mum and Dad a lift," says Polly quietly.

Somehow I don't think so. I step down and stand in front of her, feeling responsible, like I'm her older brother. She snatches Sidney off my shoulders and hides the cat down on the steps behind her.

Proceed with great caution, whispers the General from my pocket.

The engine switches off. One of the panels slides open.

There's no one inside, just shadows—

Then a pair of metal poles swings out, with a click, onto the paving stones.

Crutches.

Two human legs swing out behind the metal legs. They

belong to a tall man wearing a suit and tie under a long brown coat. It is hard to say what he looks like, only that he is white and pale, like he has never seen the sun.

He looks at us and winks.

Then with lightning speed he hops on his crutches across the flagstones towards us. He stops at the bottom of the steps but doesn't look at all tired, resting now on all four of his feet.

"Hello, children," says the man. His voice sounds foreign, but I can't work out where from. It sounds like lots of different accents all at once. "It looks like it might rain today, yes?"

I really hope not.

He swings his left crutch up towards the clouds. With a hydraulic hiss and the sound of a flag unfurling, a black umbrella squeezes out of the tip and explodes into the sky. The man holds the umbrella over our heads, which he finds really funny for some reason. "We don't want you to get wet now!"

Polly and I just look up at the umbrella that came out of the crutch, and she holds on to my arm.

"So, children. My name is Captain Skuldiss," says the crutch man. "Hello, little girl!" he continues, waggling the tip of his other crutch at Polly, which she shakes as if it was a weird robotic hand.

"Hello," she says in a very low voice.

"Hello, little boy," Captain Skuldiss says, thrusting the pole at me.

I don't take it.

Ignoring me, he carries on. "So, what are you two young children doing outside, in the good old Quarantine Zone?" He looks up at the house behind us, his milky eyes scanning the dark windows and roofs. Polly doesn't answer. The man sighs.

"Perhaps first I should tell you what Captain Skuldiss is doing, in my special van. I'm driving round and round this beautiful country, round and round the whole thing, up and down, all over the flipping place—and do you know what I'm looking for?"

He waves the other crutch in the air with excitement. "I'm looking for some animals! *Nasty* diseased old animals." He stops waving the crutch and peers at us closely. "Now I don't suppose you have seen any sick old animals, have you, children?"

We both shake our heads, perhaps too quickly.

Whatever you do, Sidney, don't move, I say without taking my eyes off the crutch.

Captain Skuldiss purses his lips. "I see. I'm sorry—I should have explained in full, told you the whole caboodle and all, my dear kiddiewinks. What is happening is this: Factorium—Mr. Selwyn Stone—he comes to me, and he says, 'Hey, Captain Skuldiss. Whatever you are doing now, stop it, and stop it straightaway.'"

"What *were* you doing?" asks Polly.

Captain Skuldiss gives her a sharp look.

"Oh, never mind, little girl! It was just some soldier's

work far away in the jungle. Some work to talk about another day, which gave me these old things for the rest of my life." He picks at the frayed leather straps wound tight round the handles of his crutches. "Let us just say I have very good personal reasons for not liking animals, especially big ones with even bigger toothie-pegs."

The Captain is lost in his thoughts for a moment, and then snaps his fingers, as if to wake himself up. "So—Stone! He says, 'Captain Skuldiss, we are very worried about this red-eye virus. It has killed so many animals, yes, so cruel and sad.' And I say, 'But this is a good thing, is it not?'" Skuldiss jabs his finger in the air. "And he says, 'No! That is precisely where you are wrong, my dear Captain Skuldiss.'" He leans in so close we can see the veins in his eyes. "'We are very worried, yes, most worried indeed, that this horrible plague'"—he beats his chest with his fist and pulls a sad face—"'that has killed so many fluffy woodland whatsits, will now kill the *numero uno* animal on this good planet. Men!'" He shakes his head slowly from side to side at the thought.

"'Very good,' says I. 'Anything Captain Skuldiss can do to help his own race of men.' So I say, 'What would you like me to do with these animals and their nasty mutating virus?'"

He whacks the front step again, harder this time. I swear I hear something crack, and I don't think it was the crutch.

"'Why, Captain Skuldiss—what do you think? Why have

I asked a top soldier like yourself to help us? We expect you to exterminate them, please. Please, exterminate these left-over animals. Exterminate them all as you might a little bug!'" He grinds the crutch tip down where he just cracked the step, as if squashing an imaginary bug.

What is the enemy intruder doing, soldier? whispers the General from my pocket.

Nothing, I say.

And then the Captain just waits for us to speak.

"We haven't seen any animals," says Polly eventually. She tries to take a step back, to push Sidney away towards the house and the still-open door.

Captain Skuldiss nods.

He points at me with his crutch. "How about you? A kitty got your tongue, has it?"

Does he know? Polly and I swap glances super-fast.

I hope you're not expecting me to run anywhere or move quickly, says Sidney from her hiding place behind us. *Because that is absolutely not going to happen.*

"You know, little boy, I'm looking at you and I'll tell you why." Skuldiss runs the cold tip of his crutch all over me, from the top of my head down to my toes. I shiver. "I'm wondering, why is he all covered in mud from head to toe?"

We just stare at him. Polly has gone as mute as me.

"Covered in mud like a dirty animal." He leans forward and sniffs me up and down, big long sniffs over my hair and neck. "Yes, he even smells like a dirty animal. So—I ask you again, children, have you seen any dirty diseased beasties?"

Out of the corner of my eye I catch Sidney trying to peer between our legs.

Sidney! Don't move!

Skuldiss prods my shin with the crutch. "So come on. Captain Skuldiss hasn't got all day. Answer me, please."

Then, without warning, he raps me hard across my shins with his crutch. I want to rub them, but if I bend over, he'll see Sidney.

"He can't talk, you stupid man!" says Polly.

"Oh?" says Captain Skuldiss, something nasty creeping into his voice. "Stupid, am I?" He takes aim with the crutch at my shins again, and whacks them—hard this time.

I open my mouth to scream, and nothing comes out. Doubled up with pain, I leave Sidney fully exposed behind us on the steps. She gives a squeaky yowl before darting towards the door—but it's too late. The umbrella vanishes back into the crutch with a flick of the Captain's finger, and in less than a second, the end has extended—like a telescope—and pinned down Sidney's tail under a clawed tip. She squeals in pain.

Polly gabbles—"She isn't ill! She hasn't got the virus! We followed all the instructions—"

"Oh yes?" says Captain Skuldiss. "Then why is she shivering?" He turns again to me, his face going darker all the time. He presses the crutch harder on the cat's tail. "Then why does she have *red eyes*?"

"NO! You don't understand!" says Polly.

"On the contrary, I understand all too well, little girl." Slowly Captain Skuldiss turns around and whistles at the van. The doors to the cab swing open and two men step out. They're wearing rubber hoods, with gas masks, rubber gloves, and waterproof trousers tucked into their boots. They're carrying guns, bigger than Polly's. They've got ropes and nets slung over their shoulders, and belts dangling with poisoned darts—the weapon of choice for these people.

Cullers.

Polly kneels down and clutches my arm tight.

The nearest culler strides over and pulls Sidney out from under the crutch with his rubber-gloved hands. She struggles but is too weak to resist, and the thug carts her away, off down the steps, heaves open the van's rear doors—and hurls her in.

Polly screams, "Bring her back! Bring her back! Where are you taking her?"

They just chucked Sidney in like she was a sack of coal. Before Polly can say any more, Captain Skuldiss levels his crutch at us. I don't want to know what else might come out of there.

"And you kiddies—you are illegally present in a restricted area. Quick march, if you please!"

But Polly is already running towards the van, shouting, "As if I would let you take Sidney without me!"

I run down the steps after her, the cockroach safely

stashed away in my pocket. Captain Skuldiss shakes his head and hops after us, as Polly and I jump through the open back doors.

"It's all right, Sidney, we're here!" Polly calls out.

At the sound of her name, Sidney stirs uneasily in the corner. *Is this how we're getting to the city?* Her voice sounds tired and confused. *I thought you said something about a stag? I'm not ready for my final journey yet.*

Our plans changed, I'm afraid. I pat her softly. *Everything is going to be all right, I promise.*

Captain Skuldiss's head appears in the van doorway. He grins. We get one last look at Wind's Edge before he slams the door shut and we are plunged into blackness. Moments later the van starts and reverses sharply, throwing Polly and me against one another in the back. But as her small hand reaches out in the darkness and wraps itself around mine, it does make me feel that I am not alone.

The van goes fast over the bumpy ground, flinging Polly and me from side to side. It is all I can do to stop Sidney and the General being crushed between us. Polly has gone quiet. She was very brave when it was just me to face off, but now I think she's properly frightened. My shins are stinging with pain that makes it hard to think clearly. But one thing is for sure—I wish I'd never left the stag and his wild.

A panel in the cab wall slides back, just large enough for us to see Captain Skuldiss.

"Smile, please!" he says.

Taken by surprise, not thinking, we both turn towards the light.

There's a blinding flash, and then another. I'm obviously not the only one taking photos of everyone I meet. He slams the panel shut.

In the darkness, circles float before my eyes. Polly clutches my hand, and then Skuldiss forces the panel open again, his white face filling the whole slot.

"So, children," he says, "a VIP animal-loving boy we have here, my phone tells me—a very special guest. What we have here, no less, is the son of another infamous Factorium employee—the son of a certain Professor Jaynes."

Perhaps it was the van going over another bump, but I feel like my stomach just went through the floor.

Polly looks at me in shock, dropping my hand like it's on fire. "You never said your dad worked for them." Her voice has a new edge to it. "Is he like this man? Is he like Selwyn Stone?"

I shake my head in the dark. I want to explain to her—but Skuldiss carries on.

"A most popular young boy, I am given to understand by my device here. Running away, making one hell of a—how do you say?—big stink. Well, don't worry. There is a call out for you, little one. Chop goes the kitty cat, and then back to Spectrum Hall you shall go." A nasty smile. "As for your little friend . . . your dear mom and pops have been arrested in Mons, little girl. For trying to collect some precious formula, meant only for good law-abiding city folk, not wicked outsidery types such as yourselves. *Naughty* Mom and Pops. So it's off to Spectrum Hall with you as well!"

He drags the panel shut and we both throw ourselves at the dividing panel, drumming our fists on it. I am never going back to Spectrum Hall—never.

"Where are they? You have to take me to them!" screams Polly. But there is no reply, just the sound of the van roaring along the road.

We lean back in silence, and after a while I can feel Polly looking at me strangely. She slides away, over to the other side of the van.

I have to explain to her, tell her—

The reason I'm in just as much as shock as she is. Because Dad doesn't work for Facto. At least he didn't when I left, six years ago—

My thoughts dissolve into nothing as the brakes scream, sending the van into a skid.

The force of it flings us hard against the wall—

And then against the door, which has now become the ceiling—

Then we're bouncing around like sweets in a tin, everyone apart from me screaming and shouting—

Until finally everything stops.

There's no noise apart from the engine hissing and whining. I feel all over to check whether anything is broken. There's a groan beneath me—something very soft and very furry splayed out between me and Polly.

Sidney! Are you all right?

There's no reply.

The poor thing feels all limp and lifeless. I hug her close to me, trying to make her warm again. Polly takes Sidney from my arms, rubbing the cat over and over, trying to get her to open her eyes, and then I hear it—a very weak and tiny voice.

What are you waiting for?

I clap my hands with relief.

Polly holds her tight. "Is she talking, Kester? Can you hear her?"

The fact that she's used my real name for the first time gives me a shock, and I almost smile. But it's not Sidney speaking.

In the pale blue glow I can just make out the silhouettes of some antennae balancing on what was the base of the van and is now the ceiling.

What are you waiting for, soldier? Open the blasted door!

Behind me, Sidney coughs like a sick baby in Polly's arms. Looking at the light squeezing between the doors, I aim a massive kick at them. To my surprise, they swing right open and a gust of wind blows in, sweeping the General off his perch.

Polly pulls herself to her feet, holding out her hand. I grab it, and she drops out of the back of the van, dragging me and Sidney with her, nose-diving straight into a ditch full of twisted roots. There's mud everywhere, over everything. Sidney has gone at once from being a white cat into a black cat with a few white spots. Polly and I are both spluttering, wiping the soil out of our mouths, her whole face apart from her eyes covered in what looks like war paint.

Now I know what I must have looked like when I broke into her house. No wonder she got her gun out.

Just above us, the General clings to a bumper, bruised but not down. The van hangs over the edge of the ditch on its side, brake lights still on, a spooky red glow over us all. Polly is just sitting there, calmly examining the different leaves and twigs, sniffing each one, stuffing them into her pockets. But this is no time to behave like she's on one of Dad's scientific expeditions. I snap my fingers at her, signalling urgently, but she just shakes her head.

Oh, my dear, says Sidney, scowling, *do try to keep up. She isn't going anywhere, is she?*

Looking closer, I can see why. Her left welly has come off, and under a soggy woollen sock her ankle is rapidly swelling to the size of a football. I hoist her arm over my shoulder and pull her up. She screams, but grabbing at roots I pull us up out of the ditch and—scooping the General into my pocket—we slither onto the road. I turn back to the cat.

You have to walk now, Sidney, so I can help Polly. That tail, whipping the air. *Come on, I know you can do it.*

She can just about, unsteadily, like she's picking her way over broken glass rather than mud and leaves. I help Polly hobble round the van as quickly as we can.

Quick march, soldier, quick march! shouts the General.

I edge up against the rear of the van. The wheels are

raised off the ground and still spinning crazily. There's a stench of hot metal and a hammering coming from inside the driver's cab, the sound of a crutch smashing—over and over again—at the van door, trapped shut by a fallen branch.

But a fallen branch didn't stop the van.

Standing just a metre away from the crumpled snout of the machine, his eyes glowing in the headlights, is the stag.

PART 4

WILDNESS

I look up at the sky to spot some unmistakable grey shapes—and a white one—turning in the air above us.

We never would, says the stag, sniffing the air as I approach. *We would never leave you, Kester—not after what you promised.*

A promise.

Before I can reply, something knocks me over, something grey and shaggy. The wolf-cub sticks his muzzle in my face, pressing his claws down into my chest.

We have rescued you, man-child! Not that you deserve it. Stag ran out from behind a tall-home and made the beast-hunter stop. He has proved he is the bravest and strongest stag in the whole world, so now you must come with us, this instant.

Polly looks first at the stag, standing tall in the head-lights, then at the huge flock of pigeons fluttering in the air, and finally at the small wolf proudly guarding them all. "What is this, Kidnapper? Are these your friends?" She pushes some leaves around in a puddle with her one good, booted foot. "You're lucky to have so many. Sidney has been my only friend since everyone left for the cities."

I just keep pushing her towards the deer. And then he says it, just like that, very simply—

Stopping me dead in my tracks.

The she-child cannot come with us. Then, firmer, *No more humans.*

I look at Polly, who has already dug the leather notebook out of her bag and is scribbling down a rough picture of the stag and the birds dotted about in the sky.

"My mother used to tell me stories about stags, Kidnapper. She said that once upon a time people believed they were gods—of the woods and trees. Do you think he's big enough to be a god?"

I don't know. But he's big enough to take an extra passenger.

We can't leave her here—who knows what they'll do? And she won't let us take her cat without her—

That is not the concern of the animals. We asked only for your help, and need only your help alone.

But she helped me. I can't leave her here. They've taken her parents.

Polly has finished her sketch and is now watching us both with an uncertain look on her face.

Wildness, barks the General, who has somehow found his way onto my shoulder, *I am proud to report that the mission to protect the boy in the human nest was a complete success. Valiantly, I, the noble cockroach, covertly accompanied the deserter—concealed in his skin of cloth—before descending and seeing off a thousand enemies with a single bite of my jaws. Then, carefully equipping the search party with essential supplies of rotten apple—*

Do you have a point, Cockroach? asks the stag, with a heavy sigh.

The General coughs. *Of course! I can indeed confirm that the she-child cares for the infected cat—which she treats as her property—and did assist us by supplying a cure for the boy's fever. She too is separated from the rest of her pack.*

The stag's soft ears tremble beneath his horns, and the wolf-cub turns his head up at him.

No, Stag—you can't! Another human—and a she-child at that! She will only slow us down with her long hair and strange blue foot. He sniffs her one remaining welly suspiciously and looks up at me. *And besides, she does not have the voice.*

I will take the cat but not the she-child, says the stag. *The cub is right.*

If you don't mind terribly, says the cat feebly, *my full name is Oh Sidney I Could Hug You Forever And You Are My Best Friend, Aren't You?*

Yeah, well, you're just a cat again now, says the wolf-cub, sniffing her all over.

Silence! thunders the stag.

The cub sulkily backs away, and the deer kneels to let Sidney step onto his back.

Then, behind us, there is the sound of wrenching metal. I turn to see the cab door busted wide-open and, sticking out of it, Captain Skuldiss's crutch waving in the air. Followed by Captain Skuldiss himself, balancing on the edge of the upturned van. He levels the crutch at us.

"Oh, hello? Hell-o-o?" he says. "Excuse me, please, children? So sorry for interrupting, but where do you think you are going with so many dangerous and diseased animals?"

I look up at the stag, begging now—

Please, Stag. She helped me. She will help us. She can talk to other humans.

Before he can reply, Polly unhooks her arm from around my shoulder and hops over to the stag on her good foot. Reaching his mammoth belly, she just hugs him tight, like they are old friends.

I look at her. She's small and hobbling, but she pointed a gun in my face at least five times yesterday.

I think we need someone like that.

I can see the deer close his eyes and sigh, but he doesn't shake her off. So Polly grabs a clump of his fur and hauls herself up onto his back, gathering Sidney into her lap.

Very well, the stag mutters quietly, * but only until we are all out of danger from these men.*

My heart does a loop of joy and I start running towards him, but Skuldiss's voice sings out across the road as I do. "I warned you, children!"

And then it happens so quickly—there's a *crack*—

I turn to see smoke curling from the crutch—

The stag is reeling back—

The tallest tip of his horns is shot clean off into the middle of the road. It lies there like a large tooth.

"That was your very nice and polite warning shot, children," says Captain Skuldiss. He fumbles in the pockets of his coat, bringing out a fistful of bullets that he slots neatly into the crutch handle.

I cannot defeat the magic from that stick, says the stag. He's just been shot, but his only reaction is to sniff curiously at the gun smoke coiling in the air. If it hurt, he doesn't show it. *Come quickly, now!*

I take a running jump onto his back. Polly leans forward and puts her arms around my waist, trapping Sidney firmly between us. As we spin round there's another loud bang and I feel something fly past my ear. The shot is a kick-start for the stag, and he leaps higher than he's ever done into the air and over the tangled hedge bordering the other side of the road, the wolf-cub yapping at his heels.

We come down with a thump in a grassy field, the stag kicking up lumps of earth as he gallops across.

My thoughts swirl like the clouds above us. I said I would help these animals. I promised to help them. Now they're being shot at and chased by men with guns—and it's all my fault. I shouldn't have left them, I shouldn't have agreed to bring Sidney and Polly—but it's too late now.

The cullers are clambering over the hedge, Captain

Skuldiss leading them. Even on his crutches he is faster than his men, as they stumble in the muddy hoof tracks we have torn up behind us.

"Please, no waiting!" He is shouting orders. "No waiting at any cost! The deer, the little dog-fox thing, the pussycat, and the birdies, please, if you could, and quick march about it!"

The stag jumps over untidy bushes and twisted wooden fences, galloping through field after field. Fields stripped empty just as Polly described; the earth torn into furrows, piled with torn-up roots. Who knows what vegetables they were going to turn into.

Despite his size, the wolf-cub easily keeps up, not even out of breath. My knuckles are white with cold from holding on, and I pull my scarf up over my face. I focus on the General scuttling back and forth over the stag's horns, like the captain of a ship tossed about in a storm, barking commands—

Faster, faster! I order you to go faster—you're big enough!

The cullers are still following us, but they are straggling, weighed down by guns and ropes, just black blobs with shiny helmets in the distance. But Captain Skuldiss is something else.

Hurry, Stag, hurry—he's catching up!

I am going as fast as I can.

Without warning, he suddenly dives off into the strip of tall trees alongside us, the wolf-cub nearly tripping us up in his rush to follow. These woods are harder to go fast in, though. As soon as we are in among the trees, the stag has to slow right down to avoid low branches and slippery ditches. Everything is silent apart from a faint roaring sound in the distance. He pauses for breath on the rim of a hollow filled deep with spiky pine cones, and we all look around at the dark wood.

Polly reaches over to the tree next to us and pulls hard at the serrated bark. A chunk comes away easily in her hand, and I can see it is covered in globules of thick yellow wax, all stuck together like a melted candle. I glare at her—we are not on a nature trail now.

But she doesn't glare back and instead simply snaps off the ball of wax, sniffs it, and hands it to me. It doesn't even smell natural. It smells more like paint than a tree.

Polly nods. "Pine resin. A special kind of pine resin. It might come in useful; you never know."

Then a voice rings out behind us and seems to bounce off every branch. Polly hastily shoves the resin in her pocket.

"Oh, children!" The voice is out of breath but strong and unmistakable. "Oh, children! I don't think you understand me."

Be brave, soldier, do not falter now—this is the hour! whispers the General in my ear.

Behind us I hear the crunch of crutches on pine cones.

"Children! I know you are playing your famous hide-and-seek."

Polly and I hold our breaths, as the stag steps gently

forward. I'm amazed at how quietly he can go when he wants to, and the wolf-cub too, occasionally twisting his head to track the crutch noise.

We push through the branches, Polly rigid with fear. I squeeze her hand tight.

We are going to escape from Captain Skuldiss.

We are finding our way out of these woods, we are going through a clearing, and now we are coming to a—

A river.

Miles wide, foaming white over rocks, flowing out beyond the banks, too deep to cross, roaring and crashing inside all our heads.

A river that is our only way out.

"It's OK, Kidnapper," says Polly calmly, looking at the heavy brown water rushing past. "We just need to build a bridge. I've built one before, you know, over the stream at the bottom of our garden. All you need is an old plank and some rope."

But this isn't a stream, and there are no planks or ropes.

Sniffing the air, the stag mutters to himself, *And then they came to the fish-road. Just as in the dream. Extraordinary.* Then he asks me a question. *Now tell me what you are more afraid of, Kester.*

I don't understand.

Tell me what you can see.

I can see mist floating across from the other side of the bank, over a fat stretch of fast-flowing water, which seems to flow faster the more I stare at it. A "fish-road," the stag called it. Not that there will be any fish left in there now.

And it's torrential. Whole branches are being carried along in a swirl of leaves and seeds, bumping over the rocks that stick out just above the surface, like the world's smallest mountain range.

Now look again behind you. What do you see? says the stag quietly.

Twisting round, I can see Skuldiss hopping towards us through the pine trees, with one crutch pointed at me and the stag. Behind him, two cullers are bent over double, catching their breaths. Captain Skuldiss is dead calm. "Please, enough of this silly running competition." He gestures with the crutch. "Hand over the animals, please."

And what do you fear the most? continues the stag, as if he hasn't heard what Skuldiss just said.

I realize what he's suggesting.

But we'll drown. I mean—the cat, the cub—

Ha! Don't worry about me! I am the best swimmer in my pack! says the cub.

Captain Skuldiss fires a shot into the air.

I might have just made the stupidest decision of my life, but there's only one way to find out. *Now!* I yell.

The stag rears up and springs off the bank into the river. Polly lets out a long, loud scream and Sidney shrieks for her life, both howled down by the wolf-cub behind us as he too leaps into the water.

For a second, it feels like we're flying—

First the sky and the ground are in the wrong place, and then before we know it, we are diving down—

With a loud, flat slap—everything goes brown.

Pushing up, grabbing Sidney, I gasp as we break the surface again, heaving for air, the wet muzzle of the wolf-cub panting eagerly next to me as he paddles to stay afloat.

"I can't believe you let him do that!" Polly screams, exploding up out of the water beside me. "You're going to be in so much trouble! You can't just do things without asking anyone!"

I can't believe we did that either. The water is *freezing*.

It might be moving fast, but it's the temperature of sheer ice. Every breath I take is like a shock, my body fighting to stay alive. I look around wildly. Sidney's head bobs just above the surface, paddling like crazy, nudged clumsily along by the wolf-cub.

That was fun! the cub gasps between strokes. *I would very much like to do that again, wouldn't you, Cat?*

In that case, gasps Sidney, *perhaps next time— someone—could kindly do us the favour—of tying you up in a weighted sack first.*

The wolf-cub frowns and steams ahead.

I glance back at the pine wood and the bank we jumped off, as the current sweeps us farther into the centre of the icy fish-road. Captain Skuldiss hops along the edge, trying to aim his crutch at us, but we're moving too fast for him to get a clear shot, and before he can, we sweep on and round the bend.

o o o o o o o o

Our teeth chattering, we feel the stag's powerful kicks beneath us and try to stay clear of his hoofs. I stretch my hands out across the water to Polly. The cold must have gone right through her: she's stopped talking, her lips completely blue. We link arms together over the back of the stag, like he's a life raft with us drifting against his sides.

It's beginning to get dark.

I scoop Sidney out of the water and coil her round Polly's neck like a wet towel. Her fur is soaking and you can see patches of skin underneath. The stag's head is barely clear of the water, his powerful legs moving beneath us as he tries to push through to the other bank across the current—an invisible but rippling line of steel that forces us back into the centre of the fish-road whenever he tries to break free.

Stay together, he says. *Whatever happens, we must stay together.*

There is silence along the banks as we spin and bump past them, but in the distance we can just hear a roaring noise that gets louder with every bend we take. Polly begins to loosen her grip and slump down farther into the water.

"I wish *I* was cold-blooded, like a fish," she says, her voice sounding blurry and confused. "Then perhaps I wouldn't be feeling so sleepy."

You have to keep her awake! orders the General. *That is an order. Wake up! Wake up!* he shouts, while surfing alternately between Polly and me, nipping at our frostbitten ears.

The wolf-cub swims up alongside us. *We will easily survive this,* he boasts, panting heavily. *I can do anything. I can run the fastest around the water at the Ring of Trees! I can play Catch-a-White-Butterfly better than any of the others in my pack. I can jump the highest off a rolling log, and I once pounced onto my father's back and held on for longer than he said any wolf had ever done. He said I was the bravest, he said . . .*

He suddenly goes quiet. I know what he's thinking about.

The same thing as me. Dads.

Then as if she was too, as if there was something in the water, as if she'd been holding it in for ages, Polly suddenly blurts out, "I hope this is all worth it, Kidnapper, and that you can help these animals! Your dad had better not be just another horrible Facto man like Captain Skuldiss or Selwyn Stone. Because if you really wanted to help animals, why would you work for a company that sends a man on crutches to kill them all?" She pauses for breath, sucking in the cold air, only just getting her next words out. "A company that has taken away my parents."

Never mind the cold or not being able to speak—I'm too angry to think. It's not Dad's fault her parents have been arrested. And as for animals, all he's ever done is help them get better. It's true that I don't know if he has found a cure yet. I don't even know if he still lives in our home anymore.

A fear ripples down through me, colder than any water. Perhaps Polly was right to look strange when she learnt he worked for Facto. So much has changed that I don't know about—perhaps he has—

She pulls at my hands, harder this time. The cat is still coiled limply round her neck.

"Come on! You have to answer! You have to tell me why your dad will help. Why is he so different to the rest of them?"

Because he is. He's always helped save animals. That's what he does.

Suddenly I'm properly angry.

I didn't send Polly's parents away to Mons. I didn't ask her to come with me. She forced her way along. Everything was going fine till we met her and her stupid cat. We wouldn't be here about to drown in this icy water if it wasn't for her! I'm rescuing her cat and all she can do is ask me these *stupid* questions. Without thinking, I jerk my hands away from hers, to say, SHUT UP AND GO AWAY!

And she does.

With a little cry that sounds more like one of Sidney's mews, she falls back, her clothes balloon around her, the cat screeches, and a current drags them away.

Stag! I yell, but it's too late.

Before he can even twist round, Polly and Sidney have been sucked farther and farther on by the pull of the fish-road.

I'll go after them! I'll save them! shouts the wolf-cub, but the harder he tries, the more the current sends him spinning in circles too.

Sidney! I cry out.

But they've gone.

The stag can barely hide his frustration—

The she-child wasn't holding on tightly enough. We should never have brought her.

This isn't her fault. I'm the one who broke into her house. And then I hear—only just—a cry from Polly in the watery blackness up ahead.

We have to help them, we have to get ashore now, we have to—

Then the steep bank is close ahead, bobbing silhouettes of tall rushes, boulders scattered everywhere—

Now! gasps the stag between short breaths. *Jump ashore! Go! I can't climb out over these rocks!*

I stick out a hand and grab the nearest rocky crag, the other firmly round the cub's neck. With a sickening lurch I'm jerked free of the stag, my legs trailing in the water. I yank the sopping wolf-cub out after me—he's heavy and still half in the water, his jaws snapping and legs wriggling—while the General scuttles along my arm and onto the rock.

There—now that wasn't so difficult after all, was it? he says.

The stag sweeps on past us into the shadows. But I can't look.

Biting my lip in concentration, I feel my way towards the shore, pulling the wolf-cub after me. His fur seems to have absorbed half the fish-road and it's like trying to drag a sack of bricks. As I haul us onto the safety of the grass, he shakes himself dry, showering me with wolf-smelling water.

Never help me again! he snaps. *I don't need your help.*

Come on. Help me, then. We have to save them!

We run along the bank. Up ahead I can see the stag stumbling onto the bank through the tall rushes, his horns silhouetted against the evening light.

Polly's cries are getting farther and farther away. And in the distance, the faint roar grows louder.

Quick! Follow the fish-road! I yell.

The stag and wolf-cub bound along the bank, with me following as fast as I can. After several minutes of jumping over small ditches and streams, I stop, heaving for breath, as they skid to a halt ahead of me. The cub is staring out into the pitch-black.

Look, he says.

I can't see anything!

You might not be able to hear them either. I can. I have the sharpest hearing in the world.

The stag's voice comes out of the darkness. *They are there—but they are moving fast. I can't see them, but I can smell them. You must hurry.*

The roaring noise sounds very close now, a bubbling commotion, filling our heads, making it hard to hear, hard to even think clearly. We race after them until we run out of bank.

Because we are no longer on the edge just of a fish-road but of something much bigger. The black water has turned white, churning and foaming, like it's boiling up, before dropping far, far away below, into nothing. The fish-road seems to stop in midair, like an unfinished liquid bridge, before tumbling down and down in a glowing curtain of mist.

A whiterforce, says the wolf-cub, in awe. *They're heading straight for a whiterforce.*

I strain my eyes, scanning until I can just make out a tiny tip of white coasting along the water, on top of a black bob.

"Kester, help me!" Polly calls out across the water. I wish I could shout out to her to hold on. I wish. She just has to believe that I am saying it deep down inside, because I am.

I wade out into the fish-road, the stag and wolf-cub splashing in behind me, until the water comes up to my waist. But I can feel the bottom beginning to fall away sharply beneath us.

Polly calls out as they start to spin faster and faster towards the edge. "Help me! You have to help us!"

I rest one hand on the stag's broad chest and feel the steady thump of his heart as the wind blows right through us.

Ask the fish-road! he yells over the roar of the whiter-force. *Ask the fish-road to help you.*

I don't understand! I shout back.

Do not give up, Kester. You have a voice. Call to the fish-road for help.

The wolf-cub takes my hand between his jaws and yanks it under the water.

What are you doing?!

He glowers at me. *Ask them! You must ask them! We cannot ask for help to save a human. But you can. You have the voice, the voice that can command all creatures. You have to believe in it.*

The voice that can command all creatures. A gift. If there were any left to call—if I knew how to call—

Help! I cry out. I can't do anything more to stop this on my own. *Please! If there is anyone there who can save a girl and a cat from the whiterforce—show yourself now!*

The water drags Polly right to the edge, spinning her round and round as if she was only a piece of rubbish. She lunges out, grabbing one of the branches wedged between the rocks, trying to stop herself and the cat going over the edge—

I close my eyes.

And I hear something—not water roaring, not the wind—but a rushing, slithering sound, speeding through the water. A rushing sound followed by a voice, and then voices. Not voices like the animals with me on land or the birds in the sky. This is more like chanting, an underwater chant.

Ommmmmm!

The wolf-cub tugs my hand. *Look!* he says. Something is tunnelling through the water, towards the whiterforce and Polly, clinging for her life to the stuck branch. The chanting grows louder in my head—

Ommmmmm! Ommmmmm!

The ripples, wavelike ropes of water dragging across the surface of the fish-road, bear down on Polly as the branch she is holding on to begins to loosen and wobble, slowly slipping over the edge.

Quick! Quick! You have to go faster! Faster! I yell at them, whatever they are. And then I see them, coiling through the water, just visible near the surface now, in the night light—long, dark, twisting lines.

Snakes.

Snakes that swim.

Water snakes, says the stag from the bank. He can see the look on my face. *Have no fear. They do not bite.*

I look over at Polly as the branch tumbles over the edge, churning in the white spray. With a little cry she lets go, scrabbling to grab a rock instead, but her hands can't grip—and the foaming water drives her over the edge of the whiterforce.

Polly! I shout, even though I know she can't hear me.

I'm running through the water, not caring about being swept away—

And a dozen long, thin lines coil out of the fish-road, so fast you could easily miss them, and I just catch a flash of yellow eyes in a spear-point head before the snakes dive under the water again, over the edge, after Polly—

Then, nothing.

I stop, bent over, heaving for breath.

They've all gone—the snakes, Polly, and Sidney.

All that's left to hear is the churning of the whiterforce and the sound of my heart. I lost them.

But just as I turn back to the stag and the wolf-cub, there's a commotion at the edge of the drop.

Black lines are appearing in the water again, pulsing strongly against the current, their yellow eyes gleaming, as they drag behind them, wrapped tightly in their coils—

A small girl who is whimpering and shaking but alive.

Slowly but surely the water snakes pull Polly towards us. The wolf-cub and I stumble through the fish-road to help, the snakes slithering between our legs as they bring her like a ship into harbour. Polly is crying softly, and as I take her in my arms the snakes begin to disappear again.

I whip round. *Thank you!*

A single spear-point head flips out of the water, looking towards me for a second, the yellow eyes blinking. *Ommm!* he says. Then, shaking his head, the snake dives back into the depths. The chanting fades away to nothing and the water is calm again, as if they had never been there.

I turn back to Polly. Her breathing is shallow, her eyes half-shut. Her voice is very low.

"It was the wrong kind of weeds on the rocks. I thought it was . . . like seaweed. I read in a book . . . that it was strong enough . . . to make nets from. I thought it might be strong enough to hold me." She turns her head stiffly and looks at me. "But it wasn't. I was wrong. You saved me."

I feel embarrassed all of a sudden. She needs to rest now.

As if she realizes this, she closes her eyes and snuggles up against the stag, also safely back on shore. We're all back, apart from the wolf-cub, who is still just standing in the water, staring into space. I pick up a tiny pebble and send it splashing behind him to get his attention.

But he doesn't even notice.

He must be exhausted. Wading back in behind him, I reach out and ruffle his damp head. He glances up at me for less than a second before turning back to stare into the darkness. I pull at his fur again, and he recoils, snarling. So quietly I have to strain to hear him, he says, *The cat. You lost the cat.*

And then—softly at first—it begins to rain.

The pigeons wake me as soon as it's light, settling on the stag, pulling seeds from his fur. At first I think they're cleaning him, but then I see they're just feeding themselves. I realize now that they're short of food too—with no leftover scraps to feed on, so many fruits and seeds destroyed. The wind has blown away the rain clouds and dried us as we slept, hidden behind the warm back of the stag. Behind us, the whiterforce tumbles down onto the rocks below as loudly as ever. Polly is still fast asleep, resting her head on her arms. The wolf-cub snores loudly at our feet, occasionally making gruff squeaks and twitching, like he's having a bad dream.

I reach out my arm to touch Polly—but I don't.

I didn't save her cat. And every step we take towards my dad is a step farther away from her parents.

I'm so lost in my head that the pigeons have to repeat

themselves several times before I realize they're talking to me. *Kester, Kester!*

What? I say crossly.

Kester—please listen. We must continue our journey with all speed.

I look at them, rubbing my eyes. *What's the point?* I can only just bring myself to say the words. *We've lost Sidney. I can't look after you all. I don't know if I can save you.*

The pigeons look at one another and give birdlike shrugs. *What is the loss of one cat compared to saving the many lives of the last wild?*

Yes, you've lost many lives, and one cat. This time the white pigeon doesn't make me smile. I explode at all of them.

Is that what you really think? How can you?

My voice must be only just audible above the crashing of the whiterforce, but in reply the pigeons flock together and launch straight up into the sky.

There's no panic—just a calm power into the air, more like they're floating up through water. Just above tree height they join up into a circle of dots far above my head. As their wingtips meet, the circle begins to spiral slowly and they start making a noise I've never heard pigeons make before. A long, low moan, which echoes all the way along the fish-road, over the roar of the whiterforce, over the rattle of the wind. And then I start to hear words, strange and fantastical words I have never heard before. Words sung in a list, repeated over and over again—

*O lapwing, kestrel, turtle dove, cuckoo, hawfinch,
redpoll, grebe, swift, pipit, whinchat, and wood warbler.*

*Corn bunting, curlew, harrier, redshank, ring ouzel,
twite, willow tit, and wagtail.*

*Bittern, grouse, godwit, capercaillie, chough, corncrake,
nightjar, and skylark . . .**

Every word is a ray cutting straight through me, like a laser.

And there is nothing I can do to stop their sadness.

I put my head in my hands.

Kester,* says the stag, standing up behind me. The pigeons' singing must have woken him up.

I just want to get away, get away from all of them. I stride off down the shore, my path blocked by a pool of water across the sandy mud. I look down, and all I can see is my own stupid, angry reflection, pink and wobbling.

Kester, turn around,* says the stag as the pigeons continue to circle and call out above. His eyes look brighter than they did. He looks stronger, fitter than I could have imagined after his ordeal.

The birds are grieving, Kester. Singing a call of mourning for those they have lost. They call out the names of those they have lost from the skies. What about you?*

I remember what the pigeons told me by the First Fold

about their calls. But I couldn't feel less like singing. He comes closer, lecturing me again.

I can see so much anger in your thoughts, behind your eyes. He pauses, but I don't say anything. *Is there anything you would like to tell me?*

Stop trying to be my dad all the time, because you're not!

You may rest assured, Kester, that I have no wish to be your father.

I beat my fists against his side. *You don't understand—none of you understand!*

Now the pigeons' wailing is waking everyone up. The wolf-cub is murmuring, giving himself a good stretch. And Polly is sitting up, avoiding my gaze as she twists two lengths of creeper from the bank into a plait.

The stag leans forward and I start, because it looks like he's going to butt me with his horns. Instead he leans in and nuzzles my neck. He's soft and warm, and it tickles.

I hate him. I hate him for doing this. He tried this by the house, and I'm not falling for it again.

Stop it. Stop it. You just want to use me, you don't care about me—

I do care about you, Kester, I care about you very much—

"What's going on?" asks Polly from behind.

You don't care about me. You had me flown to a place where I could have got this plague of yours—

But you haven't, says the wolf-cub.

You force me to help you, force me to be some kind of hero, which I'm not; I'm just a kid who can't talk. I can't do any of this. I can't save you—I can't even save a single cat. I'm not the person you think I am—

But you are, says the stag.

This virus is still here, and it's killed everything, and there's no cure, and I don't know if Dad— I stop midsentence. *What did you say?*

I said, but you are, repeats the stag, meeting my eyes.

I am what? I say back, all suspicious. Polly takes a step closer.

You are a hero. You helped us escape from the guardians—the wolf-cub growls at this—*you tried to rescue the cat, you protected her and the girl against the man with the firestick. You led us free, into the fish-road. And you might not have saved the cat from her destiny, but you used your gift to save the life of one of your own. I do not know what it takes for a man to call another a hero. But I tell you, Kester Jaynes, by any animal measure of such things, you are just that.*

For a moment I stare at him, not sure I quite heard him right. No one has ever said anything like that to me before—and then I'm crying.

As I haven't for so long.

All these animals and Polly looking at me, and I'm crying. Crying for Sidney, gone. I'm crying for Mum, also gone, and crying for Dad, whom I haven't seen in six years, the

Dad I'm beginning to wonder if I will still recognize.

Crying just because everything is such a mess, and I don't know that I'll be able to fix it.

I look at the stag through my tears. *I just wonder if I can do this—get us to the city. Everyone's against us. It's so far away. The virus is unstoppable.*

The wolf-cub runs up and nearly knocks me over. Then he stands up on his hind paws and does the grossest thing— he licks me. He actually licks the tears off my face.

I am the greatest hero on this adventure, the greatest hero in all the world, and nothing will ever change that. And you are still a smelly human. But that you have proven yourself the second-greatest hero on this adventure, I agree with the stag.

The deer grunts. *You cannot save us all, Kester. You cannot save everyone and everything.* He looks around the bank, sniffing the damp air. Almost as if Sidney might suddenly appear. But she doesn't. *If you can only save some, then that is what you must do. You see, you are a hero. Now, will you start acting like one? Can you lead us? We need to enter the world of man to find the help we need—and we cannot do that without you.* He pauses, the first time the stag has hesitated saying anything to me, and sinks down to the ground.

The great stag, kneeling before me.

You must now lead this wild to your city. We are in your hands. Then, his head lowered, he says, *Can you be our Wildness?*

A Wildness. The leader of a wild. What I thought the stag was. But now, here he is, bowing and asking me to lead them. What I thought only a stag could do.

I look around us. We are standing on a strip of pebbles, dotted in between with shallow pools, the loosely scattered stones spread thinner and thinner over a carpet of sludge as they run down towards the water's edge. Ahead, the ground rises steeply, covered with tall reeds, and I cannot see what lies beyond. Behind us, the water of the fish-road, tumbling and racing, and somewhere beyond that . . . a man on crutches, armed with a firestick.

I say the new words over and over to myself, because if I am to lead these animals, I need to start thinking like them.

The animals, insect, and birds are gathered around me in a semicircle. My wild. Waiting for me to lead.

Yes, Stag, I say. *I will be your Wildness.*

Very good, says the stag. *Now tell me again everything that you have learnt about the berry-eye from this she-child . . .*

As we turn again to walk back up the slope, something hits me very hard in the face. Something small and human-hand-shaped. Polly-hand-shaped.

"I don't care about your adventure anymore. You've lost Sidney, so you can't make her better."

Her face is red and angry.

"I want to find out what's happened to my parents. I want to go home, Kidnapper—now."

I can't speak to Polly, but I can show her I'm the Wildness now, so I step forward and put my arms around her. She struggles and thumps my chest and eventually wrestles free, but when she does there are tears streaming down her cheeks.

"Stop it! You can't make me feel better through hugs. I used to be able to hug Sidney all the time, whenever I felt alone, and now I'll never be able to hug her again!"

She sits down with a thud on the grassy bank and slouches against a boulder.

"Anyway, it doesn't matter. I can't go on with you even if I wanted to. My foot hurts too much." Leaning forward to her swollen ankle, she gingerly rubs at it and winces. I kneel down to see how bad the bruising is. Straightaway she cries out, covering it with her hands. "What are you doing? Don't touch it!" Polly smudges her tears away. "You don't know what you're doing. Wait a moment," she says, and reaches into the sodden rucksack still clinging to her back.

Riffling through the waterlogged contents, she eventually digs out her black notebook, curling and soaked right through. She unpicks the pages carefully, and I can see that the scribbled notes and drawings—of plants, berries, and seeds—are blurred and smudged by the water but still there. With that superior look on her face again, she hands me the book, open at a picture of a skinny-looking tree covered in so many leaves that it is bent right over and weighed down, the leaves drifting and trailing in a stream.

"You can't make me better with hugs, but you can make me better with this."

She's right. When it comes to swollen ankles, I really don't know what I'm doing.

"It's called a shining willow. Not because it actually shines; it's a tree. But the leaves are silvery and golden, so when the sun is out it can look like they're shining. The leaves are special. They can make bruises disappear." The tree looks peaceful. Polly looks miserable and gives a miserable sigh. "I don't know where to find one, though. And you'll need lots for it to work. We need to go and look for help, Kidnapper. My ankle hurts, those men are chasing us—we can't do this on our own."

I can sense the stag stirring uncomfortably, but he has no need to worry. We don't need to find anyone else. I can help Polly. I need to make things up to her for losing Sidney. That's the job of a leader. A Wildness. With a wave of my hand I call over the pigeons, who land on my shoulders and head, peering down at the book.

Yes. We know this tall-home, we will find it for you. We thought you were never going to ask. The tall-home that bends and shines, it is well-known for cures. But you will need more leaves than we can carry in our beaks. You must come with us.

Yes—we were never going to ask you. The white pigeon joins the others, who are already in a semicircle on the ground, their heads pecking backwards and forwards like they're doing a funny dance. I turn to the stag, but I don't need to say anything.

We will obey your command. Go with the pigeons, fetch a cure for the girl's foot. I will guard her here.

You mean she can come with us to the city?

There is a faint trace of a smile in the stag's voice. *You are the Wildness now. See how you begin to learn the power of the voice. The snakes, the pigeons, and now me—see how we obey your word.*

Then the birds disappear up the bank over the reeds and feathery grasses ahead, to search for the leaf-cure, the white pigeon calling, *Way this! Way this!*

I follow them, but the wolf-cub immediately runs after us, getting in my way and nearly tripping me up.

What are you doing? I say. *No one said anything about you coming.*

You have been declared Wildness, and I too have submitted like the stag. I must now hunt with you, always.

As we leave the roar of the whiterforce behind, a hush

falls, the wolf-cub pushing silently ahead through sheaves of tall grass. Grass that seems to be growing taller the farther we go into the marshes, as the ground gets soggier beneath our feet. It's hard work, constantly slipping into boggy puddles and stepping out again. Every cell in my brain, every nerve in my body is focused on being the Wildness now, on leading and being in charge. The wolf-cub stays by my side and jumps happily over hillocks of moss erupting out of the ground in spools of bright yellow and green, endlessly sniffing every last strand.

Why did you leave your father? Did he fall off a cliff after a great hunt too?

Not really, I mutter.

It must be very hard to be without a father. I find it hard. I'm so used to him telling me what to do. But I think I'm doing really well, don't you?

Yes, you're doing just great.

Better than any other wolf-cub without a father that you've ever seen?

Yes, much better—the best ever.

Some soil drops onto our heads, and there is the white pigeon, who has somehow managed to get filthy from the bog as well, high above our heads, hurrying us on.

So why did you leave? the wolf-cub asks again.

I look down at the ground. *I didn't want to. I got taken away from him.*

The cub seems proper shocked. *Had you committed a great crime against your pack?*

Biting my lip, I look around for something else to think about—all the rubbery leaves and pale flowers and waving grass—but the cub swipes his paw at my leg, breaking my thoughts. His amber eyes are hard, his jaw set. I don't think a Wildness is meant to have committed any crimes.

You are the Wildness now. You have to tell me.

Look, it's not something I want to talk about right now.

I turn aside and stumble on. I'm the Wildness. I can do what I like. I don't have to answer or explain anything. We wander on in silence for what feels like hours, my hands dug into my pockets, my head full of thoughts that I don't want to be there.

Finally the cub speaks again, quieter this time, wounded. *I have pledged you loyalty. Do you know what that means?*

Not really, no.

It means I will offer my life for yours if I have to. But I can only do that if I know who I am serving. You have to tell me—those are the rules of a wild.

You don't have to offer your life.

It doesn't matter. I will.

Well, thanks, that's really—

He leaps in front of me and stamps his paw, sending black mud flying everywhere. *I don't want thanks. I want to know who I am serving. What did you do? What did you do that was so bad you got sent away from your father? You have to tell me!*

We stare at each other in silence, the only reply coming

from the wind whispering between the reeds. Then there's a call from the rushes up ahead.

Found it! Found it! call down the pigeons. *Over here!*

Over there! cries out the white pigeon.

We splash on through the swamp, following their cries, and find them perched high above our heads, spread out on the drooping branches of a tree. A tree that stands all alone in the middle of a black pond, the surface covered with floating moss and lily pads. The wolf-cub and I only just stop ourselves falling in as the rushes and reeds give way to water. But neither of us can take our eyes off the tree. Here, rising out of the bog, the leaves of the tree, which hang down in bunches, pulling it right over with their weight—are bright gold. Gold and shining and twisting in the cold air.

Shining willow. The leaf-cure.

The leaf-cure that is in the middle of a swamp.

A swamp that steams and bubbles, treacly black mud stirring and oozing like oil.

I glower at the pigeons, sitting coolly on top of the tree, watching me with their beady eyes. I've only just climbed out of a freezing river—

What about this? Is this in your old dream as well?

Oh yes. They nod back.

When are you going to tell me what's really going on?

They look away.

We are only birds. We cannot explain everything that there is.

Shaking my head, I start wading into the watery mud. The swamp tugs and pulls at my feet. I try to go back but just sink deeper in, up to my knees. It gets thicker as I go deeper and deeper, pressing around me, licking my chin.

And then, I slip—

My foot stumbles on a rock. I'm falling and the mud is closing over my head—

For a minute all I can see is black, and I can't breathe at all—and there is soil and water up my nose and in my eyes—

I try not to panic, but it's hard when you can taste dirty mud on your lips as it squeezes tight around your chest, making it harder and harder to breathe, and yet—

The strangest thing. I can hear it. I can hear the swamp. There are no creatures here that I can see. No snakes, no fish, no varmints. But there are voices. Tiny faint voices, not making any sense, not forming any words, just noises and echoes of noises. Voices everywhere in the swamp. Voices waiting to be born.

It's only a moment—then I give one last push and I'm bursting up out of the swamp, wiping gobbets of mud from my eyes, gasping for air.

For a moment I just stand there, black from head to foot in bog, sucking in huge breaths of air. But I don't feel scared anymore. Not of mud. Not of the outdoors. I feel different somehow. Part of things, in a way that I wasn't before.

Then the wolf-cub shouts at me from the bank, the pigeons from the tree—and I'm plunging forward towards the shining leaves ahead. Reaching them, I strain on my toes, grabbing at the lowest hanging bunches, ripping them off.

Take as many as you can! say the birds.

Holding the leaves high above my head, I wade back through the bog and collapse on the bank, my chest heaving up and down. I sniff the leaves clutched in my hand, dripping with mud. They smell strange and woody.

The pigeons crowd round.

Place them on her ankle. Wrap them round tight. They will heal her and soothe her.

I stuff my pockets full of leaves until I can carry no more, and we hurry back through the swamp. But it is no easier to get through than before, and as we weave our way through the pools and clumps of grasses, the light slowly begins to change in the sky.

As we finally climb up the bank, pushing through the ferns to reach the fish-road again and see the long shadows falling from the trees onto the water, I realize that we have been gone for most of the day. Immediately I sense that something isn't right. Because although it is getting darker, I can still see clearly. I can see the clouds of mist from the whiterforce, the ripples of light on the water, and I can see the rocks and boulders on the shore where we left the others.

I just can't see them.

By the time I start to run to the shore, the wolf-cub is already ahead of me, leaping in great strides, skidding onto the shingle, flipping rocks over with his paw, as if the stag or Polly might be hiding under them.

You won't find them there—

I'm not looking for them! he snaps back. *I'm looking for the bug.*

General! I shout out. *General—are you still here?*

Nothing comes back—just the wind in the rushes and the sound of the cub sniffing the ground like he wants to snort it right up.

There is a scent here. Another human. I can follow their tracks.

I look up ahead at the reeds and grasses. I can't see any sign of anything, but he's determined.

Let us follow the track and the scent while it is still fresh, urges the wolf-cub.

Slumped on a rock, I slowly move a shallow pile of leaves around with my foot, trying to focus and think of a plan. And as I move the leaves around I see some white pebbles. Or maybe pieces of bone.

Square-shaped pieces of bone.

My heart leaps into my throat as I realize that they're not pieces of bone—they're tiles.

I fall onto my knees and start digging away the mud and rubbish. There are four letter tiles there, hurriedly hidden under a leaf. But the letters don't form any word I recognize.

I wonder if they're the initials of something. *May Follow Right Ahead?* But where? *My Fault Really Apologize?* Doesn't sound like Polly. *Mr. Firestick Returned Again?* That's something the stag would write, not Polly.

What have you found? What have you found? shouts the wolf-cub, jumping right into the puddle with his shaggy paws and wet muzzle, kicking the tiles up into the air. They tumble in the sky before landing back down with a splash.

You idiot! Look what you've done!

But as I crouch down again, wiping off the dirt, I realize that he's scattered them into sense.

I scoop up the tiles in my hand and clench them tight. *Come on,* I say, standing up. I follow the wolf-cub along the shore as he tracks the trail right along the bank, away from the swamp, the leaf-cure, and the whiterforce— sniffing every broken branch, every frond of leaf, for any clue he can gather. The pebbles and sand slowly disappear, buried under knotted rolls of creepers and brambles. We keep on pushing through them, until the coils and curls of greenery fall away and we find ourselves looking down from the top of a slope, where we pause to take a breath. A deep one.

Because it's as if the country we've been travelling in has just been completely flattened into the biggest and emptiest field I have ever seen in my life. All the different colours, the greens and greys and yellows, all the different leaves and blades of grass, all rolled down into one grey-brown plain of mud, stretching right into the farthest distance, where the land meets the sky.

Mud everywhere.

Here and there are ragged islands of drooping, pale brown stalks—which must be all that remain of the crops that once grew in this giant field, now just rotting into the ground.

And at the bottom of the slope, its engine idling, black smoke puffing into the air out of tall pipes, is what looks like a giant tractor cabin with a long bar of revolving metal teeth at the front. At the back is what looks like a huge green metal barn on equally giant wheels. A long chute sticks out of the back of the barn, and right below it is a ramp leading inside.

I look at the tiles clutched in my hand. A *farm* machine. A kind I once saw in a book. A *harvesting* machine. Except there's clearly nothing to harvest anymore, and no shower of grain rains out of the chute as it did in the book.

But it's not the harvesting machine that is making us run down the slope as fast as we can, Wolf-Cub and I, falling over one another, screaming and shouting, the pigeons crying overhead—it's the girl and the deer climbing into it, stepping slowly up the metal ramp into the darkness.

There's a woman too, a woman I don't know, in boots and a scarf, who seems to have smoke puffing out of her as well—guiding them in—but they're too far away. The stag hasn't heard us.

Over here, over here! cry the pigeons from somewhere in the sky above, but now our friends are inside the harvesting machine and the ramp is slowly closing up behind them. The woman is chaining it up, and I've never wanted to yell, actually humanly yell, more in my life—but nothing comes out. Then she is climbing up a ladder, back into the tractor cab at the front of the machine, and just as we reach the bottom of the slope, the tractor cabin growls and shudders, the orange lights on top begin to revolve, and the harvesting machine lumbers off over the ground, churning a spray of earth and dead crops into the air.

We chase after it as quickly as we can but find ourselves going slower and slower, our feet clogged with clay, stumbling over the freshly made ridges of earth, shrivelled stalks spread flat over each one, like tentacles.

The pigeons fly faster, over the top of the machine, but there is nothing they can do to stop it.

Then all of a sudden the wolf-cub stops. We can feel the ground shaking under us as the machine rolls into the distance, but it is getting farther and farther away, the noise fainter with every second.

What is it? Why have you stopped?

I do not think we can stop this machine, Wildness. The birds can't stop it—and I can't help you either. We have lost them.

Why are you giving up? I thought you just said you would do anything for me?

The second the words are out of my head, I wish I hadn't said them. The wolf-cub's shoulders droop and he looks down at the ground.

But there isn't time to say sorry. I look at the shimmering green block on the horizon, shrinking slowly out of view, steaming smoke into the sky. I clutch the leaves and tiles in my pocket—and realize what I have to do. I don't run after it.

Instead I plant my feet firmly on the ground and try to concentrate. To listen.

Are you listening? I know you're here! I call out.

There's no response, nothing, just the faint roaring of the machine in the distance.

I know you're here! I call out again.

Snakes in the fish-road. Voices in the swamp. There must be something, even in this dead field of stalks and mud.

Whoever you are, whoever is here—I am the Wildness and I command you to help us.

The machine is heading for the horizon. Then something runs over my feet.

I look down and squint. A single tiny, furry ginger mouse. My heart sinks.

How can you help us?

You'll want that metal beast stopping, no doubt. She jerks her head towards the disappearing monster.

Yes, I say, *but how are you—*

Easy as corn pie, my fine two-legged sir. That monster—this is what you lot call a "Kombylarbester." There's a little black tail of a wire, you see, runs down the back, under the hatch. A couple of quick chews on that and—

Well, could you—you know—just do something?

The mouse wipes her face with her paws. *Oh, I'd love to. Oh, believe you me—I would love nothing more. Problem is, see, there's no way I can actually get to the wire by myself, on account of it being a fast-moving object right at the other* end of this field. 'Cause normally, right, this is performed as a stationary procedure on the Kombylarbester, when it's not moving, at night. There's a little chute, you see, that one poking out the back there—that's the one, that's it—and we just climb down that basically. Never done it on a moving one before.*

She sucks her teeth.

And then they are above, grey dots and a white one in the sky, before I even ask. Diving down into the stalks and grabbing the mouse between their claws, so she shoots up in the air past my nose, dangling by her tail.

Hey—are you having a laugh or what? I'm not going anywhere with a blooming pigeon—

But they are gone, off into the sky, up high, and then I see—silhouetted against the setting sun—a wriggling ball drop high from their claws, still screaming loud enough for us to hear, down into a metal tube sticking out of the Kombylarbester's thrumming engine.

I close my eyes. I don't want to look.

And just as I think we've lost them forever—and the machine is about to disappear out of sight—

Everything stops—the humming, the grinding, the clacking, and the lights. Just like that. Winding down with a huge groan, like the engine itself has been given an injection to put it to sleep.

I open my eyes. She did it. The mouse actually did it. I feel dizzy, every part of me tingling and fizzing with excitement. Running back, I find the cub still in the shadows of the stalks. I give him a hug.

She did it! The mouse did it, Cub!

Maybe that mouse did play a small part in it, he says, all quiet and sad, *but I think I played the best part.*

I slap his side. *Of course you did, you totally did.*

Then we're running towards the machine as fast as we can, talking quickly, until just as we reach it, out of breath and exhausted, high above our heads a door swings open out of the metal green wall of the machine. And the driver of the Kombylarbester climbs down to meet us.

PART 5

SHE KNOWS YOUR FATHER

It's a woman with ruddy cheeks, spattered with mud and engine grease, blonde hair tied up in a scarf wrapped round her head. She takes a wedge of smouldering cigar out of her mouth, chucks it on the ground, and squashes it into the stubble with her heel. Then she jabs her finger at me.

"What you looking at me like that for, little man? I was going to come back and get you as well. Your young lady friend was very firm on that point." She flicks a bit of ash off her shoulder, pointing at the silent machine behind her, oily smoke still trailing into the sky from its exhausts. "Or at least that was my plan, till the flaming engine just cut out. Still, nothing that can't be fixed, I'm sure."

I think of the mouse wriggling about in the machine's hot pipes.

I do not like this woman or her smell, Wildness, growls Wolf-Cub.

The woman folds her arms, rocking back on her heels, looking us up and down. And then a toothy smile cracks across her face and she stretches her arms out wide as if to hug us all.

"No need to look at me like that, my lad! I'm going to help you, you daft thing. Already helped your friend Polly—found her down by the river, I did—and in a terrible state she was. You must be Kester," she says, and there's a strange flicker across her face for a second, but then she's all smiles again, bending down to face us dead-on. "You can call me Ma, if you like."

I can't call her anything, but I nod and glance towards the dead machine, thinking of the others inside.

"Fair enough. You need help, I hear. And you've come to the right place for it. I'm no friend to cullers." She twists to look at the wolf-cub, hands on her thighs. "But first, I've just got to check one thing, if you don't mind."

Before the cub can do anything, she strides forward and, straddling him from behind, grabs his head tight between her legs so he can't snap at her. He wriggles, but she's got him tight. With her other hand, she whips a silvery pencil torch out of her back pocket, which she shines right in his eyes. Ignoring his yelps, she calmly shines the torch all over one rolling eye, and then the other, before releasing him onto the ground with a thump.

"You'll do," she says.

He shakes his coat, his fur sticking out in spikes and waves like he's electrifying himself against her. *I only submit because you are the Wildness. Otherwise I would take out her throat.*

The woman smiles at me. "Oh, I don't mind his bark. Once upon a time I'd have shot him myself, just like that." She mimes swinging an invisible gun over the crook of her arm, raising it to her shoulder, aiming it right at the cub, and then firing an imaginary trigger. His growl turns to more of a whimper, but he doesn't move. She swings the invisible gun round at the pigeons on the ground, still squinting. They freeze where they stand. Ma seizes her moment and, before they can react, she is in the middle of them, quickly shining her torch into their eyes one by one—like an expert, like Dad would have done.

"Not bad, not bad at all," she says. "Fat, healthy-looking birds you've got there, my lad."

Not a bad-looking, fat bird yourself, says the white pigeon quietly.

"You can't be too careful," Ma explains, stuffing her torch back in her pocket. "I lost everything to that stinking plague: my best beasts, prize herds, these crops I had to let rot—all my wheat, barley, taters, everything."

She presses a small black fob in her hand. With a clunk and a hum, the whole back wall of her Kombylarbester folds down into a ramp.

"Right—we'd better get you in there with the rest of 'em before a blasted culler sees us."

While Ma bashes and hammers at the outside of the machine, fixing the broken cable—we crowd inside the metal cave. Straightaway the stag rushes forward out of the darkness, and the General is suddenly on my shoulder, the pigeons crowding round all of us and getting in the way and flapping in my face so I have to push them away.

I'm looking for someone else.

It's big in here and smells stale. By the cracks of light I can see the cave is full of smaller machines, jagged shadows and curves, straining at the chains holding them to the sides. And sitting right underneath one of them, her foot resting on a pile of old sacks—it's Polly. She gives me a half smile, which is better than none.

"I told you there were others who could help," she says. "That woman found us, she put me on the back of the stag, and I've told her everything and she's on our side, Kidnapper. I think she could help me find Mum and Dad, she—"

I'm about to go over to her when there's a loud rattling noise from the corner, and the pigeons explode upward crazily.

At first I think it's just the Kombylarbester restarting. Ma must have fixed whatever the mouse did, because with a loud roar from beneath our feet, the machine is suddenly lurching off over the field again. But the rattling continues—growing louder, pushing against metal, trying to get in, met by a low, steady growl from the wolf-cub. And then, with a plop, a small ginger, furry ball explodes out of a chute in a cloud of dust and rolls across the floor, spluttering.

The mouse gets to her feet and does a massive sneeze,

and then as we all stare, she puts one paw out and rotates her whole body around it. First in one direction, then the other. And then the other paw, spinning twice around again. Next she touches her tail with her nose. Finally she rolls onto her back and spins around, her tiny feet waving in the air. She wriggles back onto her front and shakes her whiskers.

No one says anything. I take a photo, and the flash in the dark makes everyone jump, blinking.

Sorry, I mutter, and the mouse looks at us all in surprise.

You got a problem or something?

No, just wondering what that was meant to be, I say.

That, my two-legged friend, was a special harvest mouse Dance of Welcome.

I've never seen a mouse dance before, growls the wolf-cub.

Well! You ain't seen nothing yet in that case, my good friends from the north. As a matter of fact, we harvest mice have over forty-six thousand different dances. We've also got the Corn Is Coming Dance. We've got the Corn Has Arrived Dance. We've got the Corn Is Really Something Now, You Should Check It Out Dance. We've got the Corn Is Kind of on the Turn Now, So Hurry Up Dance. We've got the—

All right—I think we get the idea.

She stops, looking hurt. So I hold out my palm and she hurries into it, her claws pricking my skin.

I guess I should say thanks, Mouse, I say. *I think you saved our lives.*

She bristles. *Harvest Mouse, if you don't mind. Not any old mouse.* I can just see the orbs of her jet-black eyes glistening, her muzzle no bigger than a pencil tip. *Get my name right, and we'll get on just fine. Get it wrong, and I'm afraid I will answer to no one for my actions. Isn't that right—* She looks around, behind her, and stops midsentence. As if she was expecting to see something there.

Oh, I forgot again, she says, subdued. *They all went, you see—the rest of my nest.*

Was it the berry-eye? I ask.

Harvest Mouse is outraged again. She nips my finger. *Do you mind! Certainly not, thanks very much. It never touched us. Not our little nest.* Then she is the least loud she has been since I met her. *But the problem was, you see, it took away what we was going to eat. No bee nectar, no fruit, no grubs—and then they even took the crops away.*

As she talks, her tail flicks constantly against my fingers. It feels surprisingly strong. I'm trying to make sense of what she's saying.

So—the rest of your . . . nest—they starved because of the berry-eye?

Got it in one, sunshine. You might call it a plague, but to us it was a famine. She sighs. *I've got no one left, so I was sort of hoping that . . .*

Her voice trails off as she sees the wolf-cub watching

her, his brow creased with suspicion, the stag keeping a stern silence behind him.

She is too small to be any trouble, coo the grey pigeons from their corner. *And she could be of use.*

It's decided then.

Yes, Harvest Mouse, you can come with us, in case there are other Kombylarbesters we need your help with.

Ta very muchly, my old love, don't mind if I do. Where are you lot off to anyhow?

As I tell her our story, her little eyes light up. Then, wrapping her tail around my finger, she swings off like an acrobat and twists and tumbles through the air, landing perfectly on the corner of a big old plough gathering dust in the corner.

Special Flying Dance of Acceptance on a Dangerous Journey! she cheeps.

Polly, sitting in the corner, has gone very quiet since the mouse arrived. I can guess what she's thinking about. A cat who was no friend to mice but who was everything to her. I'm trying to think of a word to make with the tiles that will cheer her up, when there's a jolt, and a sound like the Kombylarbester is turning, stopping, and turning again before finally juddering to a stop.

With a yell of *Freedom Dance!* the harvest mouse slides over the floor, wriggling her tail, and both Polly and the wolf-cub are thrown on top of me. As we disentangle ourselves, the ramp yawns open and the first thing I see is the silhouette of Ma standing in the doorway. The very end of the daylight streams past her as she beckons us to come out.

I can't believe what I'm hearing at first—sounds that I haven't heard for so long—the noise of other people, lots and lots of them, all chattering and shouting and arguing and running and walking, the noise of engines roaring. Standing on the edge of the ramp, my hand on the wolf-cub's head as my eyes adjust to the light, I think for a moment that we have arrived in the city already.

But not the city we're looking for.

Not a city of skyscrapers but one of metal barns and corrugated roofs, the huge square in front of us filled with tractors and trailers. The barn rooftops stretch out as far as we can see, glinting in the evening light. There are stacks of tyres and oil drums and plastic sacks piled high into the sky, and enough machinery—arms, diggers, claws, ploughs, sprays—to fill a whole scrap yard.

"Welcome to Old Burn Farm, my beauties!" says Ma, with another big smile.

I can see we're on a farm, all right, but not any old farm. Polly takes the words out of my mouth.

"It's the biggest farm in the world," she whispers.

"Well, come on, for heaven's sake!" says Ma. "We don't bite." I see now the "we" she refers to—a circle of men and women waiting at the bottom of the ramp, all in padded waistcoats like hers. More outsiders—lots of them. The men are wearing caps, and the women have scarves around their hair. All are carrying pitchforks and spades. But it's their eyes I notice the most—not red but hungry, big rings of shadow around them, sunken into their cheeks, and staring at us.

For a moment we hesitate and the wolf-cub's hackles rise, but then the outsiders are smiling, patting the stag's flank, stroking the cub's neck, and letting the pigeons peck at scraps of corn between their feet. Even the mouse is doing what must be a Dance of Friendship in an old lady's hand. There is a wave of chatter through the crowd, like they can't believe they're seeing actual animals again, until Ma silences them with a bellow.

"Bodger? Where's Bodger?"

There's the sound of footsteps so heavy that I think they might be leading an animal through, rather than a person—but the crowd parts to reveal someone who looks like a mix of both. He must be a person, because he has two arms and two legs, ears, eyes, and a nose, like us. But his long arms are covered in furry hair, and when he sees us he grins to reveal a mouth full of teeth as big and cracked as the stag's. The thing I notice most about him is the massive handlebar moustache, which looks like a hairy black caterpillar draped over his thick lips.

He doesn't say anything. He just grunts.

"You'll like my friend Bodger," Ma says briskly to me, wiping her dirty hands on her trousers. "He's not from round here, and he can't talk either—just like you."

Bodger just stares at us and the animals.

Ma turns to him. "Right—take this one and his girlfriend to the sick bay, please."

She doesn't sound so friendly anymore.

"I'm not his girlfriend!" Polly says fiercely. Very fiercely.

Bodger smirks. He stomps over to us, but before he can lay a hand on me I wriggle away, back to my wild. I'm not letting them out of my sight. I'm not losing another one ever again.

Ma plants herself between us, her legs apart.

"Don't worry. We'll look after them. We know how to look after our beasts, don't we?" She gives a strange smile to the crowd, who just nod, their hands tightening around their pitchforks, their jaws set. "We'll look after all of you."

Wolf-Cub jerks forward as one of the farmers grabs on to the scruff of his neck. Another throws a rope around the stag and he starts with surprise, just as a net is thrown over the pigeons and the mouse finds herself trapped under a cage. Even the General is popped neatly in a large glass jar.

No way. I dig my heels in and shake my head.

"I said I'll look after 'em," says Ma. "I've been a farmer for thirty-five years and think I know how to look after some animals." Her steady stare again. Then she raises an eyebrow. "And from what I've been told, I might even do a better job than you."

Before I can look at Polly, Bodger is behind us, his hot breath on our necks as Ma nods sharply at him. He grabs both of us by our hands and leads us firmly away from my wild.

I look back quickly at the ramp. All the animals are standing looking at me, not saying a word, like I'm leaving them on purpose.

I'll come and find you! I shout. *I promise!*

And then Bodger pushes us through a door into a barn, and they're gone, out of sight.

He drags us on through the empty barn, ignoring Polly's cries of pain as she hobbles along, down a paved passage and some crooked steps until we come to a low door covered in plastic sheeting. There's a messy red cross painted on it, and a single word:

QUARANTINE

The man-ape finally releases us, and we stumble, shaking the blood back into our squashed hands. He grunts and pulls back the plastic curtain, pointing at the door.

"Why?" demands Polly. "Why do we have to go in here? You know we can't get the virus—"

But Bodger just puts a sausagelike finger to his mouth to shush her, and then points to the sign, points to his eyes, and shakes his head. I understand exactly what he means. I can see Polly about to open her mouth again, but I catch her gaze. Now is perhaps not the best time to start an argument with a man fifteen times the size of us both put together.

Bodger fishes a rusty key out of his pocket, turns it in the lock. He nods at me and I push open the stiff wooden door. We've barely taken a step before Bodger boots us in and I tumble over Polly onto a floor of earth. As we pick ourselves up he locks the door behind us, his footsteps stomping away, back up the passage.

We're in a cramped wooden shed. It looks much older than the giant metal barn we've just come through. A few candles in glass lanterns dangle from the rough beams that make up the ceiling, and I can just make out four low beds in the dim light. Camp beds put up among heavy shovels and forks leaning against the wooden walls.

"It's just like one of our garden sheds at home," Polly says, sounding pleased. Just like the shed I broke through into her house in fact. "We'll be safe here," she says, heaving herself onto the last bed by the wall. I roll up her trouser leg and finally take a proper look at her ankle in the candlelight. Angry, red, and swollen—it doesn't look any better. She folds her arms.

"I'm sure they'll come back soon with some medicine and something to eat. I bet they've got some formula." She sounds cross. "You don't look very pleased about our new friends, Kidnapper."

I'm just wondering how normal it is for new friends to lock you in their shed. But instead of trying to explain any more, I simply kneel down next to her and dig out the fistfuls of leaf-cure I pulled from the tree in the swamp. They're drier now but still have their woody tang, and they shine in the glow from the lamp.

Polly's eyes light up. "You found them!"

I grin and slowly lay the leaves in thick layers over her ankle. But she sighs.

"You're not doing it right, Kidnapper! You need to bind the leaves really tight or it won't work."

She digs into her pocket and pulls out the creeper that I saw her plaiting by the whiterforce. Two creepers, to be precise, now bound into one long length of knotted plant rope. "Always be prepared, Dad used to say."

And we are. Through a combination of biting and tugging, Polly tears her creeper rope into lengths, which I use to bind the leaves firmly around her injured leg. At first she flinches at the sting and the burning, but slowly her breathing grows heavier and heavier. I lie down on the hard floor next to her bed, leaning against the wall, listening to her.

Keeping my eyes open is hard.

If they do shut, for once I know a river isn't going to sweep me away, and I'm not going to fall off a stag either, so I rest my head against the bed, next to Polly.

She doesn't seem to mind.

When I wake up again, it must be the middle of the night. It's completely dark apart from a single lamp flickering above our heads.

Polly is sitting up, already awake. She leans over. I think she's going to thank me for getting the leaf-cure.

But when she sees I'm awake she curls up her mouth. She's been thinking, I can tell. "I know you got these leaves specially, but"—her eyes flash at me and her voice is all choked up and angry at the same time—"everything was fine till you turned up! Now Sidney's gone. She was my best friend. You left me all alone with only animals to look after me, and then, when we heard the people coming through the forest, I still thought it might be you."

I look away. I was trying to help her—

"But it wasn't, was it? It was that woman. She was all smiling and friendly at first, promising she'd make my foot better and help us beat the cullers. Then when we got to her machine she started asking me all these questions, shining torches in our eyes—and now she's locked us in this shed." She goes very quiet. "I'm beginning to wonder if she is our friend after all."

I nod in agreement, which only seems to make her angrier.

"I want to go home now, Kidnapper, and find out what's happened to my parents—do you understand? Will you promise me that you're going to take me home?" She flops back against the wall with a sigh, staring at the shovels and forks racked up in the corner. "I just want everything to be normal again, you see. Why can't you do that? Why can't you just tell me for once that you're going to make things actually better?"

Looking at her, I wish as never before that I could talk. For a split second, I feel a muscle twang in my throat and my lips almost start to form an old shape—but then it's gone.

Polly, I say to her inside my head: I can't promise you that everything will go back to normal again. Not straightaway. But I will make it better. I will get you home again, I promise. And we can start by getting out of here. Standing up, I grab one of the shovels leaning against the wall. It's very, very heavy.

"Kester!"

I ignore her and drag the shovel towards the door. Taking a deep breath, I swing it up over my head and, shaking with the effort, smash it down as hard as I can. It doesn't do anything apart from make a tiny crack.

"Kester! What are you doing?"

I ignore her. The shovel nearly pulls me right over, but I tighten my grip, take a deeper breath, and strike again. This time I expose a long streak of bare, pale wood.

"I said, what are you doing, trying to break down a door without me?"

I turn around. Polly smiles at me for the first time since we arrived at Ma's farm. Only a fraction of a smile that no one else would spot, but I can see it.

"Come on, Kidnapper—unlike you, I actually know how to use one of these."

Then she puts her small hands around the shovel handle next to mine, and together we lift it up in the air. We bring it smashing down in the centre of the door. A plank springs out, and a cool breeze floats in.

"Again! Harder!"

Together, blow after blow, we smash the wooden door to the shed, until there is nothing left but jagged splinters jutting out of the frame. I drop the shovel on the floor, she grabs her rucksack full of letters and leaves off the bed, and together we set off to find my wild.

We head back up along the paved corridor, through the barn. At the door leading back out into the farmyard I signal Polly to stay close behind me. Empty and dark, with no tractors or trailers wheeling across it now, only silent lumps of farm equipment and their frightening shadows. I hold my breath, thinking Captain Skuldiss is suddenly going to rise up from behind them, pointing his firestick at us.

"Kester," whispers Polly.

I wave at her to be quiet. I dart across to the rusty iron scoop of an upturned digger and crouch down in the shadow of its jaws, beckoning Polly to follow.

"There's something I need to tell you first," she whispers, squatting down beside me. Tight-lipped, I shake my head at her. Now is not the time.

Then a truck door opens and slams, followed by voices and boots clomping towards us. I peer just over the top of the digger and can see some men and women streaming down through the yard.

"Kester, it's important," Polly says in her extra-stubborn voice.

I nudge my head above the iron battlements again and see where the outsiders are headed.

A giant barn with grey concrete sides and a steel door. It looks like a prison. They have just disappeared into it, swallowed up by the gloom.

Jabbing my finger ahead, I sprint out and fling myself against the side of the deserted stables next to the barn, crouching behind a half-open door. I turn back to see the shadowy figure of Polly still hiding in the digger. Waving my hand like crazy, I try to draw her across. But she doesn't move. I throw my hands up in the air at her.

"But what if someone sees us?" she hisses at me.

Looking around one more time, and then counting to five, I give her the all-clear and she starts to run, back bent—just as another crowd of shadowy figures arrives. I signal at her to halt, which she does, right in the middle of the yard. She's frozen, kneeling down, as if she is tying a shoelace.

The men and women stomp straight past her and into the shadows between the barns. Holding my breath, not daring to move a muscle, I count them, one by one, as they disappear into the darkness. Glancing back, I can see Polly actually shaking, but the people go on without even looking once in our direction.

All, that is, apart from the last one.

He stops for moment, swaying and wobbling, right in front of us. I can't see his face; he's just a crumpled-looking shadow, holding a shining bottle in his hand. He looks over towards Polly and stares at her. Then he rubs his eyes, like he can't believe what he's seeing, and hiccups to himself. Looks at the bottle in his hand, shakes his head, and chucks it over his shoulder—it lands with a muffled smash.

He scratches his head and stumbles off after the others.

Polly races across the ground towards me. We spread ourselves flat against the wall of the barn the outsiders disappeared into. Straining to listen, I can just hear distant voices and music, and another sound too, one I don't recognize. It doesn't matter. These people took away my animals. These people will know where they are.

"You've got to listen to me, Kester," Polly whispers fiercely. "I asked that woman to help us, but she made me answer all these questions while we were walking to the combine harvester. I had to tell her what we were doing—"

Good. Then at least Ma knows how massive this is, that we aren't just playing a kid's game.

"Even if you aren't going to listen, Kester, I'm going to tell you. She asked me everything, and I told her—I had to. Everything, including what Captain Skuldiss said about you."

A small warning light begins to glow in my head.

"She asked me your name and I told her. Don't you see? She knew who you were."

The alarm light in my head begins to flash and spin.

"Not just you. She knew who your dad was as well."

I look at her for a moment. Then there is a familiar voice squeaking up from our feet.

Finally! You don't half get around, you two—can you try staying in one place next time?

Harvest Mouse! I crouch down. I never thought I'd be so happy to see a mouse. She's rubbing her whiskers with her front paws, and then rearing up on her back legs and then falling down again, before shaking her tail to an imaginary beat inside her head.

The Finding a Talking Human Again After an Extended Period of Captivity Dance! she exclaims proudly.

"I forgot how small she is," Polly says, sounding a bit disappointed. I don't know how big she expected a mouse to be. Well, no matter how small, or how many silly dances she makes up, I'm glad to have her here. Polly must notice my expression in the gloom, because she quickly adds—"Sidney didn't like mice very much. But I like this one."

The mouse's tail just flicks swiftly. *Are you two going to stand there all evening, or do you want me to do my Dance of Hurrying Dawdling Children Along? We don't have much time—follow me!*

The harvest mouse hurries into the barn, and we follow her in the shadows as she weaves quickly through a labyrinth of dark passageways, towards the sound of the chatter and the music.

How did you escape? I ask her.

This old mouse can get in or out of anywhere. You must know that by now.

She darts under a heavy steel door, which we push open to find ourselves in an alleyway between two barns. The voices and drums swell in our ears, and Polly tugs at my sleeve.

"Look," she says. "The light."

What light? I think, looking around at the shadows. Then, following her pointing finger, I see it. Not just any light. Far down at the end of the alleyway, sliding long tentacles of shadow between the walls. And I realize what the other noise was.

A fire.

I told you there was no time to be lost, says the mouse, scurrying on down by the edge of the alley.

We walk out of the shadows and into a field. Not a huge plain of mud this time, but a patch of bumpy grass with rusting shards of farm equipment littered everywhere, tangled weeds underfoot. And right in the middle of it, burning a crater-sized hole around itself, a bonfire.

A bonfire as tall as Bodger—as tall as two Bodgers. Made out of logs, tractor tyres, planks, dented oil drums—anything to hand, a pyramid of flaming junk crackling and roaring into the sky, giving off showers of sparks.

We all hesitate for a second—hypnotized by the flames, the mouse's tail flicking anxiously from side to side. We're right at the back of a huge crowd gathered round the fire, a sea of backs and heads. In the glow at the front, I can recognize some faces from earlier, like the old lady who held the mouse—but I can't see Ma or Bodger anywhere. There must be a hundred or more people. Thin, hungry faces, their cheekbones casting deep shadows—men, women, and children of all ages, even a toddler stumbling around at the front, swaying to the pulse of the music.

This isn't just a few outsiders. This feels like a whole country having a country-sized party.

There's a line of girls sitting down at the front with drums between their knees, banging and slapping away, and a bearded man behind playing a pipe. Somewhere I can hear a guitar—and everyone slaps their thighs, occasionally singing along, though I can't make out the words. I can feel the rhythm of the drums drive through my body. I pick up the mouse in my palm, and she can't help but dance along too. The air is alive with talk and beats and anticipation, then the music and chatter fade away, and for a moment all I can hear is the crackling logs and the beating of our hearts. Only for a moment, though, because then the drumming starts up again, and begins to get faster—

And faster and faster—

And faster—

Everyone looks around, as if they're expecting something. Then, appearing out of the darkness, striding through the crowd, who scramble to make way for her, clapping and patting her on the back as they do—

It's Ma.

Strong and fierce, her eyes bright with the flames, she walks right into the middle of the circle and claps her hands. The music and singing and yelling stop dead—just like that. For a minute, she walks all the way round the circle, in silence. Not saying a word, just looking at everyone.

We stand back, hidden by the shadows and the crowd.

Her lips are shining blood red in the light, and her hair is swept up tightly on her head. She also has something she didn't have before—a huge knife, tucked into her belt, flashing with every step.

Ma smiles, reaches carefully into her pocket, and pulls out a cigar. In a single move she draws the knife and lops the tip off. The bearded pipe player offers her a smouldering branch pulled from the fire. She lights the cigar, takes a big puff, and blows the smoke up into the sky.

Then she begins, walking as she talks.

"First came the red-eye. We lost our beasts. Some lost pets." I glance at Polly, and she looks down at the ground, swallowing hard. Ma continues. "All the creatures that make up this countryside—*our* countryside. Not just animals neither—we lost our crops. Fruit orchards. Vegetable gardens. We lost"—she pauses, and jabs at the air with her cigar—"everything that we knew."

People mutter, but she silences them with a wave of her hand and shoves the cigar back in the corner of her mouth.

"And so came Facto. They promised to sort out the virus. To keep us safe, to feed us. To replace all the natural food that we lost. They made promises." She lowers her voice, so we have to listen more closely to hear. "What do we make of those promises now?"

An angry mutter ripples around the crowd. She repeats her question—louder, crosser.

"I said—what do we make of those promises now?"

"They're barefaced liars!" shouts a bearded man at the front, leaping up.

"I hear you, Joseph, I hear you," says Ma, gesturing at him to sit down. "They killed all the animals the virus hadn't took, but they still couldn't get rid of it. Then they forced everyone to move to the cities, said insects and bees and worms had contaminated the crops, infected the fruit and veg, declaring this land—*our* land—a quarantine zone"—more shouts and boos here—"and then . . ." She looks down, grimacing, as if she doesn't want to say the next bit. "Then they stopped giving us formula altogether."

I give Polly a nudge in the ribs, but she's staring at Ma, transfixed.

"They wanted us to starve rather than carry on living in the countryside. Where we've lived all our lives." The crowd aren't whooping at this. They're moaning.

"And for the final insult"—she spits on the fire and it sizzles back in reply—"Facto told us that their top vet—the man meant to be looking after our animals—was the man who had caused the red-eye in the first place. The man whose experiments had gone wrong and unleashed hell on the world." The crowd are actually growling now. Ma curls her face into a flame-lit sneer and lowers her voice, and I have to strain to hear her, peering through the haze of smoke, as she says—

"Professor Dawson Jaynes."

There are more angry murmurs in the crowd—people start to shout and bang tin cups against the ground. I hang my head low, as if my dad's name was written in glowing letters on my back. I can't look at Polly or the mouse—but it doesn't matter, I'm only just aware of where we are.

Because right now I'm somewhere else entirely, in my head, six years ago.

"I'm working on a new . . ." Dad had said, his voice trailing away as usual, not turning round from his computer, even though it was midnight and he hadn't eaten anything that evening. Correction—we hadn't eaten anything that evening. "This could be really . . . big." He dug his keyboard out from under the messy pile of papers on his desk, and brightly coloured shapes floated across the screen, bubbles and

twisting spirals and spiky blobs. *"Yes, Kes, this could change everything. This would really have made your mum . . ."*

Click *went the computer.*

Ma pauses, letting the words sink in, and strides round to the other side of the fire. She looks over the crowd, blazing more fiercely than the fire itself. She pounds her fist into her other hand. "They said we were finished. They left us to starve. But now we shall take our revenge."

Suddenly it's like Ma is looking dead at us and we both freeze, but then her gaze moves on.

"Because, friends, a little miracle happened out on the plains today." A round of applause. "What if I was to tell you that I stumbled upon the son of Professor Jaynes himself?" There's a big cheer. I duck down even lower behind the crowd. Ma stops pacing and slows right down.

Everyone goes deathly quiet. This is what she's been building up to all along.

"Facto told us the animals are dead. They told us all the animals are dead. But they lied." She nods, agreeing with herself. "Because lo and behold, here is the son of the man responsible, in person, with a whole troop of living, breathing animals!"

A huge cheer goes up, and the bearded man with the flute plays a little scale on it that goes up and down. Ma lowers her hands, as if to say, "Enough." The muttering fades away.

"So now," she says, the flames burning bright in her eyes, "we shall take back what is ours, what is our due after waiting and starving so long, all these long, lean years—we shall feast!"

The crowd starts to chant, very quietly at first. She's talking about food, but I have a very bad feeling in my stomach. I couldn't feel less hungry right now.

"Feast! Feast!"

We look around. Everyone is chanting. Every man, woman, and child. It begins to get louder, and louder and louder.

"Feast! Feast! Feast!"

Louder and louder the cries go, as all eyes turn back towards the tall barns of the farm.

"FEAST! FEAST! FEAST!"

The whole crowd is on their feet, shouting, stamping, chanting—

There is a convoy of men making their way towards us from the barns—

Can't see properly at first, they're carrying something, pulling something, Ma looking on, gesturing them to hurry up—

And then all the chants and drums fade to nothing in my mind, like they're happening on a different planet—

As I see what the men are pulling—

A crazed animal, rearing and bucking. Polly sees too.

"Oh, Kester," she says.

It's the stag.

He's wrapped in ropes—ropes around his horns, ropes around his muzzle, ropes around his legs and body—and he's bucking and rearing and kicking and bellowing. The ropes are held—just—by a fat man and two spotty skinheads, who struggle to hold on as the stag lashes out, his eyes rolling.

The crowd is going crazy now, surging and dancing around the stag—baiting him with shouts and cries. The last stag ever in the whole world.

Then the chanting and music grind to a halt.

There is silence apart from the crackling fire and the stag straining at his ropes—every now and then the fat man calls out, "Hi-ya!" and cracks a whip, which makes the stag rear and buck all the more. I can see he's covered in cuts and scratches.

"Don't do anything. Not yet," whispers Polly.

But I don't have a choice—because I am lifted clean off the ground by an enormous arm around my waist.

Bodger.

With a grunt he pushes his way towards the fire, trampling junk and weeds, the crowd melting out of his way. It might be night, but I feel like I have a bright searchlight shining right on me. I beat my fist against Bodger's side; I might as well be hitting a concrete wall for all the difference it makes.

He dumps me on the hard ground right at Ma's feet, and there's a burst of applause, as if he's just done a trick. Ma musses my hair, and I jerk away.

"No need to be so unfriendly, Kester," she says. "Enjoyed the show so far, have you? Did you think it wasn't for your benefit? Do you think we would have let you escape so easily?" She grunts like Bodger. "Well, you haven't seen nothing yet. The star turn is still to come."

Then, everyone watching with bated breath, she reaches into her belt and pulls out the massive knife.

"You," she says, "you're our star turn."

She hands the knife to me. It's heavy and solid, pulling down my arm with the weight. I don't want to—I can't . . .

"Go on," she says, pointing at the stag, rearing and bucking. "This is all your father's fault. And in the country, this is how we make amends. You get first cut."

My eyes widen and focus at the same time, taking in everyone and everything: the fire, shooting up to the stars, burning and hissing; Ma, her hand on my shoulder, gripping it tight; the faces of hundreds of hungry outsiders, nodding, urging me on, laughing, clapping, like this is a game . . .

Polly's pale face right at the back of them, looking at me deadly seriously, as if she knows that what I do next will stay with us forever, that everything, all of it, rests on me; and finally, the stag himself, his muscles straining, a sheen of sweat all down his side.

The fat man pulls hard on the rope wound tight around his horns, and the stag bellows in pain.

"Hold still, you wretched beast, damn you!" Fat Man yells.

What do I do now? I ask the stag, barely getting the words out, trembling with fear.

His head jerks back and forth like a puppet on a string, and I actually hear the horns flex and crack under the pressure, like trees in a storm. But his reply to me is as steady as the flames in the fire. A question for an answer.

Is it true, what I heard her say?

I don't know how to answer.

And he screams again in pain, as his head is yanked back by Fat Man.

Ma puts her hand over my hand holding the knife and squeezes it so tight that I gasp in pain. She whispers in my ear, "We'll hold him, don't be frightened." As if. Of the stag—never. "Aim for a clean cut across the throat, that's the proper way." She steps back, waiting, gesturing me to cut whenever I'm ready. "We shall all dine well tonight, thanks to you. Dine like we haven't dined for years."

How could I be so wrong? The stag was right—we can't trust any other humans. How can you ever trust someone who wants to eat you?

The girls at the front start on the drums again. The crowd begins to stamp their feet, banging cups, impatient now—

"FEAST! FEAST!"

"CUT! CUT!"

I know these people are only hungry. They haven't eaten properly for months. We're all hungry. I look again at the stag, his rolling brown eyes, his heart beating visibly in his chest, his great crown of horns—and try to answer his question.

I don't know—

Then there is only one way to find out. Do what you must, he says, gritting his teeth. *A great stag always faces his fate. Just save the wild.*

I look down at the knife in my shaking hand, and again at the stag. In his eyes there is only encouragement, nothing else. My brain is racing, thinking of everything he has taught me, but this time we're surrounded. There are no varmints here to come out of the ground and no fish-road to save us.

And as if it can sense my thoughts, as if it was wired into my head rather than strapped round my wrist, my watch buzzes angrily. I don't want to take my eyes off Ma or the stag, but I glance quickly down at the flashing pale square—

One word.

DON'T

Then it's gone, as quickly as it came, the screen black as before. There's no time to think—

"Come on, boy—don't be shy," says Ma, giving me a shove. "Don't pretend you aren't hungry too."

Don't? *Don't?* No, I won't.

I fling down the knife, which bounces and shines on the ground, resting at Ma's feet.

There's a gasp from the crowd. Ma isn't having that, though. She picks up the knife, takes my arm, and squeezes my hand around the handle, lifting it up, so the knife—its point glittering—is poised just above a plump vein running across the stag's throat, pumping faster and faster.

Make it quick, says the stag. *For I am ready.*

But I can't, I say. *I don't want to kill you. I don't want you to go—*

I made a promise, is all he says.

Ma puts her hands over mine again, and the blade—

"There, lad, I'll guide you—"

I close my eyes—

When the voice comes, it is loud and strong.

"Stop!"

It's Polly.

She's standing up, and the crowd's gaze—like a shower of arrows—has shot her way. She doesn't seem bothered. Her face set, she steps forward.

I look at her as if to say, "What are you doing? Sit down!"

She shakes her head. Everyone's looking at her, but she doesn't care.

"Kester. You always try to do everything on your own."

That's not true. I let her help me at Wind's Edge, but—

"It's my turn now. My turn to help you, don't you see?" There's confusion among the crowd now. Ma has paused, a frown on her face, but Polly is quite calm, stepping forward into the light.

"It's OK. It's my turn to be brave now."

People are asking each other questions, calling out, "Who is she?" and "What you on about, girl?"

She's not listening to them. It's like a force field, an invisible bubble that only she can see, has closed up around her. She picks her away towards us between all the sitting and lying bodies, like they are just logs or rocks. She sweeps a loose curl of hair back behind her ear. Everything is care-ful, thought through. She jabs at her chest with a passion that surprises me. "I can talk, Kester. You can't. Let me speak for you."

"All right, lass—but after we've eaten, all right?" calls Ma.

But Ma can't see the force field. Polly shakes her head, like nothing in the world will change her mind, and steps closer towards the fire. Standing right in front of the flames—everyone watching—arms folded, immovable. When she speaks, it is loud and clear, so everyone can hear.

But she only says one thing:

"You can't kill that stag."

Dead simple. Just like that.

There's a stunned silence at first. Even from Ma.

Then—right at the back, from the smoke-filled shadows, a shout—

"Don't be dumb! It's only an animal!"

Followed by a laugh, a nasty, dirty laugh. Then some people near the voice begin to chuckle as well—and then everyone begins to laugh, a ripple spreading through the crowd, like the fire itself, catching everyone it touches. Repeating Polly's words back to her—"*You can't kill that stag*"—like she'd just said the world was flat and the moon was made of cheese.

Laughs and words are thrown at her from every side. Even Ma's face crinkles up with laughter, and not the nice kind. Everyone roars and screams, slapping their thighs, heads thrown back, eyes watering, shoulders shaking—proper, proper laughing; you could probably hear it from a mile off.

Everyone laughing but Polly and me.

Ma's face hardens again. As it does, and everyone sees Polly not blushing or backing down, the laughter fades away to a blanket of silence that flattens everything. Ma turns to face her at last, her voice rough and angry.

"Why not, lass?"

When Polly replies she looks so pale, so tired and hungry like the rest of us, and yet so strong and brave at the same time. Her voice doesn't waver.

"Two reasons. One, because he's the last one ever. We're taking him, and the others, to Premium, whether you like it or not." Polly points at me. "And his father's going to find a cure for them."

There's a cry of disbelief from the crowd and Ma explodes with rage.

"I don't bloody care what you think, little missy! Take them to the man Facto says started the thing in the first place—I don't think so. And besides, what does it matter anyhow?" She slaps the stag on the flank as if he was a just a rock standing there, not a living, breathing thing. "In the end, they're only bloody animals."

But that is where she is so very wrong.

"And the second reason," says Polly, "is this." She digs into her pocket and pulls something out of it. Something small and pale, a ball of wax, squashed and misshapen by the journey, sitting in her outstretched hand.

The pine resin Polly collected from the forest by the fish-road. *"It might come in useful, you never know."*

She glances at me, like I'm meant to be doing something—and Ma squints from the other side of the circle to see what she's holding and then shakes her head with irritation, leaving the knife in my hand and striding round to Polly. "What on earth . . . ? Right, I've had enough of these children's games."

There's murmuring and muttering of agreement all around. I quickly glance at the stag. He's following her every move as intently as I am.

Polly. The girl who guarded her cat with a gun.

She keeps looking at me. Again and again.

Why? Crosser and crosser glances, like I've forgotten my lines in a film I didn't know I was in.

But I can't think. I'm completely distracted by watching her and Ma—

And then—I'm so stupid—

Like a massive penny dropping inside my brain, I realize.

I nod back, to show I've understood—

Just as Ma gets to her, Polly chucks the resin up into the air.

Everyone freezes: the crowd, heads back; Ma midstride round the fire; me; the stag; the men holding him—watching the waxy ball roll and spin through the air, till it falls straight into the heart of the fire. And everything goes bang.

The resin ball explodes inside the fire with an ear-splitting boom, sending a mushroom cloud of dirty flames up into the night, half-burnt planks and oil drums flying, hurling through the air, black clouds billowing out, everyone screaming, running for cover, coughing and choking.

I whip round and with the knife cut the ropes holding the stag. He rears up and knocks the man holding the reins flying onto his front with a powerful kick. Then there is Bodger, stomping out of the smoke, trying to grab the whirling ropes spinning in the air, and he gets a hoof right in the jaw and slams onto his back like a felled tree.

The smoke clouds grow lower, blacker, and thicker.

One sleeve over my mouth to help me breathe, I scoop up the mouse and jump onto the stag. He leaps into the centre of the fire circle, scattering the onlookers, who swear and shout as they trip over one another in the rush to get out of the way.

As we break through the moving line of people I catch sight of Polly dead ahead on the other side of the flames, waiting for us. But Ma is fighting through the smoke towards her too, wiping the soot out of her eyes, reaching out . . .

Grabbing the stag tight with my knees, spurring him on, we leap forward faster—I lean down and take Polly's outstretched hand. With every muscle in my body, I hoist her up, just out of Ma's grasp—

"Stay where you bloody are!" Ma snarls. "That's my beast now. Your father took my last ones, and I'll be damned if I let you . . ."

But I think Polly and I are the only ones who can hear her now, over the scrambling, the voices shouting, and it's hard to make out anything through the chaos. Men, women, children, falling over one another in the smoke as they run from the flames.

The stag ignores them, charges directly into the crowd, and batters straight through a run-down fence at the edge of the field like it was made of paper, landing with a stony thud back in the farmyard.

The others—quick! I yell.

He doesn't reply, just nods, and we are pounding straight through a line of connected barns, slamming into a wall of bales wrapped tight in black plastic, ripping them with his horns, as they scatter everywhere like giant boulders and then—

Wolf-Cub jumps up, jerked back by a rope tied tight around a ring in the wall. *I knew you would come for us, Wildness!*

I try to untie him, but the knot is too tight and my fingers too cold and bruised to pull it loose. Before I even turn to her, a smoke-smudged Polly is at my side.

"Here, let me," she says gently, kneeling down and studying the knot like it was another plant for her collection. Wolf-Cub watches her expectantly. "Hmm," she says, rubbing her chin. "I think it might just be a tautline hitch—"

And—like she is a magician performing a trick—the knot falls apart in her hands, and the cub is free, licking her face while she pretends to push him away.

I do manage to let the cockroach out of his jar. He rolls out in a huff, shaking the little wings on his back, those wings he never actually seems to use. *Thank you, soldier. I shall be complaining at the highest level about our mistreatment as prisoners of war,* he barks.

Polly also undoes the thick knot fastening the pigeons' cage and they fly out in a flurry, straight into our faces. Only the scruffy white pigeon is left, pecking around on his own in the corner, like he doesn't want to leave. I stick my head in.

Hey, white pigeon, don't get too cosy in here. He ignores me. I shake the cage. *Look, I've set you free for once.* No response. *Do I not even get a thank-you?*

He waddles right up to the entrance and looks around at his empty prison.

Cosy in here, thanks. And with that he grabs the cage-door hook with his beak and snaps it shut.

Strange bird.

There are shouts coming from the field. We haven't got long. I turn to them all to see the mouse doing a Storytelling Dance of Explanation about what happened by the fire. Their chatter fades away to an embarrassed silence as they see me watching, and none of them—including the stag, his eyes streaming from the smoke—will look at me.

I know what this is about, and I'm not having it.

When the stag asked me in the field, I couldn't answer. I

didn't know. Perhaps the watch was trying to tell me something. I don't know if what Ma says is true. Dad used to say, throwing his hands up, when he couldn't win an argument with Mum—which was quite often—"Well, you might say that, but as a scientist"—here Mum would groan with her head in her hands—"I can't speak about what I don't know, only what I do know. So there."

So there.

Now you might have heard that woman say things about my father and his magic, things you might not have liked. The shouts grow nearer. *I don't know if any of those things are true. I'll tell you what is true, though. You might believe in your old dreams and your calls. But I believe in something else. The only thing I've had to believe in for the last six years—my dad, and the good he does with his magic. And I can tell you this for a fact—if my father did start the berry-eye, he's the one person who will be able to stop it.*

They all stare at me.

There's a silence that seems to last forever.

And then slowly the mouse takes to the floor to do a very quiet and gentle We Still Believe in You Dance. Then the wolf-cub is licking his nose, and the General is muttering, *Well spoken, soldier. Like a true general.* Even the white pigeon at last emerges from his cage to say that he believes I'm the one person who can't stop the berry-eye.

Finally, with my foot, I start to trace large letters in the dirt of the barn floor. For Polly. I want to let her know that we're not doing this *instead* of saving her cat, but in

Sidney's memory. That I will help her find her parents once I've found Dad—but before I can even spell the first word, she puts a hand on my wrist.

"It's OK, Kidnapper," she says softly. "You don't have to try and explain. I believe you now. Also, I think he wants us to hurry." She looks up at the stag, who tilts his horns towards us, and we leap straight onto his back.

I give one last roar over the sound of the fire and the shouts heading our way—*The cullers want to exterminate you. The outsiders want to eat you. But I promise—I'm going to take you to a man who wants to help you—and once we've found him, we're not leaving till he does!*

The wild's cheers seem to drown out the cries of the outsiders running after us as the stag races out of the bale barn and we bank sharply, down to the corner of the yard, following the birds down a bumpy track, out of Ma's farm gates, and onto a road.

And we don't stop running till the light of the fire and the angry shouts have disappeared.

Old Burn Farm seems far away by the time we reach the first fork in the road. I call a halt and, wiping the worst of the soot from around my eyes, look behind me at my wild. They're all just staring at me, waiting for the next move.

Behind us lies everything that we have been through—and in front of us, the empty road.

The road that goes back to what I know or, at least, what I thought I knew.

The road that leads to Premium.

As we march down the empty road, the farm far behind us, the wolf-cub suddenly stops. So suddenly that I nearly fall right over him.

Wildness? What's that noise?

What noise?

He listens—and every hair of his fur seems to be standing on end, and then finally I can hear it too. It's like only a rumble at first, but unmistakable.

The noise of something else on the road.

A noise I recognize immediately—because the last time I heard it, we were inside the van making it.

Skuldiss.

And getting nearer every second.

Quickly I order the pigeons to find a safe route, and they fly off to scout ahead, the rumble of the culler van growing louder and louder, and I turn to see bars of headlights swooping round corners in the dark, peering over the brow of the hill behind—

Then the birds are back—

We shall follow the line of the road but not stay on the road, the grey pigeons call down. *It is the safest way.*

Yes, don't follow us, it's not safe, says the white pigeon.

We hurry through a narrow gap in a hedge, into a field of brambles that prick us with their thorns as we stumble through them.

All of us, including the stag, crouch down low behind the hedge as the cullers thunder past on the other side.

Then, like the night has eaten it up, the van's gone.

It's quiet and dark all around and my head feels light as air. Suddenly the ground seems like the place where I want to be, and I slump onto it. Polly is digging into her bag immediately.

"You're hungry. You need to eat. *We* need to eat. There might be some cat biscuits left."

But there aren't. Only a disintegrated, inedible soggy mush.

I can feel Polly thinking for a moment in the dark. "Here. Give me your watch," she says.

I can't imagine how we're going to eat a watch, but I unstrap it anyway and pass it to her. Straightaway she is on her knees among the hedgerow, shining it into every corner. I can hear muttering, tearing, and picking.

Then she is back, clutching handfuls of sticky leaves that glisten in the watch-light, shoots and wrinkled berries.

The shoots and leaves are sharp to the taste, but I can eat them. The berries too are sour—but I know they won't give me a fever because Polly has chosen them. She has even found a strange-looking root which, if you scrape off the dirt and rough skin, is snow-white underneath and lifts the roof of your mouth off with its heat—but we eat the whole thing greedily.

"You've just got to pretend it's your favourite food in the world," says Polly sternly.

With a jolt, I realize I no longer know what that is. But what catches my eye is in Polly's other hand, a bunch of formula-pink flowers that look like tiny bells made out of velvet. Not quite knowing why, I reach for them hungrily, but Polly whisks them away.

"No!" she snaps, and the sharpness in her voice stings me. "I'm sorry," she says, packing the flowers away in her bag, carefully holding them by their stalks. "It's just you must never eat these, or even lick your fingers after touching them—will you promise?"

I nod, not sure why she wants them then, but I can sense the stag and the pigeons growing restless. We finish our hedgerow dinner—Polly stuffing her bag with the leftovers—and keep on marching through the thorns in the dark, until the day begins again, with its cold grey light. Both the stag and I glance up at the sky. Swollen rain clouds are gathering and rolling.

But for now—no more rain comes.

Polly rests her head on my back, dead to the world, and

I can hear the mouse snoring in my pocket. (Probably the Stationary Dance of Solid Sleep.) Everyone looks tired—even the pigeons don't fly all the time, but take it in turns to waddle along the ground behind the others.

We head out of the brambles and onto a churned-up mud track, to the edge of a wood where the trees bend right over the path. The gnarly branches are hunched up close together, warped twigs all intertwined. Even in daylight, the path disappears into the woods in total blackness.

The stag pulls up sharp, sniffing the shoots of thorns that curl around the entrance.

Is this the only way, birds? he calls. *I do not like the smell of this place.*

Wolf-Cub slowly comes to a halt as well, looking suspiciously at the dark path ahead. Polly clutches my arm. The pigeons don't give it a second thought, though, ducking straight through under the arch of thorns.

Come inside, come inside—this is the best way. No one will be able to see us here. This hide-all will conceal us for many strides.

Yes, no one will be able to see their way inside here, says the white pigeon.

This time he seems to be the only pigeon actually making any sense. But we have no one else to follow.

The General leaps onto my head, bristling. *Have no fear. I shall be at your side ready to despatch any dangers we might face in here.*

It's decided, then.

Stag, I think we should follow the birds. They have guided us well so far.

As you wish, he says abruptly—and trots on so suddenly that Polly and I almost don't have time to duck under the thorns, which knock the General spinning to the ground.

At your side or underneath you, as you wish, he mutters as he picks himself up.

The farther we go inside the wood, the harder it is for any light to pierce the treetops twisted together above our heads, only just making it through in grey pools here and there.

But the strangest thing about the wood isn't the darkness.

It's the quiet.

It's so quiet in here, so deathly quiet, that you can hear every twig crack, every snort of breath, even every twitch of the mouse's whiskers. Soon none of us is saying a word, just crunching silently over the forest carpet, careful step after careful step.

The branches hang so low and thick, in knotted swags, that eventually we have to get off the stag and walk. Polly shivers behind me as we trudge along in the twilight, and then gives a start—tripping over something in the bracken.

She pulls out a long, strange-shaped stick.

"What's this, Kester?" she asks.

I look at the branch as she turns it over in her hands— long, curved, and yellowy-white.

The branch that's a bone.

I wave at her angrily to put it down, but it's too late, I can see her gasp as she realizes, flinging it back down.

The stag fixes Polly and the bone with his glittering eyes, sniffing the air suspiciously. Then Wolf-Cub bounds over from behind us, a smaller white stick clenched between his jaws.

Look what I found, Wildness, he says proudly, but I just reach down and carefully pull it out of his jaws. I drop it onto the ground, where it lands with a clatter.

Bones shouldn't hit soft forest floors with a clatter.

I hurriedly stand back, scuffing the ground as I do, revealing that beneath our feet, beneath the light coating of dry leaves, there are more bare white sticks, exposed and catching the light.

The floor of the silent forest is covered with bones.

I knew we should not have come this way, says the stag, looking daggers at the pigeons. *When animals know they are going to die, they withdraw so they may do it in peace.* I think of what Sidney said about making her final journey. *This forest must be where all those we have lost have come to spend their last days.*

And now I understand why we haven't seen any of the remains of other animals taken by the berry-eye. This is where they come to die.

I look around at the pillars of black trees just visible in the gloom. I shudder to think how many animals lie beneath them.

I guide the stag around to face the direction we came from. *In that case, pigeons, lead us another way, back out of here.*

But they don't move from the drooping branches above

our heads, ruffling their wings and turning their heads away from me.

It will take too long now—this wood runs as far as we can see in any direction.

Even the white pigeon stays quiet, with nothing to add. He won't look at me either. Wolf-Cub stares at the ground.

Come on, this is no time to give up, I say to the stag. But he doesn't move. Doesn't reply, doesn't even look me in the eye; just stares straight ahead.

No living animal will ever walk through a Forest of the Dead.

I look at the mouse, who does a very short and stiff Dance of Respecting the Dead on the stag's back, sticking her legs out at awkward angles in turn, before silently shaking her head. *Yes, well, I'd love to join you, but I've got this new dance I want to learn, you see . . .* Her voice trails away. The Dance of Cowardice, I reckon.

Polly touches me on the shoulder. "What's going on, Kester?" She cautiously picks up the bone again, now examining it, picking off bits of moss and leaves—then I see her begin to understand. "You mean they won't come because they're scared?"

She nods, turning the bare bone over in her hands, thinking before she speaks. "My bedroom was right at the top of Wind's Edge. And after the Quarantine Zone came, we started to get power cuts. At first they were only every now and then, but after a while, we were lucky if the lights worked at all."

I think of all the dark and silent villages I passed.

"Which meant when I went to bed, I had to go up three whole flights of stairs in the dark. Now you saw what our house was like. Every step creaked, every window rattled as I went up, and all I could think of was the strange-shaped piles of old junk under dust sheets in the other rooms as I walked past. It sounds silly, but I saw things in the shadows, heard them—" She lays the bone down again, now fully picked clean, and starts to scrape at the ground with her hands. "I just couldn't do it. Mum gave me a candle, but that just made the shadows darker, the imaginary monsters creepier. I needed her to hold my hand up the stairs until I was safely in bed. But she said I was too old for that. So she showed me how to not be scared."

She's dug away the pine needles and moss to make a shallow hole, in which she now lays the bone.

"That's what she did, Kidnapper—she showed me. By going upstairs herself, in the dark, without a candle—and then coming back down again. There were no monsters, there never were. But I didn't believe it until she showed me."

Polly starts to gently cover up the bone of the unknown animal, covering it with soil, then twigs and leaves—but I am no longer looking. She's right.

Pushing past her and the wild, I start to march on down the path, farther into the wood—and they cry after me, but I don't look back.

I made a promise to these animals, to lead them.

I have to show them there's nothing to be scared of. Alone.

I haven't gone very far away from the eyes of the wild before I suddenly feel very cold. Rubbing my arms to stay warm, I keep on walking as the path twists and turns beneath my feet. There is no wind, no other sound apart from my own breathing, faster than it was. It's pitch black, only the faintest streak of light on the glossy leaves fringing the path.

We don't have long before the red-eye claims more for their final journey, at the Ring of Trees—I am sure of that. I have to hope this will work. So I begin to listen for any sound, any cries or rustling, but there is only stillness.

If anyone out there is alive, I say into the stillness, *then come out. Don't be scared. I'm the Wildness. I'm going to take you to the city and find you a cure.*

Nothing.

I try again, this time louder. But nothing comes back, not even a whisper. So I say it again, and again, repeating my words over and over, louder and louder—there must be some left. Everywhere we have been, even though we've been told all have gone, we've always found some still alive.

Even in a graveyard. There must be. If only I knew how to find them.

All I can hear is my own voice echoing inside my head. All I can see is the deathly darkness all around. If only the pigeons hadn't brought us here in the first place, if only—

The pigeons. Of course. I don't know why I didn't think of it before.

Their call.

Slowly, trying to copy their sound, I begin to imitate the song the pigeons sang by the river after we lost Sidney. *It is how we let other animals know our deepest feelings,* they said. And that is what I will do. I know I might be out of tune, but I sing the same call, the same list of lost birds, hoping that any sick animals who might still be alive will hear, and come and join our wild.

My voice starts to waver, but I keep singing, humming where I can't remember the words. And then—

There's a scuffling sound in the bushes to my left, then another to my right.

I keep on singing, my voice growing shakier and shakier, when there is another rustle from the shadows to the left, closer this time. And then one to my right. Behind me. And in front of me.

I call out to the noises in the shadows of the forest. *Show yourself, whoever you are. We are not afraid.*

Nothing comes in reply.

Slowly I sing again, and the scuffling starts. Quick, breathy noises, moving quickly either side of the track, faster and faster.

I am Kester Jaynes, and this is my wild, I say to the scuffle in the shadows. *We are going to the city to find a cure for the virus. If you have something to say, show yourself now.*

And then there is a voice, a voice from the bushes.

A voice that is dry and cold, a voice that gets right under my skin and chills me to the bone.

I know who you are, Kester Jaynes.

Who are you?

The voice gives a dry laugh. *That does not concern you. But know this—you say you lead animals. You say you speak for animals.*

I was appointed Wildness—

Silence! Suddenly the voice is on the other side of the path—how did it get there? *You are a human. You will never speak for us.* The voice spits and stings at me with rage from the blackness. *You think you can command all creatures with your voice? You think all animals will love and praise you for what you are doing?* The voice laughs, mocking, echoing around me. *You have never been more wrong about anything in your life.*

I look around frantically in the dark. *Then why not show yourself?*

We will, Kester Jaynes, when the time is right—have no fear of that. The voice grows quiet, like wind in the trees. *Yours is not the only wild to survive. There is another. We will come when you least expect it. We will come in plain sight. You have been warned.*

The scuffling and grunting around me grows louder and louder. I take a step back, and then—the noise stops.

Hello?

But nothing comes. The wood is as silent as it was before.

And then, bursting through the undergrowth directly onto the path in front of me . . . is a ghost.

The ghost of a rabbit bouncing towards me through the bushes.

A ghost in a graveyard. But ghosts don't come right up close to you so you can touch their fur, feel their whiskers, hear their heart hammering away. See their red eyes burning. His body is stick-thin—but he is alive.

Was that you? I say fiercely. *Was that you who spoke to me like that just now, Rabbit?*

He looks alarmed.

I never said a word, he assures me in a soft, old voice. Definitely not the voice that just spoke to me. *I came here to complete my final journey. I thought my time was done. And then I heard your call.* He twitches his whiskers. *If you don't mind very much, I'm a hare—a brown hare.*

Sorry—I just thought you were—something else. Someone else. I scratch my head, confused. *But you're not a bird either.*

A call of loss is a call of loss, he says simply.

It works. It actually works.

So I try to forget about the voice in the bushes and sing the call again. As I do, the hare starts to join me, his voice reedy and thin, and he adds words of his own. More strange new names that I copy and learn to call for myself. He calls:

*O hedgehogs, dormice, and red squirrels.
Polecats, pine martens, and otters.
Pipistrelles, long-eared bats, and brown bats.*

As our voices rise and fall, out of the bushes rolls . . . a large mouse covered in sharp spikes, but with bare patches here and there.

She rubs her dry nose and turns her pink eyes towards me.

Hedgehog, she says simply. *You called.*

The hare and I look at each other, and we sing some more.

Then a whole family of long, furry, white-faced creatures, spilling out in a mess, fighting over each other, the youngest ones nothing but bones and skin, introducing themselves as polecats. They can only just stand up straight, but when they see me standing on the path singing with the hare, they start singing the call too, until we must be making enough noise to wake the dead. And we stand there, I and these animals that everyone thought were dead, singing and singing a call for those that still live to find us—and we sing till no more come.

Ha! says the General, as they all see me trudging back up the path. *The ghosts of those who sleep were too much for you, were they?*

The stag hangs his head, and even the wolf-cub looks at the ground.

No, General, I say. *But what if they are not yet asleep?*

I wave my hand, and behind me come the hare, polecats, and hedgehog—along with some rabbits, pine martens, and even a few bats flitting around our heads, some of them so small but more real than any ghost. If any of them was the creature that spoke to me from the bushes, he doesn't speak up.

Polly looks like she can't believe her eyes. Slumped against a tree, she leaps up from the ground when she sees the convoy. "You found so many! Perhaps—" But her voice trails away when she sees that a white cat is not amongst them.

Oblivious, the wolf-cub bounds up to me. *You are the best waker of the dead in the world, Wildness.*

And slowly the stag lifts his head towards me and nods. For a moment he stares deeply into my eyes, and I wonder whether to tell him about the voice in the bushes—but then I think better of it.

There is nothing to fear in these woods. Listen. I start to sing the pigeons' call again, and all the new animals in the wild start to sing the same call. My wild rejoin me and the new recruits, and they all start to sing together (although the white pigeon appears to be singing the call backwards). I even hear the General sing for the first time, as he calls out for tawny earwigs, diving beetles, and sedge jumpers, great blues and chequered skippers, damselflies, and hoverflies.

We march on through the Forest of the Dead, singing the pigeons' call.

I listen, but I don't hear any more nasty voices, and instead—

Slowly, surely, some more animals begin to come as we sing. I record each new arrival on my watch, with flash after flash. As the path runs along the leafy bank of a little stream, a toad joins us, singing out in reply and hopping along the bank. I give Polly the toad to hold in her lap, and she screams out loud. But the toad doesn't scream out or actually do anything gross. He just sits there, cool as you like in her lap, watching the world go by. When I next turn around, Polly has him cupped safely in her hands.

She is the only person not calling, because she can't hear or make the words. But every time I glance at her, the toad sitting in her lap, butterflies and wasps now buzzing calmly around her hair, she smiles and I realize she is as much part of this wild as the rest of us.

Next a pair of otters emerge dripping out of the water and slink along behind the wolf-cub. Some more birds, calling their own names in reply, join the pigeons up in the sky as the sun begins to set—shrike and yellowhammer, redpoll and woodpecker.

The bank gives way to a sandy shore, and we all scramble down to drink from the stream trickling over a bed of flat pebbles. As the stag bends his neck to the water, Polly slides straight off, scooping handfuls up into her chapped mouth. I hope that no animals came to die in this stream as well as in the forest.

But seeing me watch her, she wipes off the stray drops from her chin and shakes her head, pointing upstream.

"Look, it's quite safe." I follow the line of her hand and the silvery stream, curving round a bend until it goes out of sight—underground, bubbling through a pile of slippery rocks. "Fast-flowing, over pebbles, and direct from the ground. I'd have some while you can."

So I jump down and join her, and we gulp the fresh-tasting stream water down, then splash it over our heads, washing the soot of the fire clean away.

Back on the shore, as we rub our heads dry against the stag's furry sides, a red squirrel hops down from a tree, giving us a beady eye.

I thought you might be needing these, she says, and drops a pile of wizened berries and nuts in front of us. My stomach lurches as I remember what happened the last time I ate some food an animal gave me.

Where did you get them from? I ask.

I saved them, she replies. *Before the berry-eye came, I dug a hole and saved them for my—* She pauses for a moment, her whiskers trembling. *Well, I don't need them all now. You take 'em, take 'em all, feed yourselves and make sure you find us a cure!*

With a gasp like she is about to cry, the squirrel shoots back up the tree. I pick at the old-looking food suspiciously, but Polly is already sorting it into piles.

"We can eat those," she says, piling up some acorns, "but not those," chucking some wizened bright-red berries back into the undergrowth. I don't question her anymore but fill my face—until I can eat no more and the stag is casting his shadow over us.

Come, he says, *We must rest now. I fear we have an even longer day tomorrow.*

We both try not to notice how tired he looks as he stiffly creaks down to the ground, heaving for breath. He rests against the bank, while Polly and I huddle close together, leaning against his shaggy belly, the others lying all around.

They are not many. They are only a fraction of the names we called, but—

The forest isn't so frightening now.

PART 6
WELCOME TO THE CITY

The next morning, as we begin our journey again, it feels like the dark forest will go on forever—every single one of us still calling as loud as we can—when we are suddenly pushing through the thorns and twigs into an open field. Underneath the weight of us both, the stag pants for breath. He's growing weaker by the hour. Polly has bound the last few remaining shining leaves to his bruised and tired legs with creeper rope, but they seem to make only a small difference. Every now and then his back shudders or he trips, groaning in pain.

But what we can all see is that beyond the hedge, at the edge of the field, there is a cliff—

And below the cliff, a road—

And at the end of the road, lying spread out beneath us—like someone whipped away the carpet of green—is a plain of buildings and bridges, signs and billboards and barriers, all leading to one place—

A forest of glass towers, rising up out of the ground, like they were forced up from the earth's crust. Towers with domed roofs and red lights, blinking like eyes through the clouds, rows of windows glittering from top to bottom. Glowing homes and offices and factories of more people than have ever lived together before on this planet. Lights that are always on, pulsing day and night, rays and beams reflecting off the glass roofs and walls, rising up into the sky above, brighter than even the stars themselves.

My head is swirling like the swollen clouds in the sky above. I don't know if what Ma said about Dad is true. I don't even know if we will find him here—and even if we do, whether he will have a cure.

I know that I am taking these animals to the most dangerous place I could.

But for now—for this one moment, looking down over the glass and lights—none of that matters because I realize that after all this time . . .

I'm finally coming home. To where I belong, to where everything started.

Premium. My city.

Before we go any farther, I count all the animals.

1 stag (very tired)

1 wolf-cub (the least tired animal in the whole world, according to him)

1 large cockroach (in my pocket, asking why I didn't take a roll call before now)

1 harvest mouse (still doing the Stationary Dance of Solid Sleep)

99 grey pigeons (although hard to count exactly as they keep moving around all the time)

1 white pigeon (who has just started singing again, on his own, now everyone else has stopped)

About 12 other birds (nicer-sounding than the pigeons)

2 otters (still wet, even though we left the river hours ago. Do they ever dry off?)

1 brown hare (very old) & assorted rabbits

6 polecats

4 pine martens

1 red squirrel (good for nuts)

1 toad (who at first Polly refused to touch, and now she won't let go of)

1 hedgehog (keeps herself to herself)

Lots of flies and butterflies (different kinds, haven't had time to ask them all their names)

Not as many wasps

Various bats (who do not like flying during the day)

Beetles, earwigs, etc. (wolf-cub refuses to carry them)

Well over a hundred animals. Nearly as many as the wild we left at the Ring of Trees.

Not every animal died.

A breeze blows in over the top of the cliff, ruffling our hair, making me dig my hands inside my pockets for warmth. Over there, among the towers and lights, there are other people—working, living, and, in the middle of it all, somewhere—Dad.

I hope.

I pull my scarf tight around me as the wind starts to grow stronger.

Together we all slide down a path zigzagging along the side of the cliff towards Premium's outskirts.

Polly puts her hand in front of her face, against the wind. The toad waddles off her lap to take shelter, and she lets him snuggle under her shirt. This wind has grown cold as well as strong—it feels like it is stripping the skin off your face. With every step, it gets harder and harder to walk into, but at last we reach the bottom of the cliff.

There's no shelter down here, nothing but bare earth and chunky chips of gravel, the wind blowing clouds of dust along the top, between us and the wire fence that surrounds the city.

I look over the wasteland at the brightly lit windows of the towers. Normal people living normal lives. I can see some of them, distant figures silhouetted in window frames. Perhaps the wolf-cub can even smell them.

All the animals go very quiet.

I stroke the stag's dripping flank. He's so warm, even in this chill wind. Up above, the birds—old and new—are tossed about in the air. The General digs around inside my pockets, hiding from the gale. I look at the wolf-cub. He stands next to the stag and me, eyes narrowed, but the wind is pushing at his lips, pulling them back, blowing his fur and ears flat.

I have never known wind like this. This must be the coldest wind in the world. But we will defeat it—it is only wind!

But just as we start to see the towers close-up, the shapes of the domed roofs and the gleaming walls, the stag sinks to the ground, throwing us off in a jumble. Picking myself up, I can see his legs splayed out, his horns resting on the ground.

What's wrong?

He shakes his head, breathing like he's trying to steady himself, and mumbles something hard to hear above the wind. His side and brow are boiling up.

The others crowd round, looking—

Shaking, I press the button on my watch. Squeezing out the very last of the faint light left in its battery, I shine it into his eyes.

Eyes that now burn a deep, pulsing red.

How long have you known? I ask the stag.

I had it from the start, when I first called, when I summoned you, he whispers.

But your eyes, they looked brown, you didn't say—

The eyes are a late sign, as you know. He rolls his at me. *And if I had told you I was ill, would you have accepted our quest? Would you have let me carry you here?*

The harvest mouse, who had been clinging on to his horns, jumps off. *When the others in my nest were starving, when they were*—she pauses, gulps at the memory—*we used to do something. I don't know if it would be any help now, but—*

This is no time for a dance, Harvest Mouse.

She looks hurt.

I would never suggest a dance at a time like this. What kind of self-respecting harvest mouse do you take me for, my lad? She scratches her nose crossly with her claws. *No, if you'd keep your thoughts in your head for just a single moment—we helped them like this.* And she hurries up the stag's leg and onto his chest. The deer gives a low grumble but doesn't shake her off, as slowly, not missing a single bit, the mouse begins, with claws and teeth, to remove all the mud and thorns and twigs twisted in his fur.

I look round at the others. The stag is lying stretched out, surrounded by a circle of woodland animals.

Apart from the wolf-cub, who sits upright behind me. He whispers in the dark, *Normally this would be my chance to avenge the death of my father. I should tear his dying carcass to pieces.* The cub sounds matter-of-fact. *But I will not—for now—out of respect for you, Wildness.*

I turn on him. *He's not dying! He's not dying, OK?*

The wolf-cub shrinks away, cowering.

I turn back to the stag. *You didn't say anything. Why didn't you—*

It makes no odds now. I have survived longer than I expected. I have carried you here, as the dream said I would. The wind hits in rolling gusts, like jabs in the side, each one making us flinch. *Now you must go on and leave me here. Take the others, find your father, and find us a cure. Find us all a cure. Hurry.*

I glance up at the darkening, brooding sky. *There is no way I'm leaving you here, not after everything—*

All of that is meaningless unless you find us a cure. I will rest here until you return.

I thump my fist into the ground, spraying him with a burst of loose soil. *We can't leave you here, on the edge of the city. Who knows what could happen? Anyone could find you, cullers—or worse. You're not well enough for us to leave you on your own!*

You will go faster without me.

Then what's the point of it all? Telling me to be the Wildness, telling me to make decisions, to take charge—and then when I do, you don't listen. We can't leave you here! You'll die!

Maybe, Wildness, says Wolf-Cub, nervous I will turn on him again, *that is what he wants.*

But it's not what I want!

For the first time since we left the forest, Polly carefully puts down the toad she has carried all the way on the ground, and he waits patiently at her feet while she digs about in her pockets.

She holds out her palm to me. In the faint glow from the houses across the wasteland, I can make out the bunch of bright-pink flowers from the hedgerow. The ones she wouldn't let me eat.

I don't understand.

"Nightvale. They're not a cure, like the leaves, I'm afraid," she says. "And deadly for us. Which is why I wouldn't let you touch them." I notice she is carefully holding the bottom of the stems and not the flowers. "But a tiny drop of their juice will help him sleep a little, maybe rest and—"

But I don't want him to sleep, I want him to—

"Just give him one drop," she says, folding the cuff of my anorak over my hand, and dropping a single nightvale in. "All you have to do is squeeze the flower. He's taken us all the way, hasn't he? I'm sure he could do with a proper rest."

The others begin to drift even farther away from the stag, towards the lights, as if they have decided already.

I kneel down by him again. He is so weak I have to really strain to hear him.

You are a good Wildness. I have trained you well. But you must trust me now. This is the right thing to do. Foamy mucus drips out of his mouth onto the ground. *The only thing to do.*

I stroke his soft, wet nose and his chipped horns. He's

carried me so far. I didn't have anything before I met the stag, and now—

Oh yes, you did, Kester, he murmurs, a glimmer of a smile in his burning eyes.

Just promise me, I say, trying to ignore my tears, *that you will be all right. And I promise we will come back and find you. And we will make you better.*

Between my sleeves, I crush the bell of the nightvale flower above his open mouth, and a single clear drop falls onto his tongue—

He grunts and swallows it. Then his tone changes, just like the wind. *Go now. Before a storm comes—go!*

I need no further telling. I touch his warm head once more, stand up, and turn around to face the city fence. As I do, my watch vibrates with a last spasm of energy. I glance down and have to strain to see two words, only just visible on the dying screen:

GIVE UP

I turn off the watch. Give up? That is the one thing I am not doing, whoever or whatever is trying to tell me that I should. I feel so full of fire that I don't think a whole regiment of cullers could stop me now—the wild is waiting.

Beyond the fence there are towers, lights, people, and machines. Everything that used to feel normal. And now—I don't know how it will feel.

But without waiting another second I start striding

straight towards the fence, Polly hurrying behind me with the toad in her arms.

"Where are you going, Kester? Wait! You can't just walk into Premium with a hundred animals!"

Watch me.

We enter the city through a hole in the fence, blown open by the wind.

Then we're sneaking along alleyways, striding under shady bridges splattered with graffiti, breathing in as we slide along the narrow gaps in between buildings. Only Wolf-Cub keeps up with me, as we leave the last of the countryside behind.

Now we march up a white concrete ramp, which rises through the forest of towers and twists and turns on high pillars, raised above more wasteland far below, over slums filled with rickety sheds, caravans, and piles of rubbish. Steam and another smell rises up, the smell of something oily that makes *me* gag—and the General's antennae twitch eagerly.

Then the road swoops down again into the city proper, taking us along wide streets lined with grey, old-fashioned buildings with tattered flags dangling outside, and small withered trees in pots standing in rows, like guards. We come to a sprawling block of shops and their never-ending windows. The old hare stops for a moment and peers at his reflection in them, gawping at the faded and peeling signs plastered across the giant walls of glass.

No more shops as the road leads into the heart of the city—just the towers we saw from the cliff, shining glass skyscrapers that climb into the clouds, each one home to thousands of people, the very top floors soaring high above even the pigeons.

How do people live there? We couldn't fly that high.

Yes, how do people fly up that high?

"Where is everyone, Kester?" asks Polly, looking around at the deserted streets. "I thought Premium would be full of people. Perhaps they're scared of us."

She's right. They are. Frightened of animals, frightened of the plague they carry—perhaps people who, like me only a few days ago, have never seen a living one before now. As we walk past the towers, there are pale faces pressed to ground-floor windows—blinds hurriedly slam down, lit rooms go dark as we pass. Headlights approach us, making the polecats start in alarm, but when the drivers see the animals, they brake and reverse quickly or dive down a side street out of our way.

Ha! None dare approach the mighty cockroach warrior! says the General from my shoulder.

We continue down the street, past a silent government building that looks like a locked box, and over a bridge, taking us over the river, early morning mist still curling along it, hiding the ships and cranes moored along its edge.

The River Ams. The river that was once a fish-road.

The fish-road that splits Premium in two, between the new half and the old half. The old half. Where I once lived with Mum and Dad.

We stop to catch our breath, the animals peering through the bars of the bridge at the water flowing below. I look out farther—to my right, where way down along the opposite bank, four tall and dark chimneys stick up through the fog. I can't help but shiver, seeing them again for the first time in six years—the four towers of Factorium.

But we aren't going there. After the bridge we turn left—

Then left—left again—

To where there are no towers of any kind, just a street with houses set back from it at the top of long drives, sealed off behind fences and walls and cameras and lamps that come on as you walk past. The wind seems to have followed us, winding down the roads. And now it's not just a cold wind—

But a wet one as well.

We all look up at the clouds in the sky as spots of rain begin to explode on my hands. The rain that can mean only one thing—

The drops grow bigger and colder and wetter as we start to go past the lines of cars, raindrops now speckling the dark windscreens and shiny hoods. I start to hurry, half running, Polly pulling up her anorak hood, trying to keep up and not drop the toad at the same time as we turn round at a polished kerb, into a big circle of a dead end.

My street—it's my Culdee Sack, as Mum used to call it.

I know I should wait for the others, but I start to run.

"Kester!" yells Polly. "Where are you going? Wait for us!"

I'm not listening to her. All I can hear is the blood pounding in my head, the rain hammering on the pavement.

I glance at the different names of the houses flashing by on their shiny letterboxes, trying not to slip on the pavement growing slicker and wetter under my feet—

Until I reach the gates right at the end.

The gates of a low white house, standing on its own, the sheets of water bouncing off the glass roof that slides off down to one side, into the garden. Everything is just as it was six years ago. There are no lights on apart from the security lamps along the drive, like it's a runway. I feel like a tiny kid again. Not for the first time, I wonder whether Dad is actually going to be pleased to see me.

"Shall I come with you?" Polly's stopped a little way behind. She's struggling to make her voice heard over the wind and the rain. The toad croaks. Polly looks down at it. "Shall *we* come with you?"

I shake my head, spraying wet everywhere—I have to do this by myself.

I wipe as much water as I can off a small metal box on the wall next to the gate, and type the code into the keypad . . .

Nothing happens.

I try again, wiping more water off, pressing harder this time—and to my relief the gates slither noisily back. He hasn't changed the codes. It's only a small thing, I know, but it makes squelching up the long drive—in the glow of the security lights—easier than I thought it would be.

Because there's a knot in my stomach, tangling up, growing warm in my belly.

I find myself pulling up my sweatpants, trying to flatten my hair despite the rain, wiping the worst of the mud off my face, straightening my sodden scarf. Here I finally am, six years later, standing on the doorstep of our own home in the rain, with a girl and over a hundred animals.

I count to ten and press the doorbell.

It rings, but no one comes. I press it again.

Then a light comes on—at the end of the hall.

I can hear him coming down the passage.

Another light, a shadow appears behind the frosted glass, and all I'm thinking is, Open the flipping door—

A rattle and chunk of locks, a chain slides back, the door opens and—

"Hello, little boy," says Captain Skuldiss. "Well, this is a nice surprise. And how do you do?"

And everything goes black.

I'm back in Spectrum Hall, back in my room, right at the beginning. My window is broken again, rain and wind blowing on my face. I feel for my arms, my watch. I can't see anything, everything is dark, but I am still—alive.

I know this because I'm in pain. There is pain all over, throbbing in my head, in my arms, and in my legs. Pain I've felt before—from a metal crutch. I groan, try to move, and a thousand nerves scream at me.

Then, just as before in my room, there are pigeons pecking at me, pulling my hair, pulling at my clothes, my ears, and nose—

Wake up! Wake up, Kester! We can't do this alone! Help us!

I open my eyes instead—because I can do that.

At first I can see only the darkness of the sky above, the rain still pouring onto my face. Where has the roof of my room gone? And then slowly, painfully, I realize where we are, and I twist my head round on the wet road, to see what is happening at the end of it. To see what is happening in our drive, our street. I know it's home, but it doesn't feel like it anymore.

Captain Skuldiss is standing in our open gateway with his back to me, lit by the security lamps. He flicks his wet hair back and flexes his fingers together with a nasty crack. I hear a scream from the other side of the road.

Polly. I can't speak. I can't move.

The pigeons fuss and pull at my hair.

Skuldiss points his crutch at the sky. I flinch. But there's no shot. Instead a fierce glare fills the street. Tall floodlights that I hadn't seen in the dark, hidden in the shadows of the big houses, behind their high walls and gates, all blasting at once with a light as strong as a midday sun.

Skuldiss points his crutch again. An explosion of noise follows the explosion of light.

A van, splashing its way down the road. I can hear it screech and hiss to a halt at the entrance to the Culdee Sack. A door slides open and people are jumping out into the road with heavy boots.

I don't need to see them to know who they are.

The van we last heard on the road from the farm. Cullers.

There is no stag to stop them now. Skuldiss and the cullers' van have blocked the only way out. My wild are surrounded by high walls and gates. Pain shoots through my neck and spine, but I force myself to turn and watch.

The Captain leaps farther into the road, and Polly runs forward to meet him, the toad clasped to her chest.

"My cat's dead because of you!" she yells. "What have you done with my parents? You have to tell me!" The toad accompanies her with his angriest croak yet.

But Captain Skuldiss doesn't answer any of her questions. He just grabs Polly, the toad diving for cover under her anorak once more. Skuldiss pins her to him, one of his crutches barred across her neck, before pointing the other one directly at the wild.

The street falls quiet, not a sound from anyone, just the rain splashing down in sheets.

"So, little girl," I hear, "as you can see, Captain Skuldiss always finishes his job." He swings his crutch round and round, pointing at and naming all the different animals in turn—otters and polecats and hares—like they've ever done anything to him. Then he turns to her, and as if he's asking her to choose her favourite colour, says—

"So which one would you like me to kill first, little girl?"

Polly doesn't reply to Captain Skuldiss, but just gives a little gasp of pain, as he squeezes his other arm tighter round her neck. There is no smile in his voice now. I just pray that he doesn't discover the toad.

"Just go and bring me the dirty animal you would like to die first, and be quick about it, please." He shoves her back into the road, where I can see her facing the wild in the rain. "And remember, Uncle Skuldiss is watching, so no funny tricks, my little chickadee," he says, waving the gun-crutch at her.

I don't know how long Polly stands there, just looking, the wild staring back at her.

Eventually she speaks.

"I know I can't talk to you," she says to them, cradling the hidden toad, speaking in a voice that's only just possible to make out. "Not like Kester, I know that. But I used to talk to Sidney—a lot—and I think some of the time she understood." Her words start to wobble and break. "And I want you to know, I don't want this to happen, I don't want any more of you—"

I'm trying so hard to move, to speak, but nothing—and then before she can go on, Skuldiss swings his crutch, jabbing her in the back.

"No more talking!" he snaps. "The very clever thing about bullets, you know, is that they work on little children just as well."

Polly begins to sob, but she doesn't raise an arm or point a finger. She doesn't even look at the wild now and just stares at the ground.

Skuldiss raps a crutch on the ground crossly. "Very well, have it your way," he says. And then starts to have a conversation with himself. "Oh! What's that you say, little girl? You choose this sick beastie over here?"

He points the gun-crutch at one of the wild.

The quivering, elderly hare.

"The long-eared rabbity-thing. Very good. Are you sure?"

Polly doesn't react.

"I said, are you sure?" repeats Skuldiss, jabbing her in the backs of the legs. She stays rock-still, not giving him anything. He sails on.

"Thank you, little one. Now look how easy it is!" There's a bang, wisps of smoke in the wet air, and then, with a short sigh as if he was only breathing out, the hare slumps over onto the ground, a dark dot oozing right between his eyes, his long ears splayed out on the ground. The first animal who came and answered my call in the forest. He thought I'd saved him.

Polly gives a choked scream, like it died in her throat. "One down, ninety-nine to go," says Skuldiss.

The others begin to panic, rabbits scrabbling in all directions, polecats attempting to squeeze under gates, pine martens scrambling over walls—

I try to move, but waves of pain flood my brain, pinning me to the ground.

Skuldiss raises his crutch again, carefully takes aim, so cool, so calm, like he is taking potshots at tin cans in a fairground—and there's another bang.

My wild is disappearing before my very eyes.

I can't talk to them—all I can hear is the firing gun-crutch and Polly sobbing, the toad bellowing his heart out with her.

I slump back down. It's a nightmare and I can't wake up.

Wet feathers and claws fluster next to me.

Kester! You have to save them. Now! You have to.

It's no good. It's over. Dad's not here. I tried.

Kester, you promised. You promised the stag. You have to save them.

No. No. I'm just a boy. He's a maniac. I haven't got a gun, I can't walk—I roll over away from them onto my side. I can just see a blur of white feathers out of the corner of my eye.

I saved this from the stag. I promised it for you.

The white pigeon still makes no sense. But this time he's insistent.

Yes, we saved from the stag. For you.

And then he's pressing something against my clenched hand.

Something sharp as a dagger. Something held in his beak.

It's a curved piece of pointed bone, shot from a stag's horn.

The pigeons must have picked it up off the road—and kept it all this time.

More shots echo round the Culdee Sack.

I think of the stag, lying in the wasteland. I think of everything he said to me. I look at the white pigeon pecking at my hand, at his funny orange eyes.

I clench the horn tight and slowly raise myself up, trying to breathe.

Please hurry, Kester—please! You have to! Take it! Use it!

Still gasping for breath, on my hands and knees, I look down through our gates, beyond Skuldiss and Polly.

Wolf-Cub! I shout—but the only sound I make is a hoarse croak.

I stagger to my feet, unable to stand up properly.

Doubled over, I shake my head, trying to see straight. *Wolf-Cub!* I shout again, louder this time.

Wildness! comes the reply that I can only just hear over the shooting and screaming. *Your father looks like the man from the fish-road!* calls the wolf-cub. *And he is firing his stick at us! This is the worst cure in the world!*

That's because—he is *the man from the fish-road!* I shout back.

Then I shall tear out his eyes and his throat! comes the growled reply. *I shall overcome my fear of his firestick!*

I'm not near enough yet.

No—wait, Wolf-Cub! You are brave, you do not need to prove it now—wait for my command.

It's too late—

The wolf-cub leaps out between the animals skidding for cover, his grey body bounding across the road—towards Skuldiss and Polly—

Anyone else would run from a wolf leaping at their throat, but not Captain Skuldiss.

All he does is raise his crutch, just like that—as Wolf-Cub flies towards him, jaws bared to their max, and then I'm running too, forcing and sucking breath down through my stinging windpipe—

The wolf-cub and I lock eyes over Skuldiss's shoulder—

I know he can read the signal in my eyes, but it's too late—

He's in the air, and I'm jumping too, the stag's horn clutched in my outstretched hand, throwing myself at the Captain's back, and he lurches to the left as I tackle him, Polly running free of his grip—

But as he falls under my weight, there's a single shot— and an invisible hand slams the wolf-cub in the chest, hurling him to the ground.

Now it's the turn of my eyes to go red. Not with a virus but with rage.

Before Captain Skuldiss can pick himself up, I'm on top of him. I've got the stag horn in my hand, and I'm trying to stab him. I never knew it was possible to hate one person so much. But Skuldiss has his hand around my wrist, his grip is tight and strong, hurting me. He's smiling. Water splashes in his eyes, I'm trying to stab him, and he's *smiling*.

Polly runs over to Wolf-Cub, lying sprawled out on the hard tarmac, a dark puddle oozing out from a hole in his side. She hauls her damp and battered bag off her shoulder, and pulls out the bunch of nightvale. Protecting her hand with the sleeve of her sodden anorak, she carefully snaps off another pink bell and squeezes a tiny drop of nightvale oil onto the cub's panting tongue.

We both know, though, he is going to need more than sleep.

"What are you going to do?" she says. She speaks so quietly, I can only just hear her above the pitter-patter of the rain. She doesn't talk to me but into her chest, looking at Wolf-Cub's head held in her hands as he shivers and coughs.

"You aren't going to let him kill all the animals, are you?"

I shake my head. I wish I could explain. Wish that my eyes could hold letters, that my face was a book.

Skuldiss squeezes my wrist tighter and tighter, trying to make me drop the stag horn, but he's looking at something over my shoulder.

I turn to see his cullers running down the street towards us with their rubber suits and boots.

"It's over, children," Skuldiss says with a smug grin, as the cullers draw near. "Why bother for these nasty animals? It's either your infectious beasties or the human souls in this here city. You have to choose. Who do you want to live?"

I look at Polly and Wolf-Cub, at the houses surrounding us, houses I had thought of whenever I imagined home, which now look so unfriendly, so silent. And I press the point of the horn hard against his skin, a white spot in a white throat pushing away the blood, pushing until—

"Have you ever killed a man before, little boy?" says Skuldiss, sounding strangled and strange. "I have. And the first time is always the hardest."

His eyes stare up at me, as calm and murky as two stagnant ponds.

My hand shakes. My heart is about to burst out of my chest. I think of Sidney. I think of the stag, lying on his own in the wasteland, and of Wolf-Cub, not speaking now, not even murmuring, as Polly strokes his head and squeezes one more drop of nightvale into his mouth. I think of the old hare, of the dead and wounded lying around us.

But I can't. I can't do it.

If I thought killing Captain Skuldiss would make things better—

Would make them all better—

Then I would, I really, *really* would—

But deep down, I know it won't.

A crooked smile begins to creep over the white face pressed against the tarmac.

"You can't do it, can you, little boy? I knew it!"

Polly doesn't say anything. The wild don't say anything. The toad simply gives a broken croak.

With a lurch, a hole seems to open in the pit of my stomach, and inside I feel like I'm falling, and falling—as I realize that the stag was right.

A great stag always faces his fate.

My shoulders sink, and I loosen my grip—

Skuldiss grabs the horn out of my hand and flings it against the wall of the house, where it clatters uselessly to the ground.

"No, don't!" shouts Polly.

But it's too late.

The cullers leap on me, pulling my arms tight behind

my back, squashing my face into the road.

Polly is staring at us with her mouth hanging wide open, like she's the one who can't speak now.

Captain Skuldiss picks himself up, brushes the dust and mud off his jacket, and straightens his tie—looking naked without his crutches, standing unsteadily, holding his hands out for balance. "Children, children, when will you ever learn? Don't get involved in things you don't understand."

He laughs to himself and then quickly bends right over. At first I think he's lost his balance, but he is just pulling up his trouser leg. I get a glimpse of a scarred and mangled calf, and something else—pulled free from a strap with a flourish. A flash of steel—which now dances between his hands, catching the light. A short, flat spear. The kind you can attach to guns—or crutches.

A bayonet.

The animals shuffle back in alarm, but I hold up my head, stare Skuldiss right in the face, and smile.

"I don't think I said anything funny. Would you like to explain the joke, little boy?" says Captain Skuldiss, twirling the bayonet.

I'm smiling because of the noise.

He stares at me smugly, like he's just won the game. Unluckily for him, in *this* game, the noise I can hear gives me the courage to hold up my head and stare Skuldiss right back in the eye.

Because there are giant hoofs pounding down the street towards us, hoofs that can only belong to one creature in the world.

Polly can hear it now as well, and she's looking up at me, daring to give a half smile. Then the other animals can hear it too, and they're cheering, the toad is burping, and Skuldiss has turned round, as have the cullers, but it's too late—

A huge set of horns collides with the men in rubber suits, tossing them out of the way like they are rag dolls, barging straight through and skidding to a halt—snorting and pawing the ground—right in front of me.

His eyes are a fierce red. If Polly's nightvale helped him sleep, then he has come back stronger than ever before. Sweat foams and drips from his flank, he heaves for breath, and his horns are chipped and bent—but he is here. He came after us.

He came *for us.*

The stag, he says between gasping breaths, *saved himself for one last fight.*

Skuldiss just stares at him. He stares at the slumped bodies of the unconscious cullers. He has gone bone-white.

The stag looks at the wolf-cub on the ground, a tiny light still flickering in his eyes.

Did the man with his sticks do this?

I nod. The stag stalks towards Captain Skuldiss, who crouches down, smiling his sharp-toothed smile. "Come on, you big lovely brute," he says, jabbing the air with his bayonet. "Let's be having you."

For the first and last time, the great stag, from the last wild, speaks to Captain Skuldiss. Speaks to him in a voice he will never, ever understand.

Man, in the name of all those whom you have killed, prepare to meet your fate.

Then he throws back his head and bellows so loud that the windows of all the smart houses shake.

And I do nothing to try to stop him as the stag charges at the man who tried to kill his wild, leaping clean off the ground, his horns lowered.

Then, like that, Captain Skuldiss is no longer standing, no longer speaking, no longer killing—and the stag has collapsed on the ground beside him, bloodied but alive, steam clouding out of his muzzle. The cullers still lie where he tossed them, breathing but not moving.

I look up at the sky.

The rain has finally stopped.

I crouch down by the deer. *When it started to rain, I thought that was the storm to end all storms, that you had—*

He shakes his bloodied head.

No. Not yet. You will know that when it comes. But animals died here today. Animals will have died at the Ring. You must hurry!

But where?

Around us, the sky begins to brighten up, turning greywhite behind the aerials on the roofs of the Culdee Sack. Everything smells fresh after the storm. In the distance, there are the noises of Premium waking up. I look at the wild, collapsed in a heap, stinking of damp fur and feathers. I've brought them here—but there's no Dad, and there's no cure.

We can't go any farther.

I run to Wolf-Cub, lying in the middle of the road.

He's going cold. I kneel down and cradle his damp head on my lap, his tongue hanging out at a funny angle.

His eyes turn towards me, every word a massive effort. *I faced my fear, Wildness—did you see that?*

Yes, you did, Wolf-Cub—you were very brave.

Was I the best . . . ? But he can't finish the sentence. My hands freeze midair above him, waiting for a clear instruction from my brain.

Is it always this cold in the city? says Wolf-Cub.

I shake my head and hold him, trying to stop the blood, trying to stop everything.

Keep your eyes open, Wolf-Cub, I order. *Just keep them open.*

I look up at the grey sky and imagine crying out one question: Dad, where are you? I've brought them here, to our home—where are you? But the only noise comes from the wolf-cub, his breath fading in and out. I hold him tight, pressing my jacket against him, hoping I might be able to stop the hot blood leaking away. I feel it spill over my jacket, my arms, my legs.

Take my hand, I say, smelling his warm fur and pressing my hand to his mouth, wanting him to bite it. Weakly he opens his jaws and closes them around my fingers, teeth barely pressing the skin.

He gave his life trying to protect me, to protect all of us.

No, no, don't go, please don't go—

Then Polly is back, from wherever she went to hide. Out of the corner of my eye I can see her standing in our drive-way, talking to me, but I don't listen. Instead I just hold the wolf-cub, his body going limp in my arms, his breath gurgling in his throat.

"Kester, listen to me. I can hear a voice."

I can't even look at her.

She stomps over, squats down in front of me, and grabs me by the shoulders, her voice low and deadly serious. "Kester! Why won't you listen to *me* for once? I can hear a human voice, inside your house. There's someone else in there."

Quickly I look around for the cockroach—but he's already settling on my knee.

General, you have to take charge now. You know where to find me if anyone comes—I glance at the unconscious cullers, what remains of Skuldiss—*or if anyone comes back,* I add.

Have no fear, I will keep a safe guard over this wild. Reporting for duty!

He buzzes sharply over to the kerb and perches on the edge, overlooking all the bodies—animal and human—that fill the road.

I carry the wolf-cub as carefully as I can up my drive and follow Polly through the open door, into the big hall with the shiny wooden floor. Wolf-Cub trails dark blood everywhere.

Polly is shouting, "Hello? Hello?"

Her voice echoes off the bare white walls, the walls that I know so well, but it doesn't feel like home anymore, it feels different.

We stop, both our hearts thumping away in the silence, trying to listen, listen for the other voice in the house.

Then—I hear it too—a hammering on a door, a muffled shout. Polly wasn't hiding. She was exploring again, looking for things—and she may have found the thing I want most in the world. I know exactly where to go and hurry down the wide stairs at the end of the hall that lead down to the basement, and to a solid, shut metal door.

The door to my dad's lab.

Polly and I stop in front of the door. We exchange glances. The wolf-cub gives a tiny whistling mew.

The hammering continues from the other side of the door, but getting slower, like the person doing it is tired. I want to speak; I can feel the air bubbling in my throat, my lips and tongue trying to make a word—

The hammering stops. There's a muffled cry from behind the door.

Polly looks at me nervously. "Who's there?" is all she says in reply.

Then I hear the voice too, behind the metal—

Saying the words I have been waiting to hear for six years. But the voice is so faint—

"Kes? Kester? Is that . . . you?"

I take a step back, suspicious. How does he know it's me, through a locked steel door? I think of what Ma said by the fire. I look at Polly.

"Yes, it is," she says, without any hesitation. Then—"I'm his friend. Can you let us in?"

For a moment there is silence behind the door. It doesn't open.

There's one last thump. A thump of frustration.

"We need to open the door," says Polly in a matter-of-fact way. She tries the knob, which spins freely in her hand. Then she turns to me. "Actually, you need to break down the door."

I lay down the wolf-cub as gently as I can. Stepping back, gesturing to Polly to move out of the way, I run at the heavy steel.

I charge and charge until my shoulder is sore—

Until with a noise like a broken spring—

The door clicks open.

Rubbing my shoulder, I stare at the doorway. At the silhouette of a tall man, crazy hair and beard sticking out in all directions. I can't see his face at first, in the shadows, but then he steps out of the lab—

Through the broken door, into the light of the stairway.

My dad—Professor Dawson Jaynes.

For a moment, Dad just stares, looking past us and up the stairs. I didn't know if the city would feel normal. But I had no idea how this moment would feel. And the shock nearly knocks me off my feet. *It's actually Dad.* Still here after all this time—still with crazy hair, a crinkled shirt, and a forgetful look on his face—still the same old Dad.

My chest tightens like a vise. I properly missed him. I missed him so much more than I realized. At first I don't know if he's thinking the same, because he snaps out of his stare and balls his fist up, ready to fight. "Is that wretch still here?"

With a flash of relief I realize he means Skuldiss. Polly and I both shake our heads.

Then he nods to himself and I know he feels the same because he says it.

"Kes . . . missed you . . . so much."

And then he envelops me in a massive bear hug,

pressing my face against his lab coat—but I wrestle free. There isn't time for hugs now. I need help. Dad looks at me, then at Polly, and finally down at the wolf-cub, pulsing on the floor.

"Hmm," he says. "Is this your friend?"

"Yes," says Polly. "He broke into my house—"

Dad interrupts her with a wave of his big hands. "I meant, is *this* your friend?" He points to the wolf-cub, and I nod.

"Hmm," says Dad, kneels down, scoops him up in his arms, and hurries into his lab. We follow him in, Polly looking at me all the time.

The lab used to be all clean white surfaces and glass. It's filthy now. There are piles of paper everywhere, covered in crazy scribbles and diagrams and symbols and numbers, and unwashed plates and greasy glasses. A dozen computer screens flicker away, wires twisting out of them like ivy. The four big, sloping glass walls that look out into the garden and the river beyond are smeared with dust and grime, making the room darker than I remember.

Then the smell hits me. I thought the stench in the cockroach tunnel was bad, but this is something else, perhaps because it's—human. Polly and I both put our hands over our noses and mouths. Strangest of all—there's a bed in the corner of the lab, the blanket pulled roughly back, a bare-bulb lamp on the floor next to it, poking out of a pile of clothes and shoes. And a single toothbrush stands in a mug by the sink.

Still carrying the wolf-cub, Dad frees a hand to sweep papers and plates off the worktop onto the floor. He lays him down in the cleared space and swings a big lamp over. He's rolling up his sleeves, pulling on rubber gloves out of nowhere, and talking at Polly and me to get things, telling us where they are, in his usual, forgetful, Dad-like way—as if nothing has happened, nothing has changed.

"Swabs, bandages, and a dressing, I think—probably in the cupboard above the sink. You'll have to borrow a chair to stand on—that's it. And now, for you, young lady—what did you say your name was again?"

"Polly," says Polly, already dragging a chair across.

"Forty-eight milligrams or so of sodium diamorphate if you would. It should be in a glass bottle on that shelf or, if not, try under my chair—oh yes, that's perfect—I say, have you done this before? What did you say your name was again?"

"Polly," repeats Polly patiently, handing him the medicine.

Within minutes, the wolf-cub stops yelping, stops shivering, and just lies there sleeping. A syringe of white liquid sticks out of his leg, and an oxygen mask is clamped firmly round his muzzle, his chest slowly rising and falling.

Now Dad gives us stuff to hold and things to cut, never panicking, always staying calm, as he bends the lamp right down over the wolf-cub to see what he's doing. Then he's picking sharp instruments off a tray that Polly and I have carefully cleaned with wipes smelling of alcohol, the only clean things in the whole place—and we have to look away because of the wound.

Dad is digging around inside the cub, and then he says, "Salver," and I hand him a metal dish to drop the bloody, sticky bullet in. I think I'm going to be sick, but then he's sewing up Wolf-Cub, careful stitch by careful stitch. Dad injects him one last time, makes sure the oxygen mask is firmly on, and steps back to check his work.

Satisfied, he invites us over, and hardly daring to look we creep nearer.

Underneath the mask, the wolf-cub is still breathing. My father pats him once and then marches over to the sink, ripping off the bloody gloves and tossing them onto the floor.

"Hmm," says Dad. "Bit of rest and he should be . . ."

Six years and Dad still hasn't learnt how to finish a sentence.

He dries his hands thoroughly with a paper towel and chucks it—missing—at an overflowing bin in the corner.

We're still just watching him. For a moment, no one says anything. There are so many questions bubbling inside me—questions I can't ask. I stamp my foot on the floor with frustration. Polly jumps, and then, like that was her signal, she asks it. Like it's the easiest thing in the world to say.

The question burning in both our minds.

"Is it true, Professor Jaynes?"

Dad looks puzzled.

"Hmm?"

"What everyone said. Skuldiss, outsiders, Facto—they all said that you started the virus. That it was your fault."

And he smiles. He actually smiles. A kind of sad smile, as he shakes his head.

"Is that what they . . . ? Right. I see." He scratches at his beard. "Well." Dad gestures to the chaos of the lab. "Whatever you're thinking, whatever you've been told, whatever she thinks, it's . . ."

His voice trails away.

"Wrong?" suggests Polly.

I hope so—I really hope so.

But Dad just nods in a vague way, like she'd just reminded him where his slippers were, and places his hands on my shoulders.

"Kes," he says. "None of this is how it . . . you know . . ."

For some reason I can't meet his eye. My own dad.

He sighs and looks me up and down.

"You've grown," he says and grips my shoulders tight. "You've grown so much."

Then he turns abruptly away, like he doesn't want me to see his face. "Let me try and . . . explain," he says to the window, and starts to pace up and down, looking at the floor as he speaks.

"Science!" he announces to the mess all around him, the scribbled pages, the rows of test tubes—as if he's just revealing to them only now what they're actually here for. "That's what I believe in, Kes. In thinking things through, using the knowledge we've discovered to . . . what's the word?" He stops pacing, picks up a rubber band from the dust on the floor, and peers at it suspiciously before shoving it into his pocket. "Where was I? Oh yes! Science." He turns to us, his face lit up. "Miracles! That's what we can achieve with science. Real, living, breathing miracles."

He points to the wolf-cub, sleeping peacefully with his oxygen mask on, a large bandage around his middle. "We just saved your friend here, look."

Polly reaches out and softly touches the cub's side. Then she turns to me, her eyes suddenly full of tears. I know who she's thinking about.

Dad pauses for a moment, then goes on. "No other animal can do that, you know—help and save another one in that way." I think of the stag, lying just outside. "But we can't always. First came the red-eye. Now that was . . . savage. Total . . ." He closes his eyes and pinches the bridge of his nose, as if to clear the memory. "Unfortunately in that case, science was absolutely powerless. Even I couldn't . . . We lost so many, so quickly . . ." Dad stops in front of the operating table in the middle of the room, covered in piles of books on top of a dust sheet, and taps it. "Right in front of me on this very . . ." He sighs. "And then of course, your mother got . . . well, she got very sick indeed."

I can feel Polly glance at me anxiously. But I can't take my eyes off Dad.

"We couldn't save her either. The one person I would have . . ." He stops. Shakes his head. "I would have given anything, *anything*—but the fact is, we lost her. She was gone forever and I just couldn't . . . You see?" He clenches his hands together tightly, making the knuckles white. "So I thought . . . do something good in her memory. Everlasting . . . that was what I wanted."

He must see the puzzlement on our faces.

"A cure! I vowed to find a cure for the red-eye. A cure in your mum's name."

The lab seems to have grown quieter than before, no machines humming, and even the noise of the city from outside has faded.

"That," Dad says, "is when my troubles really started."

Dad sits down with a thump on a deck chair covered in shirts, which nearly collapses under his weight. A cloud of dust billows into the air.

"I worked harder than I'd ever . . . down here night and day. Equations and experiments, tests and models, calculations and trials. I tried everything, but every road seemed like a dead end, every breakthrough an illusion—until!" He jabs his finger in the air. "One night, I was tired and . . . perhaps just a bit absent-minded, so Factorium were right about one thing . . ." He looks embarrassed. "I did make a mistake. A very big one."

"Something big, Kes," he'd said that night. "Something big—" His fingers moving quickly over the keyboard.

My heart catapults into my mouth, and Polly clutches my hand—

"But not the kind of mistake they mean! It wasn't the beginning of the red-eye!" He stamps his foot, and more dust billows up. "On the contrary—it was the beginning of a cure."

"Wouldn't you need to test it first?" interjects Polly.

"You're quite right, young lady," continues Dad. "What did you say your name was again?"

"Polly," says Polly again, with a sigh.

"That's just it, Sally!" Dad cries. "It was only a theory. A theory in need of . . . research, proper testing—never mind making the thing." Dad rubs his hand over his face. "As a vet, I'd worked a lot with Factorium. They had big laboratories, processing plants . . . the capability! And I thought, the world's biggest food company might just want to help me save the, you know, animals? So I went straight to the top, and had a meeting with—"

He doesn't need to say. Polly and I swap looks. We both know who runs Factorium.

"Best intentions and all that." Dad rubs his hands together. "So I met Selwyn Stone. Gave him my paperwork, my samples, the lot. He was very pleased. More than pleased. They offered me a huge amount of money."

He smiles grimly to himself at the memory.

"But I never saw a penny. Because that very evening he sent round that goon Skuldiss to threaten me. You see, Stone had been bluffing. They didn't want a cure at all! Even worse, they wanted me to destroy all my work. Everything. Every last sum. And if I didn't, they would—"

I stand stock-still, not daring to move a single muscle.

Dad points at me.

"You. They said they would take you away. I didn't believe it. But that didn't stop them. A week later, they took you away, ransacked my . . ." He gestures around at the lab. "Said if I so much as thought about an equation relating to a cure, that your life would be . . ." He looks down at his large feet as if he's never seen them before. "That your life would be in danger," Dad says quietly. "And then—they locked me up too. In, you know—"

We look around at the bed, the clothes, and the lonely toothbrush. This isn't what I expected. This isn't what I expected *at all*.

But it's my turn to ask a question now, the question I've been wanting to ask for six years. I find a pen, grab a sheet of paper off one of the tottering piles, and scrawl over it one simple question:

WHY?

He grabs the note from my hand, scans it quickly, and snorts.

"Why did they do it? I'll tell you. Formula! I had invented a cure that could save the last few animals in the world, but what I didn't know was that Selwyn and his scientists had just invented formula. The magic chemical that replaces food. Stone's success now depended on there being no more animals. No more food crops, vegetables or fruit—nothing else to eat at all. And that's exactly what happened. Factorium killed all the remaining creatures left alive, stripped our fields bare in the name of protecting our health, and became very rich. Very rich and very powerful."

The sky is black outside, rain clouds gathering once more above the towers.

Polly and I are looking at my dad with new eyes. Maybe, just maybe—

Polly's face lights up. "But can you still help them, Professor Jaynes? Do you still have a cure for the virus?"

"Hmm." Dad looks out of the window at the clouds. "I'm afraid . . . the short answer is . . . no, not after what Facto destroyed. No, I don't."

No.

He can't—

I feel like I've just been thumped in the chest—

After everything—

I take a step back in shock.

Dad comes round the other side of the worktop and makes as if to hug me again, but I back away. I don't know how to feel. I—

"Kes." He stands there, hands in his grubby jacket pockets. "Wait. Let me explain."

I don't want him to. I don't want him to explain away—

Everything I believed in!

And then—

"NO!"

Just a single word, that's all it is. I say "no" to my dad. He and Polly look at me in amazement.

So I say it again.

"No."

"Kes, did you . . . ?" And then—"What did you just say?"

"No." It gets easier every time.

"No"—because that's not good enough. And not that I can say all this, but that's not what I came hundreds of miles for. That's not what I brought the animals for.

"You spoke, Kes! Oh my, that's fantastic, that's . . ."

"No!" I thump my fist on the table, and another mountain of paper slides onto the floor.

"Listen to me," says Dad, "I haven't finished—"

"No!" I say.

It's only one word. I can't say "you" or "can't." You've no idea how badly I want to, but it doesn't matter. He knows, he knows what I'm trying to say.

Everything that I've been telling myself. Telling the wild. And now—

"Listen to me," Dad says, trying to calm me down, waving his hands. "You're right, Kester, you're right. That wouldn't be . . . acceptable."

Then he points at my wrist. "Your watch, please, Kes."

My watch? I don't believe this.

"Yes, Kester," says Dad, holding out his hand. "Give me your watch, and I can show you what happened next."

Too surprised to argue anymore, I take off the watch. The screen is smeary and cracked, the plastic strap covered in mud and blood. I pass it to him, Polly and I both watching his every move.

Dad leans over and and rattles around in a jar of pens and pencils on the worktop, until he finds a screwdriver. Turning the watch flat over on his knee, he unscrews the metal back. I can see the innards of the watch for the very first time, a dark green circuit board with a straggle of multicoloured wires, and a tiny black ball buried in between them.

He pulls out a pair of pliers from his jacket pocket and clips off the black ball, holding it up to us in the light from the lamp between finger and thumb.

"A small, er, precaution. One any father would take." He sees my expression and smiles. "Any father with a basic understanding of micro-radio transmitters, perhaps."

A memory is beginning to stir in my brain again; Dad borrowing my watch, my last present from Mum. I thought it was because it was "nifty."

He leans across to the worktop again, yanking over one of the computer monitors. Then he's tapping on the crumb-covered keyboard, entering a password, and up it pops, clear as anything despite the fuzz of dust covering the screen: the photo of Mum in the garden—the photo from my watch.

Dad stares at it for a moment too. "Hmm," he says. Then he nods, moving on.

"Nothing for six years," he says, fingers poised over the keyboard. "Until . . ."

Click.

The picture of Mum changes to a satellite map of the country. There's a single bright-red dot, pulsing away in Premium, right where we are. Dad twists round to face us.

"As long as I saw that—pulsing away at Spectrum Hall—I knew you were safe. I thought maybe you might escape, but for six years you didn't move one inch."

I didn't know, I couldn't—

Dad bats away my thoughts with a flick of his hand.

"Of course, how could you? You were just as much a prisoner as me. And then, a few days ago, the dot started to . . ."

He leans in and presses some keys. *Click!* The map disappears, and then there is the photo of the General in the lift at Spectrum Hall, the first one I ever took. Out of focus, blurred, surprised—how did he—*click!* There are the wild at the Ring of Trees. *Click!* The empty First Fold. *Click!* Sidney! (I hear Polly swallow hard behind me.) *Click!* The animals from the Forest of the Dead.

"I discovered that it wasn't just sending me the location of the watch, it was copying all the data as well." Dad turns round from the screen. "I know about the animals, Kes, the ones you've brought here. I tried to send you messages, but the reception here is so weak, I don't know if . . ."

HELP
DON'T
GIVE UP

Typical Dad. Four words where ten would have been more useful.

"Do you know why, though? I'd begun to . . . give up, I'm afraid. Your mum's memory, fading away—until you started to take all those. I didn't know exactly what you were doing—but you showed me that there were animals still alive. Who needed a cure. A cure that I had once invented—but no longer had."

I begin to realize—

"At least," says Dad, "I no longer have a fully finished and working cure. But I do have something. And it's all down to you. Because once I started seeing you move, seeing your pictures, following you on the map—I saw it wasn't too late to . . ."

Dad suddenly looks tired. He looks so much older. His skin paler and more lined, his face thinner. I realize that all this time I've been wanting Dad to help me. And now, perhaps—but Dad doesn't notice my expression, and he carries on.

"In secret, I dug out what scraps of my early research I could piece together and . . . I've been working ever since. Day and night, using encryption, using every trick up my sleeve to hide it from Facto. Using your photos, studying the symptoms, making notes, working right up until the moment that . . . wretch came back. Last night."

Now Polly and I are looking at him with new eyes. Maybe, just maybe . . .

Breaking off, Dad suddenly bends down, right down to his feet, as if he was tying up his laces—

Pulling off his shoe—

Grabbing the screwdriver, tearing at the sole of the shoe, ripping the stitching, till it hangs off like an old leaf—

And sticking his hand into the exposed belly of the shoe, he brings out a glass vial. A vial that he holds up to the light, just so we can see a ray of sun pass and bend through the clear liquid inside.

We look again at all the papers, the flickering computer screens. Suddenly they don't seem like piles of rubbish anymore.

"So what have you got?" says Polly, looking warily at the vial in Dad's hands.

"One sample. A trial drug. But it's completely untested." My father examines the clear, pure liquid in the vial. "And to test it I need some living animals, with the latest mutation of the . . ." He looks at me. "Which I think you might be able to help me with. But I'm not exactly stocked up with fresh ingredients here. If you had anything that I could use—plants, herbs, that kind of . . . We might be able to er, get somewhere—"

Polly is already racing up the stairs and out of the lab, screaming to the animals she can't talk to—

"He's got a cure! He's got a cure! And I'm going to help him make it!"

And for a moment it's just Dad and me. In the lab. Wolf-Cub breathing softly.

We both look at him, together, and Dad holds out his hand to me.

I take it.

Firmly, like I never want to let go. Ever again.

Still looking at the cub, his bandages, the syringe sticking out—

"It won't be easy, Kester, you can't rush these things."

"No," I say again. But softer this time.

And Dad turns and smiles at me, his eyes crinkling up at the corners like they used to. A bright speck in each one.

"Your mother," he says. "She really would have been . . . you know . . . proud."

I want to say another word—but I can't.

There are so many in my head, sad and happy, jumping together to get out, that I can't pick any of them. Not one I can say without choking up, at least. So instead, realizing that perhaps for now, the time for talking, of all kinds, is over, I lead Dad out of the lab, up into the damp, smoke-filled air of the green Culdee Sack—to show him my wild.

It's a week later. A sunny afternoon and I'm standing in Dad's lab again, only this time it's tidy and clean. I'm looking out at our garden, stretching all the way down between high brick walls to the edge of the river, which sparkles in the light. The house looks just like it always did—except for the animals.

Some of the butterflies we saved flitter around the rosebushes, while above in the apple tree an occasional flutter of leaves gives away the pigeons' hiding place. Beneath them all, the stag lies quietly in the shade on the lawn, polecats bouncing around him, doing their best to destroy what's left of Dad's flower beds. He barely seems to notice, and is still weak, still tired, and still sick with the berry-eye. But he is also alive, and every day he takes a bit more of Dad's drug.

The trial drug Polly and I helped Dad make in the lab

behind me, using the sample vial as a prototype to make the quantities we need for all the animals.

It was hard work. First we went outside and brought all the wild into the safety of the garden. All traces of the cullers, Skuldiss, and their van had gone.

I just hope for good. I don't know how long we have before Facto send another van or another captain. And right now, I don't care. Why can't everything be normal again—like it used to be?

So next we cleaned the lab—sweeping the floor and polishing the windows till they shone like new.

Then, armful by armful, Polly helped me move Dad's stuff back up the stairs and into his bedroom. On my second trip up—leaving a trail of socks behind me—I found her kneeling on the floor, looking at a rumpled photo in her hand.

A photo of a woman with curly copper hair that had slipped out from the big pile of papers she was carrying.

Without thinking, I said, "No!" again, snatching it out of her hand. I felt more words bubbling in my throat but still wasn't ready to say them.

Turns out I didn't need to.

"That's your mum, isn't it?" said Polly quietly, without looking up.

I nodded.

She got up off the floor, still looking down.

"Do you think I'll ever see mine again?"

I put my hands on her shoulders, to show her that I absolutely promised she would, and a familiar voice boomed from behind us from the doorway. "Of course, Molly, I . . . promise too. Absolutely the first thing we do after . . . you know, we've made a cure . . ."

Downstairs in the kitchen, we found tubs of formula, good old Ham'n'Eggs and Chicken'n'Chips, one of them half-opened already on the table.

"I guess even Captain Skuldiss had to eat something," said Polly, sniffing the tub suspiciously, as if he might somehow be hiding in it.

But he wasn't—and after our first "proper" meal in as long as I can remember, we returned to the newly spotless lab. I wrote down everything about the virus that the animals had told me, while Polly and Dad went through all the leaves, plants, herbs, and berries she had collected, to see which ones he might be able to use.

And slowly, drop by drop, we made it. Dad and Polly boiled down her samples into strong-smelling syrups, sieving them into different sterilised jars. Meanwhile I sat at his computer and input all the data I could remember—how red the wild's eyes were, when the stag started shaking exactly, how heavy Sidney felt when I picked her up—and the things that no scientist in the world could ever know.

What the animals were feeling.

And then, three long days and nights later, we had a drug.

A trial drug that, as he keeps reminding us, might not fully work. A drug that we have named Laura II. Polly and I helped Dad keep precise notes of what effect certain doses have. The first batch didn't seem to have any effect at all—for example, the polecats told me they didn't feel anything, while Polly stuck a thermometer in their mouths.

We reported back, Dad shaking his head and returning to his jars and vials, measuring out everything again, until we had a drug that stopped the fever in most of the animals, and turned their red eyes a lighter shade of pink. There is still plenty of variation in the reaction to the different doses—the otters, for example, when they're not turning the lawn into a mud bath, have responded better to the cure than the polecats.

Yet all of them, hour by hour, day by day, grow stronger.

None of us will forget those who died in the Culdee Sack. Polly and I buried them at the bottom of the garden, in the shadow of the high brick wall, because Polly said that was the proper thing to do. And we dug one last hole too. An empty one that we covered up with soil and grass, and standing by it for a while, our heads bowed, finally said a true goodbye to Sidney.

"Come on, Kidnapper," says a voice behind me now. "What are you waiting for?"

I turn around to see Polly standing at the entrance to the lab in her clean clothes, holding her toad, with Wolf-Cub at her side, his bandage wrapped tight around his middle. He is still limping, but some of the old glow has returned to his green eyes. He has grown too. He is beginning to change from a wolf-cub—but not in all ways.

*Am I the best in the world at recovering from a firestick wound?*he asks quietly.

I want to laugh, but Polly's serious expression stops me.

I pick up a tray from the worktop, and they follow me down the steps and out into the garden, where the pigeons fly down from the tree to meet us, lining up on a low wall.

I look at them, every single one in turn—grey and white—because I know this is possibly the last time I will ever see them. I place the tray carefully down on the ground, and with Polly kneeling next to me, we begin to unpack its contents. Bound bags of gel batons, each one packed with a slow-release version of Laura II.

Dad and Polly made sure that not only will the drug stay fresh for a long time, but after six months, it will start to naturally degrade into the soil. Don't ask me how—all I care is that it gets to the wild.

We take out the sheaves and fasten one to each bird, tying them on tightly with ribbons. I explain carefully to them how all they need to do is pull the ribbon to release and open the bag. The gel sticks can be chewed, licked, pecked, or even swallowed whole—the effect will be the same.

The birds all nod their understanding, apart from the white one, who says thoughtfully, *Stick the bag and chew the ribbon.*

Loaded with their cargo, the pigeons turn to say

goodbye, first to the General, who has appeared from nowhere—on Polly's shoulder this time. And she doesn't seem to mind at all.

If we should meet again one day, brave comrades, he says, nervously feeling their sharp beaks with his antennae, *be so good as to remember that we once fought together on the same side.*

We shall try, say the grey pigeons.

Remember, one day we shall fight together on the same side, adds the white pigeon wisely, before joining the rest of his flock, who are already waddling down to where the stag lies on the lawn.

Goodbye, great Stag, the pigeons say. They move to leave, before turning back awkwardly. *Will we see you again at the Ring of Trees?*

He nods at them sleepily, through half-closed eyes. *You will see me again, I'm sure of it.*

Yes, we're sure we won't see you again, says the white pigeon cheerily, before being nearly pecked to death by the others. They then shuffle down to the harvest mouse, who performs a traditional Farewell Dance that seems to involve flicking every one of their heads with her tail. But as soon as she's finished she abruptly declares, *Well, I don't much like goodbyes. I've said enough in my time,* and scurries away under a bush. So the birds flock up and land on the wolf-cub's back, pecking busily at his fur, until he shakes them off with a growl.

And finally, they come to me.

I pick up the white pigeon in my hands, while Polly looks on.

Pigeons, I say, *you've got a hard journey ahead. It will take longer than you think. You might not all make it. And who knows how many animals you will still find living at the Ring.* And I stroke the birds' beak and feathers for perhaps the last time. I don't want to let them go, not on their own. But they will be faster than we could ever be. *Maybe there will be enough left for you to start again. You know my father's magic is not perfect yet—but it's better than no magic at all.*

Better than no magic at all, repeats the white pigeon softly to himself, like he is understanding something for the very first time.

I kiss him gently on the top of his head before throwing my hands up, releasing him into the air. The others follow him, flying in formation above the trees, off into the endless sky beyond. We wait until the last pigeon is nothing more than a distant dot over the horizon, until there is nothing to stare at but the clouds floating by, and then I feel Polly's hand softly taking mine and leading me back up the garden, to where Dad is now knelt by the stag, stroking his flank.

"Kester," she says, as we walk up towards them, her toad bouncing happily after us, "now that the pigeons have gone home with a cure, do you think we can go and find my—"

She doesn't finish her sentence as I freeze and drop her hand.

Because I can hear voices. Talking.

An animal voice. Talking to a human voice.

Except it isn't mine.

I race up the garden towards Dad and the stag.

They both turn to me, the stag still looking woozy from the drug, his eyelids drooping low, Dad looking startled, turning round—as he says—*as my dad says to the stag*—

Tell me, great Stag—is this in the dream?

The stag nods slowly, and weak as he is, he staggers to his feet. The wolf-cub comes to him, in his shadow, the harvest mouse and the General on his horns. I have never seen them look so serious.

My dad can talk to animals too—

Is this what Mum meant when she said, "He has to tell you?"

I'm looking at Dad. At the stag. Furious—

I'm sorry, he says. *I know I should have . . . you know, chip off the old . . . but they took you away before I could . . .*

Yes, interrupts the stag. *Yes, this was in the dream.* He turns to me, half his head dark in the shadow of the old apple tree, his horns sharp against the sky. *Wildness, the dream said the son of the man who talked would lead us over earth and rock, through water and fire, to save a wild. This you have done and we thank you for it.* He touches my hair with his nose. *But I am afraid the dream did not end there.*

There are so many questions bouncing around my head that I don't know which one to choose first, and then—

A noise makes us all turn around.

A noise coming from a distant dot in the sky, high above the glass towers. A dot that at first I think is one of the pigeons, perhaps the white one losing his way again—but if it is a bird, it's a very big metal one. Making a *whup-whup* noise, with whirring rotor blades instead of wings.

A metal bird with purple sides, a large "F" painted across the front.

A metal bird heading straight for us.

But Dad isn't frightened. He puts his arm around my shoulder as we watch it, and grips me tight.

You didn't think he'd, you know, let us get away with it . . . ? he murmurs.

The Factorium helicopter slices through the air, its windows dark and closed, the steel blades spinning circles of shadow across the river, as the sun disappears behind the horizon.

Soldier! whispers a voice from my shoulder. I look down to see the General, the cockroach who first talked to me in the Yard. *The rest of the dream begins. Are you ready?* he hisses.

I'm not sure. There's so much that I don't—

But then I look again at the brave insect on my shoulder. I think of the pigeons flying on past the glass towers. I think of the wild we're going to save. I turn round to look at the animals we already rescued. The Dad I found again. The new friends I made.

The journey we took together. Everything we did together.

The roar of the helicopter engines grows deafening, the trees sway in the rush of air, the downdraught pulls at our faces—

I reach out for Dad's hand, and Polly's. The stag stands behind me, the wolf-cub at my side.

Yes, General, I whisper back. *We're ready.*

PIERS TORDAY was born in Northumberland, which is possibly the one part of England where more animals live than people.

After working as a producer and writer in theatre, live comedy, and TV, Piers now lives in London—where there are more animals than you might think. *The Last Wild* is his first book, and he is currently writing the rest of Kester, Polly, and the wild's story.

Visit his website at *www.pierstorday.co.uk.*